T0274128

"The Chaos Grid is a breakneck ride into a brilliantly original and creative dystopian world that will floor you from page one! Brace yourself for thrilling plot twists through chaos storms, holo jungles, sleek cities, dangerous deserts, mutant animal encounters, and more."

— CANDACE KADE, author of *Enhanced*

"The Chaos Grid is one of those books that you inhale in the space of days and then spend months thinking about, because you're not ready to say goodbye to these characters that feel so real and vivid. Lewellen's brilliant debut features non-stop action, an astoundingly detailed post-apocalyptic world, moments of delightful humor, rich spiritual insights, and several twists I did not see coming. This book can live rent-free in my head forever, and one thing is beyond certain: I need more!"

— J.J. FISCHER, award-winning author of The Nightingale Trilogy

"I had a blast reading *The Chaos Grid*. This story invites you on a roller coaster adventure led by a crew of engaging characters. Friendship, surprises, humor, and monsters keep pages turning fast!"

— KATHERINE BRIGGS, author of *The Eternity Gate*

THE CHAOS GRID

LYNDSEY LEWELLEN

ENCLAVE

Escape

To my best friend and our full quiver of arrows.

Thank you for cheering me on toward the yes, even after I gave up.

There's no one I'd rather drive down the road of life with.

"'I will not,' he answered, but later he changed his mind and went."

– Matthew 21:29

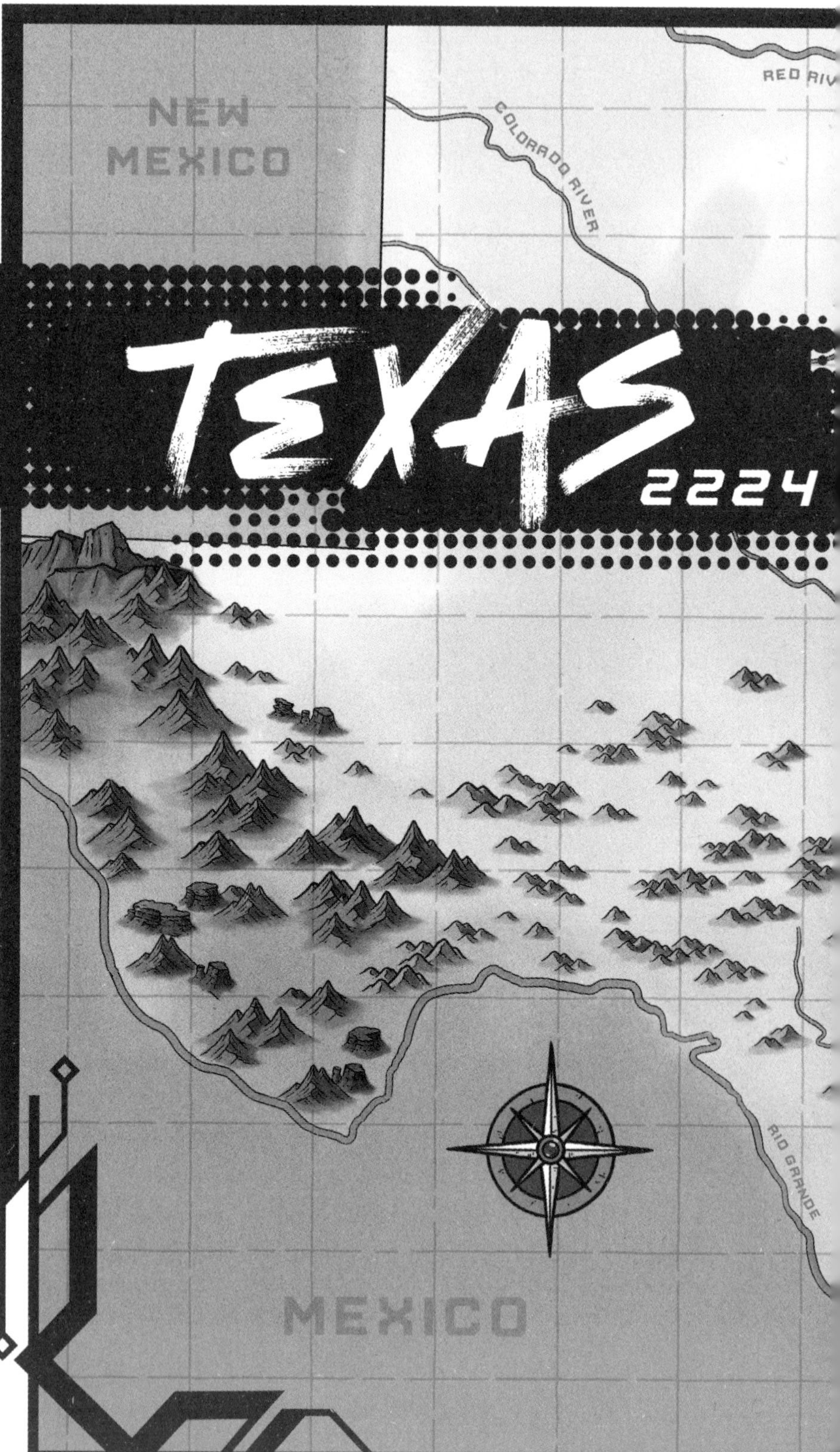
NEW MEXICO
RED RIV
COLORADO RIVER
TEXAS
2224
RIO GRANDE
MEXICO

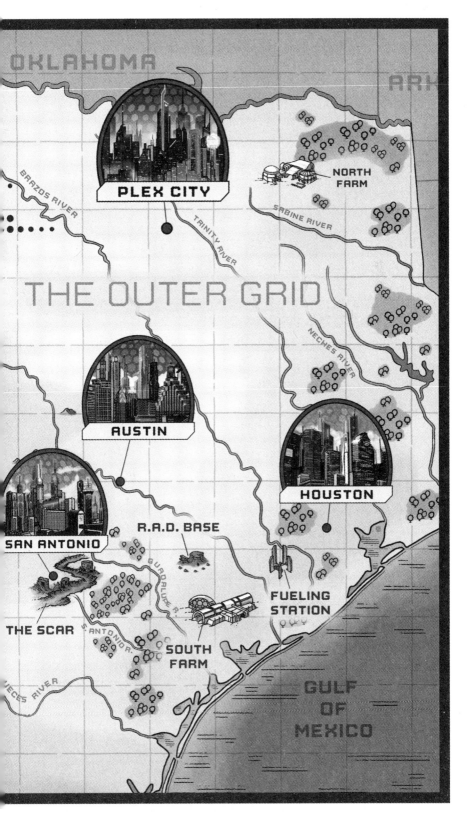

1

THE DAY PLEX CITY BURNS TO ASH

will be the best day of my life.

Its scrapers. The dome. Every inch in flames and a smile on my face. It's no secret. I've never been quiet about my hatred of the place. And yet, my aunt and uncle are bent on dragging me back there, positive I'll help them save whomever they can. But they're wrong. I will never lift a finger for those people. Not when they murdered my parents.

Today, I escape. Today, I cut the wires that have played me in a cosmic puppet show for good. Or at least, that's what I tell myself before I step into the neon-lit substation and watch every screen in the building broadcast my broken plans in surround sound.

> ATTENTION, SUBSTATION-A
> PASSENGERS, ALL DEPARTURES
> AFTER THE 5:15 TRAIN HAVE BEEN
> INDEFINITELY DELAYED. TICKET
> HOLDERS WITH LATER DEPARTURE
> TIMES, MAKE YOUR WAY TO THE
> CUSTOMER SERVICE DESK FOR
> FURTHER ASSISTANCE.

The cartoon woman in a sparkling plum uniform smiles when she delivers the blow. Sickeningly sweet, her bared teeth flash across the display screens that cover the walls. I'm sure the station designed her to be friendly, welcoming even, but she comes off like a cheap joke amidst the exploding madness around me. People who've lost their only chance of leaving the city today blurt out strings of obscenities as they shove past on their way to the ticket screens. Unable to help myself, I tap my plastic silver holo-cuff. The bright screen lights up half my forearm, and I scroll to my ticket receipt. Tension in my shoulders eases at what I find.

AUSTIN SUBSTATION
BOARDING PASS
PASSENGER: JUNIPER CONWAY
SUBSTATION-A - SOUTH AUSTIN,
TO SUBSTATION-C - BATON ROUGE:
JULY 18, 2224 - 5:15 A.M.

She said 5:15. My ticket is valid. I can still leave this nightmare. I pick up the pace on the moving platform to the check-in point. With all these people rushing to snag leftover seats, the train will be packed, and I'm not about to lose my spot. I pass through a body-sized, holographic ad for a new augmented reality game. I'd stop to watch any other time, but not now. Every second I'm not on that train is a second closer to getting caught.

The platform rolls past a porting dais—a silver slab on the ground large enough for fifteen people to teleport in on. I hold my breath and hope the circular activation lights don't flash to life until after I've moved on. But porting daises are always high traffic. White light blinks on from the dais' incoming pads. There must be at least ten people teleporting into the station, arriving much faster than the sliding glass door I came through. And paying a pricier ticket for it.

I duck behind a man glowing from his bioluminescent mohawk to his metallic leg enhancements. A synth. Like most people here, he's altered his body with as much tech as could fit. But an army of synths can't hide me.

Not when I'm a basic. Refuse the newest body upgrade—you stand out. Refuse all upgrades—or be forced to refuse them by a family who doesn't trust the tech giants—you might as well burn a "look at the freak" sign into your forehead. If who I dread comes through that port, they'll find me for sure.

My pulse hammers. The pad beams spiral up into a long white tube that touches the ceiling two floors up with a *snap-hiss*. Sterilized air jets whip my straight blue hair over my face with a chilled burst. I shake away the hip-length strands, adjust my yellow hoodie, and clench the black pendant hanging around my neck. My only lifeline.

Don't let it be Aunt Marna and Uncle Trek. Anyone but them.

When the light fades, people I don't recognize walk out. I take a breath then shove my duffel bag further up my shoulder.

We arrive at the check-in point, and I step off the platform with the crowd. There aren't any empty chairs, but a clear spot by one of the ad walls seems like an okay place to wait for the train. I zigzag to the clearing and lean against the wall. Once its ad rolls beside me, I regret my decision.

A shipper ad. The familiar jingle rings out in five ascending tones only those near the wall can hear. *Lucky me.* Its opening tune chimes light and cheery. The exact opposite of what these guys do for a living. A thin, old woman in a tight olive uniform fills the screen. Her monotone voice spews a recruitment pitch I've heard countless times.

"With natural food grown in outlying farms in its highest demand in decades," she drones on, her smile forced, "our local shippers couldn't be more needed. Shipping is not only the best means to transport food from farms to cities across Texas, it's the *only* means. With your help, we can do just that. Travel the Grid in our well-protected vehicles. Join a staff of professionals and experts to feed our great state. Our doors are always open. Here at the Texas Area Rural Shippers and Haulers, you can make a difference. We can keep you safe."

The screen fades into the next ad about the newest wrist chargers before I can roll my eyes. *Keep you safe?* That's got to be the worst tagline in history. How can anyone keep you safe in the Outer Grid? It's like this lady hasn't heard of the Global Weather Collapse. Our ancestors did all they could to fix the dying climate, but only succeeded in pulling the collapse twenty steps closer, birthing the very waste they tried to avoid. At least they gave us the domes. Halfway open, the invisible shields filter the good air into the cities. All the way closed, we're kept safe from bonkers weather and whatever else is out there. Stepping through the invisible shields that separate us from the Outer Grid is the dumbest idea—even if you're inside one of those massive shipper trucks. Sure, shippers offer something I need, a paycheck, but I'm not about to travel the Grid to get one. No, I'll get out of this city the legit and safe way. Underground.

The ad is followed up by a newsreel on the rebel attack in North Austin an hour ago. It's the reason the substation will shut down. The reason so many people are crammed into this check-in point. Twisted metal from the aftermath of a barrier outpost bombing flashes across the screen in an aerial shot. Dotting the rim of the wreckage, in the wasteland bordering the city's skyscrapers, tiny people dressed in rags flee the scene. They don't have long. The oblong, military Quell ships are hot on their trail. I've seen tons of these broadcasts. No one escapes the Outer Grid's policing unit. If the Quell wants to arrest you, that's it, you're theirs. Makes me glad they police the Grid and not the city domes.

I cringe when the reel turns to a report on the Plex. Six idiotic bureaucrats sit in a white room around a white table to discuss legalizing nano drugs within their dome. *So* progressive. Orange Pipe, the tech giant, rolls its tangerine logo across the screen's edge on repeat. It's easy to see who the leaders of the Plex work for. They seem sympathetic on the vid, wrinkled brows and puppy eyes. But they only care about their appearance, not what they legalize. Not even if it's the very thing that will crush their own citizens. The very thing to bring their dome to ruin. The very thing my parents died to—

"I said hand over your cuff, low-grade," barks some girl beside me, tearing my attention from the screen. "Don't make me say it again."

Her raspy voice sets off warning bells. At first, I'm sure the threat is aimed at me. My from-a-box blue hair color can sometimes pass me off for a low-grade synth. But when a blonde girl with a short afro is shoved halfway up the wall near me, it's easy to see who the synth with the chin-length metal hair replacements is harassing.

"The cuff. Now!" Metal Hair shoves her face inches from the blonde girl's sniffing nose.

"I . . . I can't," the girl stutters. Her hands work to break the synth's grip on her coat. The girl has a few visible upgrades, a wrist charger, and a GPS tracker. Nothing as serious as the synth with muscle enhancer wires sticking out of her bare arms. I hope Blondie wasn't planning on hanging on to that cuff. "You don't understand," Blonde Girl goes on. "I need to get home. My grandma, she—"

Metal Hair shoves her again. Her blonde head smacks the station wall. "Did I ask for a sob story? Type in your release code so I can get on that train."

I lean away, looking for a security guard. But I know even if I find one, they won't do anything. They're more concerned about mass panic over the bombing. One low-grade getting bullied by a synth isn't worth bothering with.

The wall behind me pulsates when Metal Hair lands a punch against a screen by Blonde Girl's head. I rub my cuff and tap my foot. I don't want to do this. If I lose my spot on that train then it's back to the Plex.

"B-but she's real sick," the girl pleads. "If I don't leave now, I might never see her again. Please, let me go." Metal Hair smacks Blondie across the mouth. Her plated finger upgrades slice skin on contact. Blood splatters across my hoodie—red dots on a mustard canvas. I can't stay silent.

"Leave her alone," I say, my voice low but audible. I hope my tone is enough to convince Metal Hair to back down. I know it isn't. The synth takes her time sliding her maniacal glare from Blondie to me. Her purple-painted upper lip curls into a sneer. I straighten.

"Private conversation, *Basic*," she jeers. I guess I'm not as incognito as I'd hoped. "Interrupt again, and you're next."

When she turns to harass Blondie, I wiggle my finger under my cuff. Everything inside me screams to walk away. It's not my problem. I've got a ticket out of here. I'm not blowing my one chance at freedom on some girl I don't know. But I do it anyway.

"You need on that train so badly?" The words are out of my mouth before I realize it. "Then here, take my ticket." I punch in my release code where she can see it, pull the silver cuff off, and jab it in her face. I try to hold my arm still, but I'm sure she can see it tremble. I'm not scared of a beating—wouldn't want one, but I've taken my share of hits. No, I'm shaking because I can't believe what I'm doing.

My face tenses, preparing to look like Blondie's battered mug round two. But instead, Metal Hair's sneer flips to a grin. She drops Blondie and snatches the cuff from me. "See, that wasn't so hard, was it?" Metal Hair saunters away as if nothing happened. She meets up with a group of synths near the subtrain rails, who must have watched the whole ordeal. They give her a high five before turning their backs on us. *Creeps.* Figures I'd run into a synth like that today. The one day I've got to get out of here or else I—I drop my head into my hands and pull at my hair.

What am I supposed to do now? I can't go back there. Not now. Not ever.

My aunt and uncle will be here any minute, ready to drag me with them to that gutter city, thinking they can fix it. Like it's our duty to somehow stop the place from crumbling in on itself? Well, they're not taking me without a fight. Bloodied images of my past cloud my vision. *Dad, Mom. Dead on the streets.*

"Thanks," a mousy voice says beside me. "It means a lot and . . . well, thank you."

I lift my head to see Blondie wiping the blood from her mouth with a rag she pushes back into her pocket. I forgot she was there. Worry is still etched across her brow as she picks up her bags. Understandable since she's now forced to share a subtrain with Metal Hair. I open my mouth to tell her not to worry about it when a deafening *whoosh* fills the station. The sleek subtrain blurs across the rails. Its segmented chrome body, etched in red lights and dressed from bottom to top with touch screen walls, slows to a stop with a hiss.

"Your ride's here," I say instead.

She nods, and I watch her squeeze through the crushing crowd, raise her wrist against the screen, and disappear into the train's belly.

There are plenty of empty benches now that the station's cleared out. I find the closest one and plop down. I don't know how long I sit there, staring at the subtrain filled with passengers. Ten minutes? Half hour? But soon the subtrain leaves, and the massive screen above the railway bursts with cancelation notices. The only safe way out of here is gone.

"There you are. Thought I'd missed you." A bubblegum, soprano voice startles me, and I look up. A girl with cotton-candy pink curls and blunt straight bangs flops her anime-covered duffel bag beside me. Out of breath, she bends over to gain control of her huffing. After sucking on an inhaler, her breathing relaxes. Her eyelids are smudged with matching pastel paint from brow to pink spider lashes. She's dressed in the same oversized turquoise sweater and zebra tights I saw her in at last night's school's-out party. A party that must still be going on. At 5:15 in the morning.

"Nope. Still here." I sigh.

"Well, good," she says. The scent of black licorice taints her breath. She reaches into her bag to draw out another strand of the candy and tears off a chunk with her teeth. "For a second, I thought you were going to do something dumb. Tell me that's ketchup on your jacket."

I fling my blue hair over the yellow fabric to cover the bloodstain. "You knew what I was doing when I messaged you, Tori," I say, changing the subject. "Why else would you be here?" If anyone can interpret *l8r* as *I'm about to board a subtrain and skip town*, it's Tori.

"Hey, you're the one who went on and on about buying a one-way ticket out of here. I was hoping you were kidding. But you didn't answer, so here I am, missing Anton's party."

"Missing what part? When the cops show up? You didn't have to follow me," I say when she takes another bite.

"Oh, right, 'cause I'd be a *great* friend, hanging out at Anton's while my best friend goes off risking her life." Her smacking chews muffle words spoken behind glossy black nails.

I bite back a laugh. Here I am, sitting in an empty substation getting harangued on responsibility by Tori, the girl who frequently parties till the crack of dawn.

"A subtrain to Baton Rouge is hardly risking my life. I'm seventeen. Think I can handle living on my own."

"Oh, really?" she says. "Do you even watch the news? There were three bombs in the past four months, Juna. All near substations. Can't you just wait for them to at least catch these guys?"

I rub the bridge of my nose. We've been over this so many times I've lost count. I'm beginning to think Tori doesn't care about logic as much as she doesn't want me to leave, period. Which is sweet, but what choice do I have? I've already tried hiding out in the city several times. My aunt and uncle found me in hours. I'm going. But where I go, I hope, is up to me.

"Tori, they're leaving soon," I remind her. "I don't have time to wait for some Gridders who've only injured—what?—two people to be locked up. My aunt and uncle are determined to ship off to the Plex. The *Plex*. So, either I go with them, or I find a way to . . ."

My voice trails into nothing as what I said births an idea so dumb, I must be more desperate than I thought. *Ship me off?* Ship . . . I can't believe I'm considering this. A trip through the Outer Grid? Might as well jump off the nearest high-rise. And yet, joining the shippers is a move my aunt and uncle won't expect. Plus, I'd get a paycheck and a for-sure ticket out of town tonight. Exactly what I need. Assuming I survive the Grid.

Tori says something, but I only catch the tail end. "And what does it matter? They only threatened to take you to the Plex for the summer. Maybe it's changed since you were there, and maybe—"

"I'm not getting into this again," I say, interrupting her. "I told you what happened in that cesspit. I'm not going back. I don't want to spend ten minutes there, let alone a whole summer." Mind made up, I stand, throw my bag over my shoulder, and head for a map terminal.

"Juna, wait, Juna!"

I slow my pace. She's going to follow me anyway. No sense in making it hard on her. The terminal is a waist-high black cube that was surrounded by people twenty minutes ago. Now, as it stands cold and empty, I wave my hand across its surface. It takes a second, but soon, a sea of colored lights flickers above its surface with a big blue dot inside South Austin's subtrainstation flashing *you are here*. I type *TARSH headquarters* into the search bar. A red circle pops up far to the left—a good forty-minute walk from where I stand—and a blue line winds through the streets connecting the dots. I scan the area for a port station when Tori groans beside me.

"TARSH? You can't be serious."

I ignore her and dig through my bag. "I think I have enough for a port in cash." Even if I do, it'll be the last of my funds. I shouldn't be spending it on anything. But I know a forty-minute walk will cost me more. I find the ragged gray wallet under a water canteen and shuffle through crisp bills.

"Yeah, that'll do it," I say and move to the porting dais I passed earlier, Tori trailing close behind. I reach the dais and hesitate. My aunt and uncle will worry. But I can't—I can't go back there. Besides, I'll be gone for a couple of months at most. I'll contact them once things relax and I'm out of the city. I type in my location on the prompter, insert the last of my cash, then step on one of the pads. The prompter dings to begin a ten-second countdown.

"Tell me you're not doing what I think you're doing." Tori glares at me, arms crossed.

"I'll miss you, too, Tori," I say. "You're a good friend. Don't worry. It'll just be for the summer. I'll be back before you know it. Promise."

Tori rolls her eyes and mutters to herself. Then, with a wave of her holo-cuff over the prompter, she pays for a port and stands on the pad beside me.

"Don't think you're getting off that easy," she says. Before I open my mouth to argue, the port comes alive, swallowing us both up into probably the worst decision of my life.

WHITE LIGHT SPINS AROUND US,

sizzling my skin and hazing my vision. Soon, the porting light fades from white to midnight. I blink to adjust my eyes from the port effect. When my sight returns, TARSH headquarters stares back at me, flashing a sign in red letters.

TEXAS AREA RURAL
SHIPPERS AND HAULERS
– CLOSED.

"Closed?" I cry out. "It can't be closed!"

I've seen the ads, loads of them. This thing is supposed to be open twenty-four seven. Not closed on the *one* day I need it. This can't be happening. And yet, the flashing sign on TARSH's strange building is impossible to miss.

I've never seen a structure like the shipper's headquarters. It's only three stories high and sits between two thirty-story scrapers. More horizontal than vertical, the thing looks like a scraper fell over and someone cut doors on its side. No strips of neon or bright screens decorate the exterior walls. Painted black, only the closed sign and a speckle of lit windows brighten the surface. If not for the pink sliver of artificial sunrise outlining the frame, I'd mistake it for a dark gap between two towers.

"All right, Master Escape Artist," Tori says beside me. "Now what?"

I take a second to think. If the lights are on, then somebody's inside. I pull up my bag and step off the dais.

"And . . . we're breaking in," Tori says, and continues when I don't answer. "You know, I'm terrible at picking locks. But I'll bet someone back at Anton's knows how. We should go ask."

I crack a smile. If there's one thing Tori is, it's persistent. That's why it was so easy to make friends with her a couple years back when I moved to South Austin. I still remember the determination in her mismatched eyes when she sat beside me in calculus. After the entire student body ostracized me for being a basic, only one person dared speak to me. Social status never did deter Tori's friend-making skills. Instead of shunning me, she insisted we were best friends by the end of the day.

"You can go to Anton's if you want, Tori," I say. "I'm not stopping you."

She spurts a humorless, "Ha." We both know she's not leaving my side.

We reach the Shipping headquarters' front wall, and my spirits die. Not only is the place closed when it's not supposed to be, but there isn't even a front door. I run my hands over a metallic beveled surface and search for an entrance. As far as I can see, there's no lit-up frame, no sliding glass, not even a crack in the wall. How anyone gets inside this place is beyond me.

"So, you're going to punch the wall and crawl in?" Tori asks from beside me.

I give her a look of exasperation then sidestep her. "There's got to be a door here somewhere." I move down the length of the building, running my hands over its surface till I find a good place to knock.

"Welcome to the Texas Area's Rural Shippers and Haulers' Austin Branch," a female voice blares from above, almost giving me a heart attack. The same crusty woman from the ads appears on a screen to my left several feet up. I must have mistaken the screen for part of the metal wall—black blending into black. But there she is, the woman I'd seen so many times, pixie-cut white hair, vomit-green suit and all. She may have said welcome through her strong southern drawl, but her tight, lined mouth and sharp, squinted eyes say anything but. At first, I think she's a recording. But then she lifts her chin and lowers her gaze to meet mine.

I look to Tori, unsure what to say.

Arms crossed and leaning against the wall, she juts out her hand for me to get this over with.

I suck in a breath. "I'm here for the job. I heard you need new shippers and thought—"

"If you've come to our hub to join our company"—the woman no longer looks at me—"I regret to inform you our representatives are currently working on a supply trip. We cannot take any applicants at this time."

My shoulders sag. A crummy recording.

Tori tugs on my jacket. "Sorry, Juna. Can't say you didn't try." She tugs again. "Let's get out of here."

My failure threads its way from my head to my heart. We move away from the wall to the sidewalk and then toward sparkling lights and my one-way ticket back home. I can't ignore thoughts of the Plex. Visions of streets blanketed in thick rain, walls collapsing, and snarling faces. I can't go back.

I take one final glance at the shipper station when the torso of a man appears on-screen behind the woman. I slow. The man bends till his face shows. He's younger than I guessed—a year or two older than me max. He clenches his teeth, showing off a jawline sharper than most city skylines. Dark stubble on his jaw. The rest of his deep bronze skin is smooth and flawless. His wavy black hair spills over a pair of chrome shades as he whispers in the woman's ear. When he's finished, he tilts his chin to nod at me.

"You! You, there!" calls the woman in the suit.

My body jerks at her voice and I slow.

The woman flies from her seat. "Stop! Don't go anywhere. We'll be right out." The screen disappears in an imploding circle of black.

Tori joins me when I stop. "What in the—" she says, more to herself than me. "That lady was really there?"

I open my mouth to reply when a sickening crunch of metal has me throwing my hands over my ears instead. Both Tori and I hunch over till the piercing sound dies. When I straighten, a burst of hot air shoots beneath a door wide enough for two subtrains to fit through. No wonder I couldn't find the entrance. It's the size of half a city block. The gust sends blue hair into my mouth and eyes. As I struggle to get the mess behind my ears, my heart skips a beat. The grating sound finally stops altogether, and I free my face from the tangled strands.

What I see slackens my jaw. The door sits open as high as my shoulders. Under both sides, beefy men in charcoal uniforms grip chains attached to the door's frame. They tilt their massive bodies back till they reach a forty-five-degree angle. Their exposed arms slicken with sweat while they tie off the chains onto hooks on the door they opened.

Manually.

My mind rattles. It's not automatic. Everything's automatic. How can they not have an automatic door? City maintenance would have fixed a broken door long before it got bad enough to make that awful sound. Yet, somehow, these shippers are using a manual front door. No *failure to comply* notice scrolling across the wall. No workman busying away to fix it. Just a functioning, manual door.

My nerves jitter. The voice in my head I've been telling to shut up for days yells at me to run. I shake it off and refuse to budge. This is what I want. What I need. Anything is better than the Plex.

Green suit lady's assistant, the curly-haired guy I saw earlier, ducks under the door and steps toward us. His eyes are glued to the holo-pad casting a purple glow on his chiseled face. He's shorter than the men holding the door, but that's not saying much. Those goliaths would dwarf a stack of scrapers. I'm sure if this guy stood next to any others our own age, he'd tower over them by a few inches. Judging from the way he fills out his uniform, I'd bet he'd hold his own in a fight with any of them.

I can't tell what he's looking at behind the single-lensed sunglasses curved across his face. At five in the morning—outside in the dark. Really, his holo-pad isn't *that* bright. It's bulky, opaque, and about five years out-of-date, but not blinding. Shades on at this hour declares "partier," but the rest of him doesn't fit the type. His hair is so dark it mirrors the artificial sky above. But it's too natural a shade to be genetically altered. Now that I think of it, I can't see any glowing tech enhancements on his skin or any visible modifications. If I didn't know any better, I'd think he was a basic. Which is odd. In every city I've been to, I've only known four basics. All of them related to me.

He swipes his fingers across his holo-pad, and the lights blink out. He folds the thing in half then stuffs it into his pocket before looking us over.

"Here's the deal," he says. His voice is low with a hint of a Mexican accent. And there's a grit to it, like he either wore it raw with overuse or he's getting over a cold. "We're going on a run right now. All the training you'll get will be on the job. Do what you're told and you'll be fine. You get paid when—and if—you finish the job."

"I . . ." I start, but Tori grasps my sleeve and gives me a quick shake of her head. Her raised brows match the unease in my stomach. Something's wrong. They blow me off one second and offer me the job without speaking to me the next. And the more I look at those men behind Glasses Guy—no visible tech on them either—the more I think they're basics too. Tori's right. We should leave.

The guy gives an impatient click of his tongue. "Look, we've got to get going. If you're coming, good, but if you're planning to wuss out, don't waste my time."

Wuss? I blink, sure I heard him wrong. But when he tilts his head and shifts his weight to the side, I know I heard him right. I stiffen.

"Juniper!" Tori gasps. I snap to and turn to her. "It's them." She shakes her holo-cuff in front of me. The small icon of my aunt and uncle flashes on her forearm. Blood drains from my face. "They want me to turn on my porting pad in my garage so they can pick you up in person. Did you tell them you're at my house?"

Cold sweat breaks across my skin. "I might have said something like that on my note-screen." *Great.* My awesome idea to pretend I was at Tori's for the night backfired. "They say anything else?"

"Only that we need to say our goodbyes."

The ground drops out beneath me. I struggle to hold myself up at her words. Words I've heard dozens of times before in dozens of cities. My aunt and uncle are through with their threats. We're moving to the Plex. Not for the summer. For good. And we're leaving today.

I take a deep breath, trying to calm my shaking body. "Don't answer," I say. They can coax anything out of Tori. If they do, I'm done for.

Her face scrunches, like I suggested something dumber than joining the shippers. "Don't answer? Like *that's* not suspicious. They're going to find out you're not at my house, then they'll track your cuff or mine back here. If they find you at a shippers' station, they'll flip."

I hate this. Even if they decide to track my cuff to Metal Hair in Baton Rouge, I know they'll follow Tori's cuff first. It's how they caught me three weeks ago. I'm out of time, and I have no other option.

"They won't find me," I say. "Because I'm leaving now." I turn back to Glasses Guy and lift my chin. Forget the bad feelings about this place. I'm all in. "Let's go."

"SHIPPING IT IS, THEN." GLASSES GUY

cocks a grin that shows off a pair of deep-set dimples. He leans over and taps Tori's holo-cuff. "You can't take that."

She rears back, bringing the bracelet wrapped in fake jewels close to her chest. Her eyes dart between me and the Glasses Guy. "My cuff? You're kidding." Her eyes dart to me. "He's kidding, right?"

His head shake is final. "No city-tech past this point. Either it stays or you do."

Tori's mouth drops. "How do you expect me to get places? I can't exactly pay for a port without it."

He bursts into laughter. Running his hand over his face, he mumbles something to himself, then takes a step closer. "You've got legs? Use those."

Tori's nostrils flare and her mismatched eyes burn. The roots of her hair blacken like burnt bubblegum, matching her sizzling mood. I take both her hands and spin her toward me. Growing up in a poor neighborhood, Tori is unable to upgrade beyond a low-grade synth. Hair-color-on-a-whim enhancers and eye color gene modifications are as far as she goes. That punk had no right to talk to her like that. This path might be my choice, but it doesn't have to be hers.

"Go back home, Tori," I say as calmly as possible. "You're a great friend for coming this far, but you don't have to follow me."

Her mouth tightens. "I do if you're going to jump headfirst into the *Chaos* Grid." Her emphasis on the slur is impossible to miss. She searches my face, maybe in hopes some sense has cracked my resolve. I hold firm, and she sighs. "But since you're going anyway, and you need me, whether you think so or not, I'm going too." She pulls out of my grasp, types her release code on her cuff, and slaps it into Glasses Guy's hand.

"Estupendo." He flashes a quick smile as he stuffs her cuff in his pocket. "You'll get it back when we're done. This way." He disappears under the door and we follow.

A part of me is glad she couldn't bring her cuff. It makes it that much harder for anyone to track us. But no matter how much of a front she put up, I can't ignore the shake that was in Tori's voice. I move closer to her side.

Stepping into the station, the air thickens with humidity. I wish I hadn't worn this jacket. The place is at least twenty degrees warmer than the climate-controlled city outside. The men holding the door drop the chains till every hint of neon light vanishes. Metal crashes on concrete with a *thunk*, cementing my decision.

"Hurry up," Glasses Guy calls. He's a good fifteen feet ahead.

I couldn't move faster if I tried. The sheer strangeness of this place slows me to a crawl. It's not like I haven't seen exposed beam ceilings or massive interiors before. I've lived in at least fifteen different domed cities. But every warehouse I've seen is sleek, new, covered with holo-screens and tech. This is different. Older. Hotter. Mustier. Like we shrank down onto an overheated circuit board made of junk parts from the 21st century. Rusted beams cover the ceilings. Manual doors are on every wall. And cardboard boxes sit stacked around us like a maze.

Glasses Guy leads us into an elevator that's so plain it's got to be a base model. It's stifling in here, not at all air-controlled. I can't believe I stepped into this human oven. He pushes some protruding buttons by the door. The elevator lifts with all the speed of a porting line during a power outage. With no news screens to watch, we're forced to stand in unbearable silence. Glasses Guy doesn't seem bothered. He stares ahead like he's the only one there, chin raised and bobbing his head to a song only he hears. Tori's eyes dart around, and she flicks her backpack strap. I twist my hair in and out of a braid.

After forever, the elevator stops with a *ding*, opening to a space at least four stories up. Glasses Guy is out first, leading us down a narrow bridge that connects one side of the warehouse to the other. Giant hooks sail across the ceiling on metal chains the size of my arms. Coming to a stop, one of them makes a terrible squeal then descends past me at breakneck speed. Like an idiot, I grip the railing and stretch my neck over to watch it drop at least fifty feet down.

It was a mistake. A big mistake. The room spins. My muscles tighten. I push away from the edge. With legs now turned to jelly, I struggle to stand. Through my blurring vision, I see Tori come at me.

She links her arm in mine. "Hey, you alright?"

With her steadying me, the spinning slows. I nod.

She squints at me with doubt in her eyes and tightens her grip. "Pretend it's all one level, okay? We're almost on the other side. You can do it. Remember, flat, bright, and you can see it all." She begins to breathe loud and steady.

I follow her rhythm. The moment we step foot on the other side my lightheadedness fades. "Thanks," I murmur. Should have known that hook would sink deep, deep, deep . . . I slow my breathing more to shake off my jitters. Stupid bathophobia.

She shrugs. "No problem. Told you, you need me."

Glasses Guy opens yet another manual door and waits for us to catch up. "Razor will get you started. After you," he says, ushering us in. Looks like he might have some manners after all. But the closer I get, the cockier his smile grows, like he won a bet getting us here.

We step into a small room with a strange brown desk taking up half the space. I'm not sure what it's made of. Wood? I think that's wood. Whatever it is, it's old and covered in papers. I thought the entryway had a stale odor. This place stinks like a hospital waiting room that's got a serious mold problem. The flickering ceiling lights reflect off the tall steel cabinets lining the blank walls. Papers stick out between the cabinet's drawers every which way. Behind the desk, the old woman in an olive suit with a silver "T" covering the left side of her chest raises her eyes from a stack of papers. She pushes a pair of rectangular glasses up her thin, hooked nose and stands.

"Come on in, y'all," she says. Her southern drawl is thicker than the accent she uses for her ads. Even that was like wading through audio peanut butter. Hardly anyone strays from the stale city accent we all use. It's both strange and impossible to ignore. Still smiling, she dismisses Glasses Guy with a flip of her wrist before settling back on us. "Sorry for earlier. We're in a rush and didn't have time to gage our situation when y'all arrived. We don't usually get the best candidates at our door. Not easy to tell at first glance. But they're a little too, well, synthetic for this line of work, if ya'll know what I mean."

I have no idea what she means. But she sticks out her bony hand as if her explanation is enough and she doesn't care if we understand.

"Marge Razor," she says. "TARSH Hiring Director."

"Juniper Conway," I say, shaking the woman's hand. Though she's tiny, her grip is tighter than most guys I know. "And this is my friend—"

"Astoria Kinsley," Tori finishes then also shakes the director's hand.

"Y'all have a seat." Razor points to two black plastic chairs on our side of the desk, waiting for us to sit before returning to her chair. Her face sours while she shuffles some papers on her desk, until she pulls out an antique black pen from under one of the papers. "Ahh, there we are," she says, clicking the bottom of the pen to her chin. "Now, about the job. As you can tell, we have urgent openings for shipping aids. There's not much to the hiring process, and not much to the job. Extra, natural bodies willing and able to go into the Grid is what we need. Can either of y'all drive a car?"

I swallow, embarrassed I didn't think of this little—though not little—glitch in my plan. "Um," I start, unsure how to tell her I've never gotten behind a steering wheel my entire life. Or that I've only seen ground vehicles as subtrains, in history vids or shipper ads.

"Hold on," Tori says, cutting me off before I expose my ineptness, "we have to *drive* one of those things?" She jumps from her chair, spider-lashed eyes wide.

Razor holds up a hand. "Heavens, no! All our drivers are well-trained rig operators. Those positions take months to fill." She chuckles. "We couldn't train y'all in a day if we wanted to. No, I ask because if you've driven a car, you might have some idea of what it's like in a rig. It's slower than city porting. You'll need patience getting where you're going."

Tori sits and I exhale.

"Patience won't be a problem," I say and mean it. My aunt and uncle have moved me to so many domes, I can't count the number of delayed subtrains I've waited on.

"Glad to hear it," she says, pushing her glasses as far up as they will go on the bridge of her nose. Her chair squeaks when she leans back. "The work we need you two for won't be until later in the run. You'll be helping where you can. Loading crates, strapping things down, and unloading when you get to hubs. Think you can handle that?"

I nod and Tori rolls her eyes before doing the same.

"Perfect. I'll need some identification to get started."

Instinctively, Tori and I hold up our left hands for a palm scan. Razor disappears behind her desk only to return with the most outdated palm scanner I've ever laid eyes on. Which is saying a lot for a girl whose aunt had her hacking palm scanners since she was fourteen. But this tablet with a cracked black screen for the scanner would give me a hard time finding its interface at all. Of course. *Why would this backward warehouse have updated palm scanners?*

With a rag, Razor wipes the screen on the clunky device, which does it no favors. A little hesitant, I place my hand against the smudgy, dust-caked glass. She taps her side of the screen, and we wait for as long as it takes my arm to go numb. Then she moves on to Tori.

Satisfied the thing worked—though I'm not—Razor nods and stands. "Before we get started, read over and sign the application forms." She pushes some papers and two pens toward us. "I'll be right back."

I pull the yellowed paper as close to my face as possible. It's been forever since I've read something not on a screen or my holo-cuff. The light blue writing almost disappears into the paper, and

I can only make out half of the words. But the part about the pay is more than I expected. Enough to set me up for the month break between runs if my aunt and uncle leave without me. My eyes glaze over the technical terminology until I get to the age restrictions. Seventeen and older—no guardian permission needed. Perfect. Finding the line for my name, I jot down my signature and set it back on Razor's desk.

Tori bites the end of her pen. "You sure about this? I mean it says we'll be out there two full weeks. Look at all those dots," she says, tapping the map on our application. "They ship food to the whole lower half of the state and—" Her voice trails as she looks into my eyes—dead set and ready to go. "Sooo . . . we're going no matter what." She sighs and signs right as Razor returns.

She takes our forms, nods, then grabs a hand-sized wooden cube and slams it on our papers. I bend forward to read the words APPROVED now marked in red. Razor tugs on one of the steel cabinets until a long drawer pops out and stuffs our forms inside.

"The work is straightforward," she says, without looking at us. "But there are a few things you'll need briefing on before you go." There's a creak from behind, and she lifts her head. Standing in the doorway is her assistant, arms crossed and leaning against the frame. "Dax, help our newest shippers get accustomed and ready for the next run."

"Will do," he says. "This way."

I stand, torn between the excitement of signing myself closer to freedom and the dread of her assistant's company. I try to stifle my disappointment, but a huff must have escaped by the way he chuckles when I pass.

We move through a long hall and into yet another large room, jam-packed with hundreds of cardboard boxes moving on squeaky conveyer belts. Eye-watering aromas overwhelm me. I partially cover my nose and try to adjust to the potency of natural food. A TARSH worker nudges me as we pass. He and some other workers carry boxes of natural food that fills the air with more welcoming aromas. Peaches, berries, and—are those strawberries? I salivate. I should have eaten before I left.

Dax raises his hand, stopping us right beside a waist-high table with green vegetables piled up on top. Taking a step back, he cocks his head, and gives me a look over. I fight the urge to throttle him.

"How big are you?" he asks when he's done sizing me up.

"Excuse me?" I say, bumping into the table. A few leafy greens fall off their piles, and I bend to pick them up.

"I asked how big you are," he says. "You aren't skinny, and you're tall for a girl. Doubt you could fit in a small. You wear what, a ten? I'm right, aren't I."

For a second, I stare. This guy can't be for real. My mind goes blank, unable to put together a coherent thought. "What does my clothing size have to do with anything?"

"Well, if you go out there in those fancy clothes, *Princesa*," he says, having the nerve to flick the string on my hoodie, "you'll fry."

Princesa? Who does he think I am? I'm not dressed in rags, but it's not like I own a personal scraper in Westlake. This is the only nice jacket I have, with or without the bloodstain. And while he may not see the holes in the liner, anyone who's barely glanced at a fashion feed knows it's not couture. I'm definitely not a princess.

"It's in the one-twenties in the Outer Grid right now," he continues, without explaining the dumb nickname. "One step outside this building in that city outfit, and you'll wish you were dead in five minutes. Our suits are the only piece of city-tech they'll allow out there. Trust me, you'll be grateful for every second it's on you. So, either give me your size and I'll get you some better clothes, or you can sweat like a pig the whole ride."

I crush the fallen vegetables between my fingers. This won't be the first guy I've decked.

"Look, if you think you can talk to me like—" I start, but Tori snatches my hand and pries the mangled plants from my grasp. She gives me a chastising look, and I clamp back on my retort. *Fine. I'll play nice.* It's not like I'll have to stay here with Razor's assistant for long.

"Eight," I say, letting off some steam in a long exhale. "I wear size eight." I've never told any male besides Uncle Trek my size. My cheeks feel like they're on fire. I pray this guy doesn't notice. I doubt he misses anything. He's probably getting a sadistic kick out of my surrender. Well, joke's on him. I don't want to die out in the heat—I want to die right now.

"There. That wasn't so hard, was it?" His focus turns to Tori.

"I'm a two," she offers before he asks.

"Perfect. Stay put." Tugging on his jacket, he disappears between the workers.

My muscles relax at his absence, and I lean against the table. I drop my bag at my feet. I swear the heat in here shot up ten notches.

"If he's going, I call not sitting by him," Tori says, leaning beside me.

"Oh, thanks," I say dryly. "You'd let *me* have that pleasure, huh?"

She shrugs. "You two are already hitting it off so well, I'd only get in the way."

I wipe my forehead with my jacket sleeve. "If by hitting it off you mean I'd end up clocking him, then I guess you're right."

She pushes my shoulder, and we laugh. I may have not planned for her to tag along, but I'm glad she did. Friends like Tori are hard to come by. Especially in a city prone to outcast anyone who can't follow the latest synth craze. Keeping up with these people is insane, and for me, impossible.

The reminder of my social status makes my insides cringe, and my stomach growls. I reach back, snap off a leaf from the vegetable behind me, and fold it into my mouth. Expecting the thing to taste like grass, I'm shocked when sweetness explodes across my tongue. *What is this?* Still chewing, I go for another leaf.

"What are you doing?" Tori asks, annoyed.

"You've got to try it." I hand her some.

She swats my hand away. "Or not. This place gives me the creeps. We don't even know anyone here let alone what that is."

"Maybe I can help," says a male voice behind us.

I jump off the table, whip my head around, and drop the leaves back where they came from. A tall guy with buzzed, blond hair is watching us with bemused gray eyes. He's dressed in a sleeveless charcoal uniform with a neon green "T" on his shoulder. From his oval baby face, I'm guessing he's about eighteen.

"My name's Zane," he says, flashing an ivory smile. "So, now you know someone." He flicks the leaf I dropped. "And that? That's poisonous. Probably shouldn't be eating it."

"What?" Tori and I exclaim together.

With the back of my jacket, I scrub my tongue, getting every flake off.

That is, until we notice Zane standing there laughing. "Kidding, kidding. Calm down, it's just a sweet leaf hybrid. Not poisonous, relax."

I stop wiping my tongue and glare at him. "What kind of a joke was that?"

He holds up both hands. "Sorry, couldn't help myself. Not every day we get newbies. But you probably shouldn't eat things around here if you don't know what they are. Anything on this table's fine, but some of this stuff will make you sick for a week. Here," he says, tossing me a green fruit from the table near him. "If you're hungry, eat that. We've got plenty of food to keep you well fed through the entire trip, so don't worry." He extends his hand. "Let's start over." He gives my hand a shake—quick and firm—then does the same with Tori.

"I'm Zane. Rig Seven Driver. Dax sent me to help you two with your things. But as usual, he didn't tell me your names."

"I'm Astoria and this is Juniper," Tori says before I can reply.

Zane's gaze drops down to her, and he smiles. "Beautiful names too," he murmurs to himself. "Pleased to meet you both. Here, let me get those." He points to Tori's bag, and she hands it to him. Then quickly grabbing mine, he slings them both over his shoulder like they weigh nothing. "All right. This way."

As his back turns on us, Tori grabs my arm and pulls me to her. A spark flickers in her eyes that I've seen time and time before. I know exactly what's going on in that pink-haired head of hers. This guy is *so* her type. *Wow*, she mouths to me, confirming my guess.

Oblivious to our silent conversation, Zane continues giving

information. "We sure are lucky you two came when you did. Three of our crew caught something awful yesterday. Been throwing up all night. One's a girl even." He slows to a stop, and we almost bump into him. "Not that it matters if she's a girl or not," he stammers, looking at us with red-tinged cheeks. "Except that, well, you two are girls, and the job can be rough. You know, for anyone. So, I thought it would be good you knew girls can do it no problem is all. Unless you weren't even worried that it might be hard on you. In which case I should shut my trap." He slides his hand over his face and starts walking again.

Tori grins and lifts her shoulders, all excited and giddy. I can't help but agree. Zane's flustering is cute. Hopefully we'll both get on his—what did he call it?—rig. We exit the food room and enter a narrow space filled with grated blue lockers stretching above our heads. The few people in here, some the burly men who opened the front door, stop what they're doing and stare as we walk in. After a while, they go about their business, still eyeing us.

"You can put your stuff here." Zane pounds a locker door with the side of his fist. The blue metal swings open with a squeal. "TARSH provides everything you'll need during the run. But if there's anything in these bags you can't live without, as long as it's small, you'd better get it now." He slides the bags off his arm and holds them out to us.

"Just one thing," Tori says. She digs through her bag and pulls out her inhaler. Her cheeks flare to match her bubblegum locks, then she puts the white device in her zebra pocket.

"That it?" He looks at me and I shake my head. "Perfect." He takes our bags back and stows them into the locker.

When he clicks it shut, Dax appears on the other side as though he'd been standing there the entire time. He tosses some clothes at me, and I catch them on sheer instinct.

"There," he says. "Those should fit. The girls' changing room is over there to the left. All you'll need is packed in the trucks, so hurry up and get dressed. We'll meet you back at the food processing room in five."

"Uh, thanks," I mutter, but he's already moved past us, not waiting around to see if we'd follow orders. "Real people person, that guy."

"That's the boss for you," Zane remarks, giving a quick nod in Dax's direction.

I blink. "Boss? He's a teen. I thought that Razor lady was your boss."

He shrugs. "Razor runs things here in the warehouse, not out there. Anyway, nineteen, twenty-nine, forty-five, none of that matters in the Grid. He does the job better than anyone. And he's dead serious about the five minutes, so you'd better change, and quick."

Flashing his pearly whites again, Zane leaves to join Dax, or the boss man. I feel my face scrunch at the thought of taking orders from him. Even so, I follow Tori through a steel door with an engraved "W" on the front.

I don't waste time. Who knows if Dax will up and leave us? I wouldn't put it past him. Quickly taking care of personal business, I hold up the charcoal pants he threw at me and puff out a skeptical grunt. *Like that's going to fit.* With one leg in and then the other, I pull it all the way up, no problem. I bend down into a stretch, amazed at its comfort. I move on to the flimsy chartreuse thing that's got to be a shirt—or a dishrag. I'm not sure. Pulling it over my head, it takes forever to find the armholes. It's a sea of green mesh fabric. *Ah, there they are.* My arms slide through, completely exposed, and I tug the bottom till it hangs loose at my waist.

As I reach for the green apple I'd placed on a bench near me, cold air sweeps over my skin. Goosebumps prick my arms. I rub the shirt's material between my fingers. Somehow, without hum or vibration, this shirt pushes cool air over me as I move. I look closer and notice a subtle scale pattern covering every inch of fabric. I bet that's what's cooling me down. I tuck in my shirt and slip on the thin jacket with a pale gray "T" across its shoulder and down the left side. At first, I thought it'd be just as hot as my hoodie, but the thin, scaled material gives it much better airflow.

"I look stupid." Emerging from her stall, Tori pinches up the shoulders of her poncho-like covering then lets it go. I take a bite of the fruit and scan her from top to bottom. I don't see stupid at all. Her dark gray uniform with a giant gray "T" slapped on her poncho is scale-patterned like mine. It's way too big but looks cool with the front tucked in her high-waisted black sash.

"You kidding me? You look awesome. All pink-haired-short-girl-assassin," I say, slicing the air with karate moves.

She makes a face. "Right. 'Cuz that's so me. At least yours fits," she says, reaching under her poncho-shirt to tug up her pants. "Come on, let's go. Don't want to be late for our trip through a barren wasteland."

When we reach the food preparation area, I spot our two guides standing by a door clear across the room. They don't spot us at first. Dax laughs with Zane, nudging him like they're best friends. Total opposite of how he acted around me earlier. But the second his gaze lands on me, his smile fades and he stares—brow furrowed.

A wave of heat crawls up my neck. I fiddle with the bottom of my jacket. "Tell me I'm not wearing this backward," I whisper to Tori.

She gives me a not-so-subtle once-over. "You're not wearing it backward."

"Then why is he giving me that weird look?" I ask, tossing the fruit core in the nearest garbage incinerator.

"Who knows? Maybe we went past his sacred dressing time limit."

On cue, Dax looks at an antique watch on his wrist, elbows Zane, and then strides out the far door. With a nod, Zane gestures for us to follow. They move fast. Lights flicker above us as we tear down narrow halls that twist and turn. Tori pulls out her inhaler, bringing it to her lips. These guys weren't kidding about being in a time crunch. A siren pulsates through the air. The voice in my head blares at me to turn back when everything happens in a blur.

We round the corner to see a large room erupting in chaos. Men run up ramps, tossing boxes into the backs of giant green vehicles. I remember seeing these beastly machines on shipper ads. I count six or seven trucks in all. With people zooming past and almost knocking me over, it's hard to tell how many of the vehicles cram in here. The tires on these things are almost as tall as I am. My intimidation level spikes. In front of the trucks, wide doors crack open to let in the artificial red dawn. Or . . . is that the *real* sun? I've never been this close to the edge of the city to see it.

I don't have time to make sure. Zane waves us to sprint toward one of the trucks. In seconds Dax is beside us, shouting orders.

"That's it!" he yells at no one in particular. "Close her up. Let's move!" He looks over at Zane then pats the rim of a tire. "You taking that one?"

Zane nods. They don't clarify. I assume he's talking about trucks. But when Dax grabs my wrist with a crushing grip, his meaning is so clear I want to jump out of my skin. Tori's going with Zane, and I'm not.

"Then you're with me, Princesa."

"WAIT, WHAT?" I YANK MY ARM WITH

no success. Dax has me in a death grip, dragging me away from the only friend I have in this frenzied warehouse. Worse yet, I'm the only friend Tori has here. Guilt seizes me in the gut as Tori disappears into the green truck after Zane—her eyes wide.

"Hang on," I protest when we round the next truck. "You can't separate us. Tori's here because of me. I've got to go with her."

Dax ignores me, moving faster.

"I said wait. I don't want to leave her." I tug again but he's too strong. "Are you listening?"

We reach the front of the metal giant. He pulls down a lime-colored ladder attached to the truck's side, releases my wrist, then waves me up.

I cross my arms and push my heels down till they are one with the concrete. I'm not going anywhere until he answers me.

His mouth tightens into a line, then he exhales through his nose. "Or you can stay here, I guess. Either way, there are still only two open seats. One on Zane's rig and one on mine. But I'm leaving now." His face is now inches from mine. "So, if you want a paycheck, you'll climb up there and sit your entitled rear in that chair. Clear?"

He spins away and rounds the truck before I can react. Entitled? No. Desperate for a paycheck and a way out of town? My shoulders slump. Escape is my real motivation, and it's a strong one. I'm sure Tori will be fine. The girl could make friends with a holo-ad. She can handle Zane.

She'll be fine, she'll be fine, my mind repeats the entire climb up the ladder. Once on the exposed side platform, I grab the railing to steady myself. *So, this is a shipper's truck.* The ad on my tiny holo-cuff screen did it no justice. Spacious doesn't begin to describe the platform, and I'm not even inside yet. This is the first moving ground vehicle I've been on aside from the subtrains. The thought pins me in motionless awe.

"Hey," Dax says about three feet to my left. Holding open the tinted door to what I think is called a cab, he beckons me to him. "This way." He's back in his seat before I make it to the door.

With a quaking rumble, the truck shakes to life. My knees buckle. The vibrations shoot up my legs straight to my heart. This is nothing like a subtrain. I stumble into my chair, grasping at everything I can to keep from falling over. My body tenses. Dax pulls levers and twists knobs like *he's* the machine. I refrain from death-gripping anything I can on this earthquake on wheels. Dax is cool and calculated—probably done this hundreds of times.

"Ready?" he asks, both hands on a wide-rimmed wheel.

"No," I say, fumbling with the strap for my seat. Everyone in the ads wears these things. Dax has one buckled across his chest too. All this jostling makes it hard to stay in the seat, and we haven't even left the station. "But I suppose we're leaving whether I am or not."

He laughs, then leans over and helps me click the strap in. "You catch on fast."

With one more lever cranked, the truck lurches forward. The force slams me against the seat, hard. My fingers claw into the metal armrests. We roll out of the shipping station's exit onto rocky terrain. The jagged concrete forms what was once called an expressway, or highway, I can't remember which.

Most roads were torn down soon after short-distance teleportation made moving ground vehicles obsolete. The only paved streets left connect the shippers to the Outer Grid. Though, from its horrible condition, city maintenance must not care about them.

Dax pushes a button by the rows of what look like vintage TV sets in front of us. Blurry images flicker across their screens. The top row shows different angles from outside the truck. Seven faces pop up on the row below, the last one Zane's.

"Status," Dax barks.

"All seven rigs rolling and accounted for." Zane's voice competes with bursts of static fuzz.

"Good." Dax lowers his sunglasses to the tip of his nose, shielding his eyes with his hand. He leans over the wheel then shoves the frames back up his face. "And our other problem?"

"Our scanners show the dome barrier's still open, sir," says a brawny, red-bearded driver. "But the warning light's still flashing hot. Fields will close in five."

Dax slams his palm on the wheel and curses under his breath. "Five? You sure, Rook?"

"No doubt," Rook says with a drawl that makes Razor's accent sound like she was raised in New York. "Countdown's tickin' away before my eyes."

"Then hail them. We need another minute or two."

The ginger shakes his head. "No go, sir. Hailed 'em twice already. They ain't responded to either."

Dax runs his fingers through his dark curls. The other drivers stay silent. They eye him every few seconds, worry etched across their faces.

"Keep hailing them Rook," he lets out at last. "Don't stop till that clock turns back or we're on the other side. Everyone has full permission to gun it. We're getting under that barrier, boys, with or without help."

My eyes go wide. "The barrier? As in the *city* barrier?" I fly as far forward as the belt will allow, angling my gaze up to the clouds. As I feared, a webbing of blue light sparks in and out of focus. Hexagonal patterns ignite across the morning sky on a transparent canvas. Like a blanket of electric rain, it begins its descent toward the ground.

How? How is this happening? The Quell already cleaned up the rebel attack this morning. The barrier shouldn't be closing now. Unless this is a drill. I rack my brain, trying to remember this morning's report. *New summer upgrades. No scheduled rain. A West End high-rise going up next Friday.* But nothing, not a word, on a routine barrier lockdown. The city would have told us. They always tell us when they lower the protection dome to test its defense capabilities.

Then it hits me. My face drains of blood. "This isn't a drill," I say, my voice shaking.

Dax doesn't respond. He's pressed against the wheel, his foot flat on the pedal. The acceleration glues me to the leather chair.

"Tell me we're not driving into a rebel attack." I need him to laugh it off.

His intense expression doesn't crack. Jaw tight, he drives on, indifferent to both the danger beyond and underneath the barrier. I'd throw my hands over my face if they weren't digging into my chair.

"Are you crazy?" I try to keep my voice from shaking. "That thing will crush us. Can't we wait here till it's up again?"

"No time. It could be down for weeks if we do. We'll make it," he says then clamps his mouth shut as if his words should both comfort me and make them true.

I push up on my seat and lift my eyes back to the sky. We're close. The barrier's bottom edge flares in warning. We won't make it. The dome wall is too wide and falling too fast for seven mammoth rigs to clear before it crushes us.

A heart-thumping electronic drone overpowers the rumble of the truck's engine. As we speed forward, the unbearable drone swells. Minutes burn into seconds. Before I know it, we're completely under the collapsing dome face. No longer transparent, the barrier blots out the sun with a ceiling of flashing midnight. Ahead, a thin strip of sunlight shrinks into a deadly line. My toes curl as all my muscles contract. So, this is how I'm going to die—like a bug squashed under the city's boot. With one last gulp, I twist into my chair, preparing for bone-crunching pain.

But instead, the air pressure around me shifts in a whoosh that pops my ears. With my body slammed against the seat, I look up at the sound. Dax yells out like an ancient movie cowboy, followed by relieved cheers from the TV screens. Blessed sunlight pours in from all directions. I let out so much pent-up breath I double over. I close my eyes to calm the jitters raging inside me when the loudest guttural boom I've ever heard flings them open.

I jolt forward. "What was . . . was that the barrier?" I've never heard it close like that before. Not in Houston, or the Plex, or any other domed city I've lived in.

Dax nods, finally acknowledging my presence. "No sound dampeners on this side, Princesa," he says then mutters, "There's a whole lot of *nothing* on this side." He flips a few switches and checks some circular monitors. "Everyone make it through?"

"Rig two rolling, sir," says Rook. "Thank God."

"Rig three's still alive. That was mighty close, sir."

As the drivers check in, I gaze out the front window. What have I gotten myself into? Minutes in and I'm not only separated from my best friend, but also nearly crushed to death by a massive dome wall. Not to mention Dax is right about what's out here. Absolute squat. The rocky, coal-black highway extends as far as I can see. Both sides house dilapidated buildings and dead or dying trees. And everything—every square inch—is covered in yellow-brown dirt. Paradise, for sure.

At least we didn't run into a rebel stampede. I'll take a long boring drive through a scorching wasteland over an ambush of murderous thugs any day. I've seen the newscasts. Rebels bombing city outposts. With their explosives, wild eyes, and infatuation with slaughtering all things cyber, they'd be a blast to meet. It definitely could be much wor—

An enormous, winged animal circling above us pulls me from my thoughts. Weird. I didn't think I'd see any grid beasts so soon. I thought the strange, mutated creatures lived much further in. But the giant black bird is there, right outside the city. Or at least, I think it's a bird.

It grows larger by the second. My breath stills. That's not a bird. Not at all. What I took for feathers are many metal plates jutting out the sides of a ship. Bright red rings explode from the ship's belly, orbiting the craft in a gyro motion. I shrink into my seat as it lands in our path.

"Dax? Dax!" I shout, interrupting whoever was next in his check-in.

"What in the—" Dax yanks the wheel.

The rear of the truck whips to the side.

I grip the strap across my chest, but my body lurches to the left. Thick clouds of dirt billow out beneath us. I struggle to make out anything through the haze when Dax slams on the brakes and I jolt forward. An inescapable squeal slices my eardrums. Everything around me shakes. I squeeze my fists till they hurt.

And then we stop.

I'm thrust against the belt and then smacked back into the chair, the wind knocked from my chest. It's a good while before I can breathe again. The dirt dissipates into a hazy layer of film on the shield. The other trucks must have kept their distance as none of them hit us. Dax flips a switch near the wheel, and two blades swipe across the shield, clearing it from the debris.

About fifty feet ahead, the two-story ship spins to a motionless halt. I squint. Through the toppling rings, I see a circular emblem on its side. I recognize the "Q" with the three sideways slashes of red in the emblem's core. It's not the awful tangerine circle of Orange Pipe, but equally as menacing. My heart goes cold.

"Tell me that's not what I think that is," I manage to whisper.

"A Quell ship," Dax answers, like I wish he wouldn't. "But we've got worse problems," he says then bangs on the TV set closest to me. I look from his paling face to the screen he's beating. Screen seven. Zane's screen. Tori's screen.

It's the only screen full of static.

"RIG SEVEN? COME IN SEVEN. ZANE,

you'd better answer." Dax knocks on Rig seven's TV screen over and over, but it does no good. Tori's screen is silent. Still swirling with gray and white static. Each bang of Dax's fist sends a chill down my spine.

After about the tenth bang, my shock subsides and I come to, clawing at my belt lock. I've got to see for myself. To make sure my best friend didn't get smashed by a thousand-ton dome wall. I've almost got the strap unlatched when Dax's hand crushes mine.

"Hey, hey," he says, holding on till I look up at him. "Don't even think about it. We've got Quell eyes on us now. You step outside without their say so, and they'll shoot you dead."

I inhale a shaky breath. I know he's right. The Quell is yet another reason not to cross the waste aboveground. City police are pushover babysitters compared to the Grid's Quell. Or at least, what I've heard about them. I don't want to test the rumors, but my heart and guilt refuse to concede. "Tori—she had to make it through. I have to check."

"No. You have to stay seated," he states. "You're no good to your friend dead." He squeezes my hand to emphasize his point then releases. "What's going on back there, Cyrus?" He turns a knob by the sixth screen. "Rigs two and three are blocking my rear cams. Tell me you have eyes on Zane."

The man with deep brown skin and a maroon bandana around his neck swipes beads of sweat from his bald head. "Naw," he says, his voice a low baritone. "All I see is black metal and red lights. Quell ship's right up my six."

"They've pinned us in real good," says Rook. "Ain't responded to a single hail, then jump us like flies on manure the second we're through that wall. Gotta keep us all in line, else we make 'em look like pitchforks without tines."

"Watch it, Rook," Dax snaps. "You're on an open channel. Everyone, stick to protocol. Keep visuals running but go to radio silence until we're cleared." Turning the knob till it clicks, Dax sinks into his chair, running a hand over his jaw.

I pull some strands at the nape of my neck and braid. My eyes lock with the black and white jumble on screen seven, hoping it'll come back to life. My thoughts singe with images of Tori, the barrier, and body parts mangled in metal and blood. Like fingernails screeching through my brain, I cringe at the possibility. But I shake myself out of it. I've got to focus elsewhere before I explode with anxiety.

I tilt my head to watch the Quell ship settle. The blades I mistook for wings fold down on both sides to keep its egg-like frame from rolling over. A thin panel slides out from its sleek black body, forming a ramp to the cracked road below. Through a puff of smoke, a slender being, followed by several massive ones, emerge onto the ramp. I stare at the battle-clad androids moving toward us. Bodies decked in metal and wires, they're nothing more than robotic war machines. No one can be *that* synthetic and still human.

Part of me is thankful. I've only heard stories or watched newscasts on my holo-cuff about the Quell. Never encountered one in person. The other part wishes I knew what to expect.

"What do they want with us?" I ask, hoping Dax has dealt with these guys before.

"Don't know," he says with a shrug. "Give me a speeding ticket?"

I cough a dry laugh. *A speeding ticket?* We're not in a skycab, and there's no one else out here. Why would anyone care about traffic laws in the Grid? "Yeah, I doubt that," I say. "You aren't carrying anything illegal in these trucks, are you?"

He answers with an annoyed frown.

"What?" I toss up a hand. "They're called the Quell. And they look like robot monsters. Don't think they're here to wish you a happy birthday is all."

Dax pulls up his sleeve to look at his vintage watch. "Our rigs are checked and rechecked dozens of times over before each run. We're not dumb enough to drag illegal anything into the Grid. I've no idea what they want, but we're about to find out."

The thin Quell agent plants itself outside Dax's side of the rig. The rest follow suit, making it clear which one is in charge. From my angle, the leader's body looks feminine, appearing to have a curvy hip. Outstretching its arm toward us in one sudden move, it spreads its fingers wide. Within its armor-plated palm, a red, circular light pulses bright. The truck rattles. Dax's door flies open. Metal slams against metal.

My hands cover my ears too late. The ringing in my head echoes then fades. Lowering my hands, I catch the tail end of a female voice calling us outside.

". . . of this truck are immediately ordered to evacuate the vehicle for questioning." Her two-tone voice is thick with auto-tuned electronic notes. I've heard false voice boxes several times— usually in synth singers. They have a slight harmonic double pitch that makes it sound like someone is speaking in two keys at once. But I've never heard it with such a grinding edge.

"I will only ask once," she finishes.

"You heard the lady." Dax unstraps his belt and moves out of his chair. He turns toward his open door. "Hope she's got my birthday present down there." He hops out of his chair and doesn't wait for me to follow.

I swallow the lump of fear rising in my throat at meeting deadly machine people and unlatch my buckle. Coming around the space behind our seats, I step out onto the platform behind Dax. My face roasts in the sun's rays. Heat wiggles up in waves off the dry ground like snakes sucked into the sky. Each breath invades my mouth, hot and thick. I wonder how it's possible to survive this climate, when a rush of cool air slides over my skin from beneath my clothing. It glides past my face, making the air easier to breathe. I remember the sensation from when I first put it on. It's temperature regulated. No wonder Dax insisted we wear this. I can't imagine what I'd be going through in my yellow jacket right now. I wish I had time to relish the small comfort, but Dax is already on the lowered ladder, gesturing me to him.

I take one rung at a time, stalling as much as I can. But the rungs aren't infinite, and I'm forced to step off the ladder. The moment my feet touch the ground, I move close to Dax. He may be a jerk, but at least he is a human jerk. And one that seems to be trying to keep me alive. It's more than I can say for robot lady, who ripped our truck door open without touching it.

A few feet away, ten or so Quell form a semicircle around us and the truck. The line of shipper trucks zigzags back toward the city. I stand on my tiptoes and try to catch sight of Zane's missing truck. Of any sign at all that my best friend is alive. One truck. Two. Three. The gap disappears with synthetic bodies blocking my view. Soon, their figures mesh into a sea of geometric pewter plating and blinking lights.

The female-shaped robot wastes no time approaching us. There's something printed in bold white lettering across its collarbone. EVOLEN-6. It might be its name or title as none of the others have writing on their bodies.

I stare at my reflection on its slick, crimson helmet. I wince—the petrified look on the girl staring isn't doing me any favors. Bringing my shoulders back, I try to put on my best I'm-not-afraid-of-you face. I seem a smidge tougher. The Quell agent doesn't flinch.

It brushes a finger over the side of its head. The shiny red plating from chin to forehead slides up, letting out a whoosh of air. Underneath, a human face appears—an average, fleshly, human face. Well, not *average*. Her choppy sable hair frames alabaster skin so flawless it might as well be glass. Her eyes—two oceans of black with hallowed disks of electric blue in their center—don't hold a speck of compassion. And her synthetics have me staring. Wires protrude from her chin to collarbone. Blue cyber tattoos replace her brows, and the rest of her is full metal. She's a total hardsuit. I've heard of hardsuits. People who've had so many military augmentations they're more machine than human. I'd never actually met one.

"Driver," she says, fixing her creepy robot eyes on Dax. "Tell me. Are your signal receivers broken in that moving heap? Or did you deliberately ignore our warnings of a full-scale barrier lockdown?"

Dax crosses his arms and meets those eyes. I don't know how he does it. This lady has got an intimidation factor of a billion, and he's standing there unfazed.

"No, *ma'am.*" He stresses the courtesy title in contempt. "Our receivers work fine. But looks like our hailing system is all jacked up. My communications man hailed your base more than once for extra time. And what do you know, that wall still came crashing down."

It takes everything in me not to smack him. Never thought I'd die vaporized via sarcasm.

EVOLEN-6 lifts her sharp chin. "A nonresponse and the barrier continuing its descent should have been answer enough. What was so important to risk outright rebellion and death?"

I glance at Dax, curious to know the answer.

He laughs, as if the reasons are obvious. "We're two full days behind schedule on a shipping run to the south farm. Who knows how long this unscheduled lockdown could last. Missing this run means millions go without natural food across the state. *You* may be okay with synth food, but I'm not about to let thousands of people with synth allergies starve."

I recoil. His response makes sense, even makes me feel better about going under that barrier. But his smug delivery stinks.

A snarl curls EVOLEN-6's blood-red lips. "Heroic. Except the part when you and your crew brought city-tech into the Outer Grid."

Dax hesitates. "I don't know what you're talking about."

So, he *did* smuggle something out here. I can't believe it. And after the hard time he gave Tori and me about leaving our city-tech too. My jaw tightens so hard it pops. What, did he think he wouldn't get caught? I almost round on him, but EVOLEN-6 jumps in first.

"You don't?" she asks. "And yet, all your vitals say you do. What is your name, driver?"

Dax hesitates longer this time before answering. His body leans as far away from the Quell agent as possible. "Daxal Garza, TARSH Supervising Shipper."

She acts indifferent to the title. "Well, Mr. Garza, consider you and your team fortunate. While I should drag you in for questioning, the barrier is down. Not only that, but I've got a rebel outbreak to deal with in the north." She steps closer, imperious. "Don't think because I can't spare enough men to haul you all off to our outpost we're letting this insurgence slide. I take it you'll be able to perform your precious delivery minus one city-tech smuggling truck?"

Confusion flares across Dax's face. And then something dawns on him and his jaw drops. "My seventh rig? You *took* it?"

At his words, emotions mix and swirl. Relief. Dread. Anger.

"Tori," I whisper.

"Don't act surprised," robot woman continues. "If you're the head of your operation, then you know the consequences of breaking the city-tech ban. After we take that truck apart bolt by bolt, we will interrogate your crew. Only when we're satisfied they pose no threat, will we return them to you. Keep your signal receivers on for our hail. And when you get it, I suggest you comply." She cuts a path through her minions straight to her ship.

My world breaks into slow motion. Each step the woman takes, each ragged breath escaping my lips, is like a century passing. Those machine people are leaving—getting in that gigantic ship of fear and taking my best friend with them. And I'm letting them go.

Something like an electric shock sparks through me, charging me from my stupor. My limbs move without permission. Before I realize it, I'm there, grabbing machine lady, yanking her around. It's a miracle I'm not dead.

"No! Please, you can't take her." I hope I don't sound as pathetic as my ears let on.

EVOLEN-6 cocks her head to the side, sending a train of loud pops from her neck. She examines me head to toe and back again.

Her nostrils flare and her tattooed brows dip into a V sharp enough to cut steel. It's only then that my brain catches up with my mistake.

The hardsuit raises her hand, her fury clear and mortifying. I flinch but am unable to move away. In one terrifying breath, she whips the back of her hand across my temple. The world topples over itself. A lightning bolt of raw pain courses through my face. Limp and ragged, my body crumples against the dirt. A jumbled blur of Dax's boots runs toward me. But before they reach me, my vision fuzzes and fades to black.

A DULL ACHE THROBS AT THE BASE

of my skull when I wake. It takes forever to open my eyes. When I do, I'm met with a blur of gray and blinding white. I blink away the haze, and the ground beneath me shakes. My grogginess vanishes. Flat on my back, my fingers dig into a leathery surface. It's not dirt, not rock, and not the Grid I collapsed on. I bolt upright. The sudden movement sends the room into a spin. Assuming I'm in a room—on a fault line. When the spinning fades, pressure explodes in my head, ready to crush my brain to goo.

I groan, pushing my palms against my temple.

"Afternoon, sunshine," says a raspy male voice beside me. I lower my hands and blink again, the haze still somewhat there. Deep gray blurs sharpen into a dark form-fitting jacket with a light "T" across the chest. Still wearing his shades and sitting in the driver's seat of his rig, Dax glances at me then out the front window again.

"Wha—what happened?" My words muddle into a soup of confusion.

"You don't remember?"

"I think I . . ." I slide my hand through sticky blue hair strands to ease my aching neck. My fingers brush a lump beside my ear, and pain spiderwebs through my whole head. "Ssss," I inhale sharply, holding my breath till the throbbing fades a little. "Feels like a porter malfunctioned me into a wall."

Dax laughs dryly. "More like you got your lights knocked out by a Quell officer on a power trip." He reaches into a rectangular cavity of what I think is the dash.

"I what?" The hardsuit's metal fist flying at my face flashes through my mind. I wince. "Oh. Yeah. How could I forget?" I let go of my neck. I must have gotten that lump when I hit the ground. I run my fingers over my left temple where EVOLEN-6 struck me. It's tender, even more so than the lump. When I check my hand, I'm grateful it's not spotted with blood. I bet it's dark purple by now. There are plenty of metal surfaces in this cab, but they're all covered in grime. Every part of my reflection is a discolored blob.

"But how did I get here?" I ask. "I remember being on the ground and . . ." I skim my surroundings, losing track of thought. Unlike Dax's seat, my chair is flat, more like a bed. A leather strap is tight across my waist, securing me as the truck jostles and quakes.

Outside, the real sun has climbed to the top of the sky. Like a beacon on an invisible scraper during a blackout, its rays light up everything they touch. Broken trees and sparse vegetation sprinkle both sides of the ragged highway. Their shadows seared to nothing by the blazing torch above. Even in the chilled comfort of the truck, I can sense its warmth—remember the few seconds I baked beneath it. As a kid, I spent hours imagining what it'd be like to stand under the real sun. I had no idea. The Grid is nothing like the controlled cities. Sheltered from the elements, the cities are lit with a 24/7 artificial glow. Now that I think about it, I've only seen the real sun in the movies and documentaries my uncle watches. During last week's mandatory family time, we watched a two-hour docu-feed on the ancients and how they used the sun's position in the sky to tell time. Uncle Trek said it was useful info. More like useful for a nap.

And then it hits me. "How long have I been out?"

"Four and a half hours." At least I think that's what he said. Either he's forgotten how to enunciate, or he's stuffed his face full of food. "Our medic, Slate, bandaged you up. Got you back in the rig right after the Quell left. You've been going in and out of consciousness since Houston. Unloaded all the trucks without you, and we're headed back to the farm now."

My brain fogs over. He spoke more clearly that time, but nothing he said makes sense. "Did you say four and a half–" I start then stop as I watch him shove, well I don't know what it is, into his mouth.

"Hours? Yep." He wipes his cheek with the back of his sleeve. "You missed the real pretty part too."

"Oh, really?" I listen to him talk with a full mouth. "What are you eating?"

His thick brows rise over the rim of his glasses. He lifts a super fat sandwich thing and spins it around like it's on a revolving display.

"Want a bite?" At least he swallowed first.

I lean as far away as I can without falling out of the chair. "No. Pretty sure my mouth can't fit over that . . . that . . ." I gesture at the monstrosity.

He grins. "That what? Never seen a sandwich before?" He's killing it in the understatement game.

"That's not *a* sandwich," I inform him. "It's a whole plate of sandwiches smashed together. How can you eat that?"

He takes a bite so giant it seems impossible. I shudder. I can't tell everything that's on that thing, but it reeks of pickles, peanut butter, and baked beans. A mess of fruit chunks and plant leaves spill out the sides. And the whole thing–peppered meat, white sauce, and all–sits three inches thick between two slimy doughnuts. To top it all off, my rebellious stomach growls. It gives him an unspoken cue to offer me Frankensandwich again.

I shrink away a second time. "No, I'm good."

He shrugs and wraps it back in the paper it was in, using his knee to steer. "Guess it's no synth food, but hey, your loss. There are some bars in that cabinet by your feet if you want something else. It's not like we're stopping for anything."

Of course we aren't stopping for food. Even if one of the rare run-down buildings we pass was a restaurant, the chances of someone manning it are as high as me finishing off Dax's sandwich. I unbuckle my waist and crouch down. Instinctively, I run a finger over the cabinet's smooth pewter surface. Nothing happens. After a few tries, I look back at Dax, frustrated.

"No city-tech in the Outer Grid, Princesa. There's a handle on the side."

I let out a puff, annoyed by my deep dependence on tech and how fitting his irritating nickname sounds right now. In my defense, the handle by the cabinet's edge is a small crevasse and near invisible. A fact that barely eases my embarrassment. I've got to get used to this low-tech world fast. Being a newbie burden is about as awesome as taking orders from my aunt and uncle.

I reach in and retrieve a bar that looks filled with food. I open the wrapper and am met with a sweet-smelling brown square. Taking a bite, I scoot back in my seat, determined to fix this flat chair without Dax's help. Engraved circles spread across the armrest remind me of tiny touchpads. An angular lever also rests by my hip.

Low-tech. Think low-tech. I skip the probably-not-touchpads to pull the lever. The top half of my chair springs up and smacks my back. Proud, I chance a look at Dax. His half grin fades the second I see him. My own delight lingers longer than it should. It's a lame victory, but the only one I've had lately, aside from escaping my fate.

I take another bite of whatever this stuff is. I enjoy the fruity tang, then instantly feel guilty I can't share it with Tori. How did things go belly-up so fast? I'll never forgive myself if anything happens to her.

"The Quell," I say, breaking the silence we've lulled into, "you think they'll keep their word? Bring Tori and Zane back safely?"

Dax grunts. "Doubt it."

His words hit me as hard as the Quell's fist to my face. How can he say something so horrifying with complete nonchalance?

Those glasses turn my way and he sighs. "Look. I'm not going to water it down. The Quell have my rig, and you can't trust the Quell in the Outer Grid. Anyone who's traveled the highways knows that. Best you can do is stay out of their way. And you never, *ever* break the city-tech ban." There's an accusatory bite to his tone.

Heat burns my ears. I know exactly what he's getting at. "You think this is *my* fault? Don't know if you've noticed, but I've been sitting on *your* truck the whole time. It's not like there's a porter in here to flash over and sabotage my best friend."

"Never said *you* did anything." His meaning is clear.

"Tori? You think Tori smuggled city-tech onto Zane's rig?" It's such an insane thought that I can barely contain a laugh. He doesn't try to deny it, so I go on. "Here I am thinking I'm the one with the head injury. You took away everything we came with, remember?"

"Yeah," he says, "and I also swept each truck. Twice. They were spotless. It's you two we didn't get a proper scan on." He runs a hand through his hair. "Besides the fact that you're both low-grade synths, I know nothing about you."

Low-grade. Well, that's Tori for sure. As for me, queen of boxed blue hair dye, I bet he'd choke on that sandwich if he knew how low-grade I am.

"Can you think of anything we missed," he continues, "concealable upgrades she might've had on her? Or something she brought?"

I count to ten in my head before answering. This guy's ability to listen is pretty much nil. "Unless those hardsuits consider pink hair city-tech, then no. You took everything." I say the last part with as much oomph as I can muster, hoping it sinks in. But I'm sure all I did was make him mad.

Silence stiffens the air between us. He leans over the wheel, his shoulders touching his wrists. The scowl on his face steams out anger hotter than the heat waving off the asphalt outside. I wiggle in my seat, uncomfortable in any position. I don't think what I said was *that* bad, but I don't know. Aunt Marna always said I've got a tongue sharper than steel.

The suffocating quiet grows until I'm about to burst. "Look," I say, trying to come up with an apology that doesn't negate my position. "All I'm saying is, you may not know my friend, but I do. If she had an upgrade, I'd be the first to—"

"Shush," he quiets me, leaning toward the window.

"Okay fine. Never mind then. It's not like I was trying—"

"Quiet," he chastises me again. "You hear that?"

I clamp my mouth shut and hear nothing but my irritated breath and the engine growl. Seconds pass before a high-pitched squeal whizzes by my ear. I turn. There's nothing out my window but hills of dirt, waste, and burnt trees. Each sight more static than the last. Another squeal sounds in Dax's direction. I whirl around. He leans forward to push a flashing button by the rig monitors.

"Tell me you ain't hearing that boss," says Rook from the screen below, his audio popping on with a click and a buzz.

"I hear it."

The rest of the crew eyes him with nervous glances through the boxes. His response must have been far from settling.

"Shouldn't we be stopping then?" asks a girl with a burgundy-bobbed haircut in the middle screen. She leans in front of her tattooed driver. "Get off the road. Find shelter or something?"

Find shelter? Whatever's got these shippers in a panic, it can't be good. My mind races to the worst thing I heard happens in the Outer Grid. A Weather Flux. I bite my lip, hoping I'm wrong. Weather Fluxes are the biggest reason to stay out of the Outer Grid. Monsoons change deserts into swamps overnight through chemically gorged rainfall. Ice storms ravage the south, dropping hail big enough to kill a grown man. Earthquakes form mountains in the blink of an eye. They've drilled the stories into us since kindergarten as a warning. But I don't know a single teacher who told us what to do if we found ourselves *in* one. I guess the school system never expected any of us to come out here.

"Sir?" probes the tattooed driver when Dax doesn't respond.

Unaltered, Dax shakes his head. "No, we keep going. The fueling station's only a few miles from here. We can't afford to stop."

The squeals intensify, now carrying bone-rattling low tones that rocket my pulse. I cover my ears, unable to escape the noise.

"But sir," says Rook, shouting over the squeals, "we're in the direct path of a whaler call. If we keep going it might—"

"What would you have me do, Rook?" snaps Dax. "Hunt through these buildings, hoping one of them is big enough to hold us all till it passes? Even if I did, that whaler's path can change any second. We're just as dead out there as we are here. No, our best bet is the station garage." He pushes a button that kills the audio feed between rigs and slams his foot down.

"What's going on?" I shout, my back glued to the chair. "What's a whaler? Why are we running from it?"

"Not an *it*, a *they*," he replies. "Whalers are a hunting tribe. And we're running from what they're about to drag up."

My temples throb in confusion. The dread in his tone makes me think I should be terrified at his words, but instead, I'm more lost than ever. I've heard about whales in school—giant fish or mammals that once swam in oceans and now live in zoos I've never visited. Maybe whale means something else out here, because there's not a single drop of water in sight let alone any ocean. Then again, Dax's lips purse tight and a plethora of anxious looks rise from the screens beside me. I've got a bad feeling I'm the one in for the shock.

But then relief softens Dax's face. He mouths something I can't hear over the noise.

"What?" I shout louder.

"The fueling station." He points toward the horizon. "We're almost there."

A handful of rectangular towers cluster together at the far end of the road in a tight pack. Equidistant from each other, they form a circular crown of intact buildings. Sunlight reflects off their surfaces in shimmering burnt orange against the cerulean sky. Beautiful. Elegant. Like buried bars of gold sticking out of the sand. Dax was right. There are at least *some* pretty parts in the Outer Grid.

As we drive closer though, the earth beside the road bulges. I blink. I didn't know I could see mirages while in a truck. But when I look again, it's there, worse than before. Everything around us is flat—the dirt, the road, even the old buildings. Everything, except for one growing hill I swear wasn't there seconds ago. The swelled earth cracks like an egg. The few dead trees on the hill rise then snap at the roots.

"What is that?" I point a shaking finger out the window. I'm not sure Dax can hear me over all the shrills. Right as I take a breath to warn him again, silence encases my voice.

Only the ghosts of squeals, whistles, and hums linger. Even the rig's rumble hushes. It's an uncanny quiet.

Dax mutters a curse to himself. He shifts his leg. The truck slows to a halt a city block or so from the fueling station towers.

I'm afraid to ask but do so anyway. "What's wrong? Why did we stop?"

He pushes himself back into the chair, wincing. "Brace yourself."

I don't ask. I clutch the armrests of my chair until my knuckles whiten. The earth shakes, and the rig teeters. In an explosion of rock, roots, and tree limbs, a beast that only lives in nightmares breaks through the ground.

A terrible mixture of fear and awe surges through me. Out of the earth, an enormous, oil-slicked beast with claws for fins bursts through the dirt. Time slows. Several stories high, the thing the size of a subtrain transcends. The engorged imposter bird blots out the sun. Up, up, up, it goes, until it touches the sky. Then, turning its spike-covered head, the creature plummets right into the road in front of us.

Chunks of concrete soar at my face.

THUD, THUD! CRACK! CRACK! CRACK!

Huge pieces of road explode from the mutant whale's reentry spot and spiral at my face. Rock after rock hits the windshield with violent jolts. Though none break through, they fracture the glass into sickening webs. I throw my arms over my head. I can't escape the chaotic rain of concrete pounding the shield.

Dax pushes the button on my belt and yanks me off the chair. He's on me in an instant, unsnapping his jacket and covering us both. He pushes a button buried within the jacket's lining before shoving me down further. I hear something like metal colliding against itself come from his back. I have no idea what made that noise. Not with my head stuck between my knees and his torso.

The windshield bursts with an ear-slicing blast. Pieces of glass and rock rip into the rig. They clang against whatever metal Dax wears for cover. But it doesn't shield us completely. One shard slices the skin on my calf. Pain spikes up my leg. I utter a squeaky cry. My eyes squeeze together, and my inner vision tunnels into a kaleidoscope of dancing black shapes.

Then everything stills. We stay there for ages. Breathing, shaking, praying. I don't know how long it is before my muscles relax. I push up, but Dax's presence resists me. I try again, harder.

"Oh . . . sorry," he says. I hear him click the button in his jacket again. As the metal retracts, glass falls to the floor, and he eases away from me.

I struggle to move from the cramped position. There was barely enough room for the both of us down here, and my legs are twisted around my chair.

"Is it gone?"

Glass is everywhere, covering the hood of the rig with its cratered dents, the floor, my seat. I'm forced to stand, hunched over as my head grazes the roof.

Dax nods, shaking off the debris from his jacket and rising. "They never stay in one place when they're hunted." He looks out the broken window as if expecting something to drop from the sky. "Whalers should be here soon."

As if on cue, the piercing whaler's call echoes his words. Only this time, its makers follow the sound. Hoots and cries trail a cloud of people zooming past us on their rickety flying machines. They head straight toward the hole in the road. I'm not sure how their crafts move with such precision, as old and rusted as they are.

Strange vehicles and stranger drivers. Garbed in layers of earth-toned rags that flap in the wind, the whalers remind me of rebels. Only ten times wilder. Mohawks, dreadlocks, and colorful feathers blow about on the heads of men and women alike. Many of them wear giant goggles of every shade over their eyes or around their necks. Some whalers sport pale, striped paint on skin as diverse as the rainbow. Others are wrapped up to their eyeballs in torn cloth like mummies. Unique yet unified, they swarm over the wasteland.

But how are they flying? The city-tech ban should extend to everyone except the Quell in the Outer Grid.

"How can they be—" A burst of air punches through the rig and whips blue hair into my face before I can finish my thought. I'm knocked back. My calf slams against the edge of my seat. Pain shoots up my leg. I clench my teeth, bending over to cover the wound.

Outside, one of the whalers flies his craft above the broken windshield. His maroon vehicle pushes hot air onto the dented hood and through our cab. Its engine chugs in guttural rumbles. With a single seat and a pair of handlebars underneath a bug-crusted shield, the craft holds a lone driver. A driver who doesn't mind sitting on a pile of caked dirt. I can't tell if it's dirt or old paint swirling over the inverted trapezoidal frame.

Who knows? All these vehicles are faded. And not all of them fly. Some ride atop vehicles with a single tire as big as a rig wheel, spinning to a stop like a twisting coin. Others hang off machines resembling ancient pirate ships more than trucks. Whalers lean this way and that off the sides as they grip on ropes attached to massive sails. A few ride paneled homes smashed onto outstretched wheels, smoke billowing behind them. They yip and holler and trill their tongues, waving long poles with feathers tied to the ends.

The whaler in front of us, a lanky man with sunbaked skin, releases his grip from the handlebars. He pulls down a tattered bandana that covered his lower face. Sitting tall on his craft, he grabs his grimy goggles and slides them up onto his dusty hat. He must not take his goggles off much. The skin around his large eyes is a much lighter shade of brown than the rest of his face. His nose bends to the side, like it's been broken more than once. A white strip holds it straight at the bridge. His gaze slides past me like I'm background noise. But his lips twist upward when he spots Dax. He chuckles to himself then leans back, looking at Dax with smug surprise.

"Well, looky here." His raspy tenor voice bounces over the hum of his engine. "If it ain't our state's finest delivery service. Hope our hunt on *our* territory didn't cause you too much trouble, *city* boy." He leans over his handlebars and extends his pierced lower lip in a fake pout. I have no idea why he's emphasizing certain words. It's like he's having some weird inside joke with himself.

"We're fine," Dax snaps. "My truck though . . . it'd be better off if a terra cetus hadn't landed in front of it. But you already know that."

Gray hat man gives the rig a look over and shrugs. "That can happen. Don't worry. It's only cosmetic."

Dax gives a harsh laugh. "Cosmetic?" He shuffles through the glass-and-debris littered cab and waves his arms. "You call this cosmetic damage? I've got no windshield, an interior that's torn to shreds, and who knows how badly that thing messed up my engine."

The man's tongue toys with one of the many white rings looped around his lip. He cocks his head to the side. "Could've been worse."

"You're right," Dax says with disdain. "You could have forced that terra cetus right on top of us. Instead, you pushed it there for a cheap warning shot. Don't give me that territory line. These highways are protected transit, and you know it."

I cringe. Is he out to make enemies of everyone he meets? Even if he is right, antagonizing this guy doesn't seem smart.

The whaler frowns, narrowing his dark eyes. "Outer Grid's a tough place. Maybe you should turn around and take them trucks to a wirehead in that city you came from. I'm sure they'll know what to do with it." He pulls his goggles back over his eyes and twists his handlebars, ending the conversation. The rusty hovercraft roars and flies off to join the tail end of his tribe.

Dax grunts. Then, as if nothing happened, he brushes off his chair and flicks some switches. My head fills with questions faster than I can form a sentence.

"Who was that—how did you know him? That monster thing! It's not possible. It's not—why didn't you tell me? Someone should have told me."

Dax ignores my incoherent rambling, continuing his tasks. "Thank you, Dax, for saving my life," he says in a terrible, high-pitched imitation of me. The normal pitch resumes. "De nada, Princesa. Glad that rock didn't smash up your pretty face."

I blink at the word *pretty*. Every question I had bursts into as many pieces as the glass on my chair. I turn my back, willing my flushed cheeks under control. He's right. If it weren't for him, I'd have glass sticking out of my face right now.

"Thanks," I mutter.

I hear his fiddling stop. When I check to see if he's still there, his one-sided smirk brings out two, deep-set dimples. He's enjoying this. My embarrassment burns into irritation.

"Sorry," he says, and dips his brows in fake confusion. "What was that?"

I force a long breath through my teeth. "Thank you," I say, loud enough so I don't have to repeat myself again. "For helping me with the rocks."

His smirk spreads into an all-out smile. "It was nothing, Princesa. Don't mention it."

I grind my teeth. There it is again. *Princesa.*

"It's Juniper," I say through tight lips.

"What's juniper?"

"My name. My name is Juniper. Not *Princesa.* I don't even care if you call me Juna. If we're stuck together on this trip with kidnapping hardsuits and giant fish moles, then you can at least call me by my name. I get it, I'm a sheltered city girl who knows nothing about the Outer Grid. But maybe you could, I don't know, *teach* me about it so I won't be such a pain in your neck when something weird happens that might get us killed."

He stares at me, mute.

"What?" I ask.

"Nothing," he says at last. "I'm just surprised you know what a mole is."

I narrow my eyes till I can barely see out of them.

"Okay, okay," he concedes, hands raised in mock defense. "It's called a terra cetus. Monster whale of the dirt. Ever heard of the grid beasts?"

I nod. In all the cities I've lived in, teachers told two stories about the Outer Grid. One about Weather Fluxes and the other on the mutated animals known as grid beasts. Weather Fluxes, I assumed, to keep us from venturing beyond the protective barrier. Grid beasts because they had to tell us.

Every now and again, a beast made its way into city limits, needing to be explained. A lizard with butterfly wings or a frog covered in feathers, showing up in bedrooms and restaurant floors make people nervous. Especially when man's best friend was robotic, and the only natural animals live in controlled zoos or farms.

Since every one of my teachers told the same story, I believed them. They said the Weather Collapse caused all the problems. That the government tried to fix the climate by assaulting the sky with chemicals, which made things worse. I didn't question when they said everything outside domed cities during the collapse mutated, and only the small grid beasts survived. But now, I fear how many other lies I've been bottle-fed.

"I didn't expect any of them to be so big," I say.

"No, I'll bet you didn't. City's been regurgitating that lie since the moment they tried to play God." He sits then motions for me to do the same. I brush off the glass and rocks, picking up as many shards as I can, then sit and fasten the waist strap.

He sticks a small, flat, metal stick into the neck of the wheel and twists. The engine sputters, shaking the rig like it's about to fall apart, then dies. He tries again and again with no luck. Clicking his teeth, he leans back, defeated.

"Whalers hunt the biggest beasts out here," he comments without looking at me. "Some for food. Most for sport." He goes for the stick again, his next words coming out strained. "And a few to spook a pack of shippers who've invaded their turf . . . come on!" Dropping the stick, he slams a fist against the wheel.

"Hey," calls a man from outside the truck. "Y'all in one piece up there?" Covered from thick neck to toe in shipper gear, Rook stands in the dust, red-bearded face lifted up to us. It's so weird full-grown men would take orders from a nineteen-year-old. Two other shippers join him, one covered up to his dark sideburns in black tattoos. They assess the damaged hood, shaking their heads.

Dax stands, raising a hand to grab the roof's rim so he can lean out the broken shield. "We'll survive. Can't get this thing to start though. Mac?" He focuses on the tattooed man who lifts his head. "I'll need a tow. Hook me up?"

"You got it." Mac and the other man disappear around the truck.

"You sure you're okay, sir?" asks Rook.

"Said I am, didn't I?" Dax answers, rubbing his forehead.

Rook tugs at his beard. "All due respect, that terra cetus about crushed you—"

"I'm *fine*." Dax's tone rises, sounding a whole lot like Uncle Trek right before he grounds me for a week.

"But sir," the ginger presses. "First the trouble with the Quell and the barrier, then we lose Zane, and now this? Not to mention that red sunrise. It's like something out there don't want us on this run. Some of the men have been talking, and they think this trip's ripe for a—" He coughs, glancing my direction. "Well, I think you know what. Something ain't right, and if there's a chance of a . . ." He spins his finger in the air as if the motion alone finishes his sentence. The implication is meant to fly over my head. "Well, the men are getting antsy is all."

Sheer frustration tightens Dax's jaw. "Then the men need to man up and stop jumping to conclusions one day in. We've made it through worse. No one's calling anything a chaos storm just because we run into some lousy luck. Now go back there and tell everyone we're getting this truck fixed, finding Zane, and finishing this run. Understand?"

Rook straightens, like Dax's little speech made everything right with the world.

"Perfectly, sir." He's around the truck before I can blink, replaced by the rumble of Mac's truck passing us on the opposite side.

Dax releases the rim and flops down in his chair. He lets out an exasperated breath then stares out the window. I wait, expecting him to explain that cryptic conversation, knowing he won't. *Might as well yank it out of him, piece by piece.*

"Thought you said the Quell won't give Zane and Tori back," I say.

"No. I said I doubt it. But just because they don't hold up their end doesn't mean I'm giving up on my crew. We'll get them back." He's so matter-of-fact. Like going against an armed unit of super soldiers is a kid's game. But at least he wants to save Tori. I hope his plan involves more than positive thinking.

The truck lurches forward, chained to the back of Mac's rig, and I'm forced to sit. We circle around the giant crater left by the terra cetus. It's empty of all whalers now. I assume they went off after their prey.

I catch a glimpse of the flaky-layered chasm descending into an inky pit. Swirls of dirt fly in and out of its mouth. Either my eyes are messing with me, or the hole is breathing. Alive. A monstrous cavity, salivating at the thought of swallowing its prey. Bile jumps up my throat.

I force myself to look away, to push my phobia down. I need to think of something else. Something to take my mind off the pit.

"So, um, what's a chaos storm?" I glue my eyes on Dax and not that hole.

He glances at me then reassures me almost sympathetically. "You don't have to worry about it, okay?"

How can I not worry about anything out here? There's a massive hole right next to us that wasn't there minutes ago. We could slip into it at any second. One tire, then two, and in we go. End over end, we'll sink into never-ending nothingness. My stomach twists. I'm making myself sick. I look out over Mac's truck. The golden towers of the fueling station grow with each moment we move toward them. My stomach spasms slow the further we get from the hole.

"I don't know about that," I say. "It's got Rook pretty jumpy. Besides, so far, I've had to worry about everything out here. Crushing me. Eating me. Kidnapping my best friend. So, tell me, what's the worst thing that'll happen to me in a chaos storm?"

Not sure why, but Dax twitches at the question. An awkwardness settles in, and he has me wishing my question back through my lips. No way am I prepared for what he's about to say.

His face goes expressionless when he answers.

"We maroon you."

THOUGH THE MIDDAY SUN IN THE

Outer Grid is impressive, the sunset here is mind-shattering. The sky, void of anything but haze hours ago, is now decorated with eggplant purple clouds. They float across a backdrop of fire orange. In the small spaces between each puff, warm colors bleed into one another in a giant splash of light. My fingers itch to paint it—capture its beauty across the digital landscape of my holo-pad. Which I left back in my bedroom. My only option is to remember the tangerine sun as it descends behind the fueling station's towers. For what, I don't know. I'm starting to doubt I'll live long enough to ever tell anyone about this place.

Especially if everything going wrong is God's doing.

Is that what this is? Tori taken away, that monster fish nearly killing us, now a chance these people might maroon me? Is this a way of forcing my hand? Well, it's not going to work. I'm not going back there. Ever.

The thought sours my mood. I pull my knees to my chest. From my vantage point on this hill, I watch the crew tinker away on Dax's rig in the valley-like crevasse of the station. The station consists of a stand-alone garage, five shining towers, and a broken-down hut.

I've counted six attendants so far dressed in ill-fitting governmental rags. Though they obey Dax's orders, they don't seem as impressed with him as the shipper crew is. Doesn't surprise me. Most people don't enjoy someone barking controlling orders. Glasses Guy is allergic to the word tact. Or respect. Or decency.

Beyond telling me there's a possibility they might abandon one of us on a whim, he didn't once explain the chaos storm. The second we drove through the fueling station's gates, he shut down, refused to answer my questions. And then, when I walked over to help on the truck because I don't think they're paying me to warm a seat, he shooed me away. Said fixing a broken rig isn't part of my job description. *Whatever.* He knows I'll ask more about this chaos storm and doesn't want to tell me. But it's not like he can avoid me forever.

"Rough first day?" Climbing the hill with blankets in one hand and a lit cigarette in the other, Mac makes his way toward me. His long, black hair flaps in the wind over his various neck tattoos.

"You could say that." I squint up at him to keep the swirling dirt out of my eyes. "It always this . . . um . . . eventful out here?"

"It's the Outer Grid," he says with a nod. "Expect the events." He stops a few steps short of me, puts the cigarette back in his mouth, and rolls the blankets under his arm. Holding out his free hand, he bends. "I'm Mac. You're Juniper, right?"

I release my knees and reach up to shake his ink-covered hand. "That's me."

For some reason, my response makes him chuckle. But he catches himself before I have time to guess why.

"Sorry," he says, "it's just, wow—he actually knows your name."

It's not hard to pick up his meaning. "You mean Dax?" I catch a glimpse of the person in question arguing with a station attendant. "You mean he didn't call me Princesa?" My tone drips with sarcasm.

"Ah. There's the nickname. Dax rarely uses real names on newbies until at least their second run. *If* there is a second run." He finishes the last part under his breath.

I frown. *Typical.* "And that's supposed to be normal?"

"Fair enough." He nods. "But think of it this way, you know how shippers run all those recruitment ads? It's because they're desperate. Razor does her best to keep our numbers up, but low-grade synths are hard to come by. Even harder to keep employed. Outer Grid will chew you up if you don't bite back. High turnover and slim pickings make it hard to get to know anyone past the job.

Took Dax three weeks to stop calling me *artwork*. But he already knows *your* name." His tone is thick with implication.

I don't care what kind of turnover they have, getting to know someone's name shouldn't be that hard. And I'm not sure I like whatever Mac is suggesting.

"He's probably having an off day," I retort. "One insult short of his normal jerk self."

I cringe. I shouldn't have said that about the boss to a coworker I just met. Who knows how strong his loyalties lie? But instead of defending Glasses Guy, Mac smiles.

He points at my leg. "Terra cetus give you that?"

Moments after we got to the station, Slate, the shippers' sweet medic, and the only other girl on this trip, patched me up.

"Yes," I say dryly. "I'm collecting all *kinds* of memories out here. Giant earth-dwelling whale beast is my favorite by far."

Mac laughs. The hoarse laugh of a guy who's smoked a pack a day for years. "I'll bet. That guy can put on a show. Glad you're okay. Here." He tosses me one of the blankets. "Doesn't look like we're getting out of here tonight. Most of us are sleeping in our rigs. But since Dax's truck is getting worked on, you'll be spending the night in the station house. I guess that's where they put up visitors."

He points to the hut clear on the opposite hill. My heart sinks a little. Its floppy roof looks like it'll cave in if I look at it too long. That, and these strong gusts picking up by the second aren't doing the place any favors.

"You sure it isn't going to collapse on me in my sleep?"

He grins. "No, probably not," he says, heading back toward the station garage. "Anything still standing in the Outer Grid is made of sturdy stuff."

I'm not sure I'm okay with that statement. Does he mean it's safe from earth whales, or something worse? He's only a few feet from me when I realize my chance to ask about the something worse.

"Hey," I shout, "what's a chaos storm?"

He freezes, taking a long drag on his cigarette before turning to face me. With a sigh, he puffs out a cloud of smoke and looks to the sky. "Rook bring that up?"

"Yeah, but Dax was the one who gave it a name. Even though that's all I can get out of him. Well, except for the whole marooning business."

Mac scratches the back of his neck. "He would tell you that," he mutters. "Remember how I said new recruits are scarce? Means we get workers from wherever we can. Most are Gridders—born out here. 'Bout as low-synth as they come. We dig them up from broken rebel factions near the border. They denounce any rebel alliance, but none of their superstitions.

"Lot of them believe there's this cosmic force out there. It controls everything and makes trouble for people who upset it. Enough stuff goes south on a run, and these guys deem it a chaos storm. After that, we roll stones to see who ticked the cosmic force off. When we find the guy, we maroon him. That's that."

That's that. Like marooning someone for superstition is no big deal. The things I wish I knew before signing up with these guys.

"And you believe in this force?" I ask, hesitant.

He sucks on his cigarette before answering. "Not sure what's out there, but when you've seen as much as I have, you're not surprised." He studies my face and sees something that makes him add, "Don't worry. Chaos storms are legend. Most of us have never seen one. Just don't do anything to tick off the big force out there and you'll be fine," he says. Whirling his finger upward, he winks at me.

I lower my eyes and rub my fingers across the ridges of my triangular pendant. When I look up again, he's gone, leaving words meant as a joke to churn in my gut. If only he knew who I ticked off by coming here. Someone who cares way more than an inert force. I stand and finger back the hair thrashing in my face, tucking it behind my ears. Hopefully, a chaos storm is as rare as he says. I don't want to think about roughing it out here on my lonesome.

The trek across the station is short but chilly. I rub the goosebumps pricked across my exposed arms. The temps must have dropped at least fifty degrees in the last hour. Loose debris of paper and rock blow about in swirls. I'm careful to avoid airborne pebbles in the eyes as well as the men working on Dax's rig. I'm even more careful to steer clear of Dax, which isn't difficult. Since his argument with the fueling station attendants, he's all but disappeared. Good. I guess. Except I'd like to know if I can snag the jacket I left in the truck.

Now that the sun has completely dipped below the horizon, moonlight shines on my path to the rickety hut. I know Mac said it'll hold together, but I don't see how. Sitting atop a hill, the shack has one rotted wooden door, a couple of broken windows, and leans far to the right. The uneven deck boards creak beneath me as I take the first cautious steps forward.

An odd smell like foul laundry or week-old garbage stifles the air. I clap my hand over my mouth. Still not used to manual doors, I stand near it, expecting the thing to open. Seconds of standing like a fool later, I remember where I am and reach for the doorknob. Lot of good that does. The frustrating piece of junk won't open. I turn the knob and pull, but no luck.

I go to give it one more tug when a male hand slides between me and the door, sticks a metal rod into the knob, twists, then pulls it open. Startled, I flinch back. Standing way too close to me, Dax grins wide.

"After you," he says, all sugar sweet.

Oh, no. He is *not* bunking with me. "Why are you here? Got tired of harassing the station attendants?" I ask.

He shrugs. "Yeah, well, I've seen more hospitable Quell hauling off rebels than those punks. At least a hardsuit won't ask you to sleep outside in the Outer Grid. That, and they've got some awful turnover here. Half those guys can't tell a monkey wrench from a crowbar. I'll probably have to fix the whole thing by myself in the morning. But I'm exhausted. Hope they don't foul it up before we get some shut-eye." He moves past me and through the doorway. "Outside," he says to himself. "Pfft, I mean really." He looks back at me. "You coming?"

It's not like I have much of a choice. If Dax, Mr. Outer Grid Master himself, won't sleep outside, there's no way I can. Taking a deep breath, I follow him into the darkness. "Tell me there are two separate bedrooms in here."

A bright spark explodes from Dax's fingers. Holding a tiny, burning stick, he puffs his lower lip in a fake pout. "Aww, you don't want to share a room with me?"

I give him my best get-lost face, but my cheeks burn so hot I doubt it's doing the trick. Maybe it's too dim in here for him to notice. He grins again, and I wish we were still in the dark.

"Have it your way." He turns from me to fidget with something on a desk. "There are two bedrooms on opposite sides of the cabin. Or at least there were last time I was here."

The fire from his stick splits in two, one flame now lit atop a half-melted candle. He continues his work, lighting candle after candle till the room is bright enough to see. I expect an onslaught of yummy scents. Filling rooms with the smell of apple was all we ever used candles for back home—that and the rare blackout. Instead, the place doesn't smell any different than the sour fuel and grease of Dax's rig. That and a weird scent I can't place but makes me wish I didn't have a nose.

Cans wrapped in pictures of food, like I've seen in the natural food stores, line the lime-shelved walls. Boxes of every shape and size litter the floor. And in the few spaces that aren't cluttered to chest height, small boats lean against the wall.

"What is this place?" I ask.

"Used to be a guesthouse. But now I guess they use it for storage. The station attendants live in the apartments over the garage. They built this cabin for shippers who have to stay the night. But we try not to do that. Fuel up and get to the job as fast as possible. Been a long time since I've been here." He blows a puff of dust off the desk, messes with some knobs on its surface, then coughs. "Since anyone's been here."

There's a sizzle then a pop. Under one of the metal circles on the desk's surface, Dax lights another flame. He then inspects the labels on the shelved cans. "Looks like it's tomato soup for dinner tonight."

So, what I thought was a desk is actually some kind of heating station. One that's like the computerized heating stations we have back home. He bends down and digs out an empty pot to put on the burner. I'm surprised I didn't recognize it. It looks like a heating element on one of those retro cartoon vids I watched. I pull down a couple of cans and set them on the counter beside me.

"Great," I say. "I'm starving. How can I help?"

He pauses and frowns, like a whole bunch of stupid fell out my mouth. Not that I blame him. I doubt he gets very many city girls asking to help warm his dinner. But I'm not that bad of a cook. Besides, it can't be *that* different from back home. He pulls a bizarre metal tool out from a drawer and tosses it at me.

"Ever use one of those?"

"Um . . ." I toy with the handles, trying to make sense of it. It's got little metal disks covering its surface I'm sure are meant to help open the cans, but I've got no idea how. It's like a weird metal torture device mixed with a baby rattle. Our can openers look nothing like this and use lasers to get the job done.

"Don't worry, Princesa, I've got you." The use of that nickname again grates me. I tear my eyes from the Grid tool to let him know how much I want to hear him calling me that. But I stop when he closes the distance between us, and his hands encase my wrists. His body glides behind mine. Frozen in place, my heart jumps to double time. In one fluid motion, I'm completely in his grasp.

Though my muscles stiffen at his touch, he adjusts the tool in my grip onto the can. I'd revel in the victory of guessing it's a can opener if it weren't for his calloused fingers brushing my skin. I can't breathe with him so close.

"Clamp it down. You'll feel the seal break." His hand tightens around my fingers.

Though he keeps on with his tutorial, I couldn't care less about the can. Instead, I chance a look at his profile. His frames are so thick I can't see anything behind them. There's a bluish reflection on his cheeks—maybe from the lenses or something else. I tilt my head. More of his face comes into focus. I can almost—

His head jerks toward mine. With a jolt, he releases me like I'm made of fire. His fingers fly to his frames. "Keep turning that till it opens, then heat it up." He pushes his glasses further up the brim of his nose. I have no idea what I did, but already he's clear on the other side of the hut, moving some boxes from a doorframe. Fine. It's better without him so close. I dump the contents of the can into the pot.

Minutes later, we eat in silence. I stand against the cabinets, as a table is nonexistent. The soup, though filling and welcome, does nothing to distract me from Glasses Guy standing across from me. He hasn't looked up from his bowl since I handed it to him.

"All right," I finally say, setting my bowl down. "What's with the sunglasses? You've worn them since this morning."

He takes another spoonful of soup then slowly pulls the spoon from his lips. "People say they make me look mysterious and handsome." He cocks one brow above his frames. "Do you think I'm mysterious and handsome?"

I flush. How am I supposed to answer that? His knee-weakening dimples aren't helping. "You're something else, that's for sure," I say, but doubt I hide my embarrassment.

He laughs at that. "Come on, I'll show you your room." He sidesteps me with the panache of a synth dancer in one of those reality vids, leaving me speechless.

Deep down, I know he's conned me off of the topic. Half of me wants to push the matter—find the truth behind his glasses. The other half fears what blush-inducing act he'd pull to keep me at bay. Opting for the safest route, I follow him. He's already disappeared through the door by the time I'm halfway there. I step over box after box, but the further I get from the candles, the dimmer the room grows. I'm positive I've cleared the next box when my foot hits an uneven board, and I lose my center of gravity.

I fly forward, hitting the ground hard on my hip and palms. Blunt pain throbs from my wrists. I hold them up and angle them in the dim light. My skin is broken in jagged rows, but no blood that I can see. I get to my feet to join Dax when a soft glow emanates beneath my uniform shirt.

My heart plummets. I pull up the chain around my neck. Blue light flashes from my pendant. The cracks along its onyx surface glow as tiny gears within its body spring to life. The almost musical staccato clicks chill my blood.

Oh, no. Not again. Not out here.

It's not city-tech. Not exactly. So, I'm not worried about breaking the ban. I'm worried about something else. I stagger back, knocking my heel against whatever it was I tripped on. The light from my pendant illuminates a handle on the floor. My necklace burns bright. I don't want to reach for the handle beneath me, lift it open, or see what's inside. But I can't help myself. My body rebels against my mind. The rectangular wooden door opens with a screech to stairs below. The pungent stink of the hut slams into me full force. I tug my flimsy shipper shirt over my nose and cough as my eyes water. I don't want to keep going, but I need to make sure I'm wrong. *God, please let me be wrong.* A few stairs down, I descend into darkness. And then my eyes adjust, and I see it.

Exactly what I feared. What my parents' pendant warned me of. In this damp dungeon below the hut, stacked in piles from the rocky earth on up, are bags filled with the translucent blue nano drug—the Freeman's Governor. And where there's this much Freeman's, there's always something way worse nearby. At first, I don't want to look, to ignore the truth.

But how can I when there are two dead bodies rotting at my feet?

MY MOUTH DROPS. A SCREAM

gurgles in the back of my throat. I clamp my jaw shut, afraid of who might hear. The two carcasses, slumped and covered in black blood from chins down, are tied back-to-back. Shadowy splotches line their arms and legs, as if from torture. It's so dark in here. The light from my pendant and the Freeman's does only so much. The bulk of the bodies are the only way I can distinguish them as male.

"Princesa?"

At Dax's voice, I drop my pendant down my shirt and encase it with my hand. Now the only light in here shines from the pile of contraband and through the cracks in the floor above. I stumble up a few of the stairs, unsure where to put my feet.

"Princesa? Where'd you go?" Dax calls again.

My jaw locks so tight I can't respond.

"Juniper?" Alarm edges his voice. I twist back, and he's there, at the top of the stairs, candle in hand. "What in the world? How did you get—whew! What's that stink?"

"Dax?" I say finally, voice shaking. "How well do you know these fueling station guys?"

He tilts his head at my odd question and takes the first steps down. His torch begins to illuminate the horror around us. "Not well enough apparently. I've never seen this place before. What is it, a basement? There must've been a full staff turnover since I've been—*holy*—"

He reels back, and I cover his mouth with my hand before his outburst alerts anyone. His voice vibrates my skin. I've got to press hard to keep the sound muffled. A few seconds later, his breathing slows, and he nods at me. I assume that means he's not going to scream again, and I let him go.

"Knew those guys were hiding something. Telling us to sleep outside," he says, his voice breaking a whisper. "Now we know what—hang on." Bending down, he moves toward the corpses.

"What are you doing?" I can hardly handle another second down here, and he wants to move in closer?

"I know these two." He reaches for the dead man on the left, actually grabs his slickened black hair, and then lifts his head.

I'm sure the guy once had a normal face. But now he's so disfigured, I can't tell where his swollen eyes end and his broken nose begins. A jagged gash along the man's throat stretches open at Dax's tug. Something white and puss-like spills out. I shiver. Flies swirl and buzz in the candlelight. I about lose my dinner. But thankfully, Dax lets the man's head drop.

"Yep," he says, his voice throaty and squeamish. "That's Hoyt, all right. Same neck tattoo. And I'm pretty sure the other one's Ajax. They are—*were* the real station attendants. From the looks of it, they've been dead for a while." He brings his wrist to his mouth and steps back, looking like he's struggling to keep his dinner down too.

"Question is," he goes on, "if these guys are down here, sliced up and rotting, then who's up there working on my rig?"

It's the exact question I don't want answered. Especially when the answer involves Freeman's smugglers. But I'm not naïve enough to pretend this isn't happening either. These guys are beyond dangerous.

"I'm guessing whoever they are, they've got something to do with all that," I say, pointing to the piles.

Dax follows my directing. His candle lights up the clear cases filled with stacks of Freeman's. The light bounces off their tiny, bioelectronic circuits.

"That what I think it is?" he asks slowly.

I nod, afraid to say the name aloud. "Thought city-tech was illegal in the Outer Grid."

"Yeah, well murder isn't smiled upon either, but here we are." He looks up at the floorboards above, and his head moves side to side like he's searching for something. "Ah, there it is," he says, pointing to a crack between boards.

I squint, move close to his candle, but see nothing more than wood. "There's what?"

"City-tech dampener. Blocks Quell tracers for miles. It's webbed all over this place. Blocked most of the smell too." What is he talking about? I can't see a thing. He looks at my confused face. "But it's hard to see. I'm only spotting reflections of it myself."

I move around, squinting, and catch a thin glimmer of a honeycomb shape above us. I guess that's what he's talking about, but how he can see it all over the place is beyond me.

He lowers the candle and exhales. "So, we're dealing with homicidal Freeman's smugglers who probably have more of this stuff hidden away in that garage. Where my rig is. Great." He runs his hand through his hair. "And seeing as they don't have problems killing people, they're probably users too."

I cringe. I had formed the same conclusion seconds ago. Freeman's, the nano drug designed to "free" a person from mental blocks, comes with two nasty side effects. It not only destroys inhibition, guilt, and morals, but it's addictive. *Highly* addictive. But when users are hyped up on Freeman's, usually the blue marks across their skin gives it away.

"I didn't see the marks on any of them though," I say.

Dax stops his pacing. "No, you're right. Their skin was clear."

"Which means they're probably using now. Which also means . . ."

"Come on." He pivots around me toward the stairs. Grabbing my wrist, he pulls me with him. "We're not safe here."

The air outside the hut has turned frigid. Breath puffs past my lips in erratic balls of pale smoke. With a firm grip on me, Dax takes me down the deck stairs, letting go at the base.

"Go to the road where the other rigs are," he commands, but only loud enough for me to hear. "Find Rook. Tell him the place is crawling with Freeman's smugglers and we're leaving now."

I don't have time to register his words before he sprints off in the opposite direction. "Wait, where are you going?" I yell.

"They've got my truck," he calls back. In seconds, he's gone, down the hill and toward those maniacs in the garage. By himself.

I stand there agape. Idiot! I don't know what kind of ninja skills he thinks he has, but taking on a garage full of men hyped up on Freeman's is a little more than a one-man job. More than a two-man job.

I should know. I've dealt with users more than I care to remember. And way more than Uncle Trek will let me forget, not with the hours of rigorous training he put me through. *Always be prepared for that moment your life depends on it*, he'd say. Well, my life wouldn't depend on it as much if he and Aunt Marna stopped putting me in life-threatening situations.

I turn toward the road. Maybe Dax has dealt with users too. Maybe he knows what it takes to stay alive. And maybe he's about to be slaughtered. *That stupid truck can't be worth this.* Half of me wants to run after him, prove he can't fight these guys off himself. But the other half knows I'd only be getting us both in deeper water.

I race down the hill to alert the other shippers. I'll bet we'd at least outnumber them. I pull out my pendant and clutch it tight. *We can do this ourselves. I won't have to use it.*

The ground begins to level out when light shines through my fingers. I slow my pace and look down. My pendant is ablaze. *Oh, no. No!* Frantic, I scan behind me. Towers, the hut, darkness, no one's there. *Thank God.* I turn back, ready to sprint, and crash face-first into a rock of a man.

My feet trip over themselves. Whatever center of gravity I had vanishes. But I don't hit the dirt. Someone's meaty hands wrap my waist and clench my hair at the roots, preventing me from falling back. With my hands covering my nose, I try to wiggle free with no success.

"Look what we've got here," he croaks. "If it isn't the blue-haired little shipper girl." I struggle to make out his features through the blur of pain. All I can see is a hazy broad man with short, spiked hair and a bulbous nose. There is one trait though that's impossible to miss. Tiny cracks in his pasty skin let out the Freeman's bioluminescent reaction in a circuit-board pattern.

The marks of a user.

"Found out our little secret, did you?" he goes on, inching closer with each nasty breath reeking of spoiled fish. "Told that little snot to sleep outside. But I guess he only gives the orders. Doesn't take them. You though," he says, squeezing my waist, "I have better plans for you in my bed. Fact, we're heading there now. If I like your performance, we'll figure out what to do with you in the morning. Sound good?"

Adrenaline and disgust pump through my system.

"How about we figure it out right now." I let go of my nose. With as much force as I can manage, I slap both hands hard against his ears. He drops me. I use his shock to my advantage. Grabbing his face, I shove both thumbs in his eyes till he cries out and stumbles back.

My attack might have done the trick, but I don't want to hang around to find out. I take off, panic spurring my movements. I'm lucky it was just one user. Who knows if there are others lurking nearby?

The light from my pendant softens as I run, blanketing the station in terrifying darkness. I've never been anywhere outside that isn't lit like a torch in city neon. But here, there are only clouds—dark masses rushing across the blurred white moon. Wind howls around me, low and thunderous. Dirt and gravel churn in heavy gusts, pounding my skin like tiny missiles. My legs burn, but I will them to keep up the sprint.

A little further. I can make it.

About a dozen spheres of red shine a few yards away. Shipper trucks. Their green-ridged bodies are a relieving sight. It's not long before I'm a few feet from the last rig in the line. I make my way to the truck's front ladder when my pendant flickers and flashes. Every muscle in my body tenses. I look down at my necklace. I should be watching where I'm going. My foot slams into a big mound in the dirt. I topple forward and land on my aching wrists.

Dust envelops me in a cloud that sinks into my lungs. I push up on my elbows, fighting to breathe through sporadic coughs and hacks. My hand covers my mouth to keep more dirt from flying in. But the second I regain composure; I move my hand away to see my fingers covered in blood.

Palpable confusion renders me immobile. My wrist, nose, and leg still ache, but I don't think I've cut anything. I look back at the mound I tripped over. My pendant casts its aqua light on what I missed. My breath stills. Blood and black ink splatter over a horrific canvas of shipper clothes and flesh.

Mac. Oh, please no. Mac!

I SCRAMBLE TO MAC'S CRUMPLED

body and fight to keep from hyperventilating. Every first aid lesson Aunt Marna taught me is swallowed up by terror. Blood pools over the right side of his chest. His clothes are singed and there's a burning odor wafting around us. I don't know what kind of weapon they shot him with, but whatever it was, I'm sure it punctured his lung. My fingers hover over his wounds, completely unsure of what to do. I don't think I can move him. But we can't stay here. I force in a steadying breath. I've got to calm down. *Get the bleeding to stop. Dress the wound.* Aunt Marna's words ring in my ears. I'm not sure they're what I need, but they sound good, and I go with them.

"Hang in there, Mac." Placing a hand over the wound, I search for anything that can cover the hole in his chest. Although, I have no idea how I'm going to secure whatever I find to stop the air from collapsing his lung. And if there's an exit wound out his back, what good is it going to do? I'm going to need two of whatever I can find. But nothing's here.

Mac's hand grabs my arm, tight and shaky, giving me a jolt. Blood drips from his mouth. "They're going to take the trucks," he rasps, then sucks in a deep wheeze. "Fought them off but they told—*huhh*—told me everything, before they—*huhh*—"

"Shush," I say. "Don't talk. Just stay still."

"Tell her—" With his other hand, he pulls out a rectangular piece of paper from his shirt pocket and shoves it against my chest. "Tell her—she was right—there is a cure—the users know—she has to find it before them—*huhh*—"

I flip the bloodstained paper over. There's an image of a

beautiful girl with long, jet-black hair cuddling Mac. She's almost as tattooed as he is. With her inked fingers, she pulls him tight. They're both smiling. Happy.

"No, Mac," I say, choking on emotions. "*You* tell her. We're going to get you out of here. We just have to—"

He tightens the grip on my arm. "Promise me."

"I . . ." How can I promise him that? I barely know him, let alone where to find her. "What's her name? How can I find her?"

His eyes roll back, and his head drops.

"Mac? Mac!" My two fingers go to his neck. "No, no. No! Don't you die."

God, please, don't let this happen.

I try again, but it's the same. No pulse. Tears slide down my face. My insides tighten. No, I won't accept it. If I can find Slate, she'll know what to do.

My pendant blinks again, then locks on to a steady stream of blue. Male voices cackle in the distance. Or right next to me. I don't know. The wind is deafening, and I can't think straight. Afraid they'll find me, I gently let go of Mac and back up against one of the rig's giant tires. I cover the light of my pendant with my non-bloody hand and shove the picture into my pants pocket with the other.

"Come out, come out, shippers. It's time to play," a thunderous male voice hollers, wild and off balance.

I stretch away from the protection of the tires. Four or five silhouettes climb the rig next to me. Freeman's marks spider across their weapon-filled hands. The one at the top aims his barrel at the cab door. But instead of gunfire, a growing electric charge hums through the howling wind. It gives a loud pop, and the door flies open. The two men behind him reach in and pull out a shipper. He's the deep brown skinned bald man who Dax called Cyrus. They toss him to the deck floor, laughing and kicking him in the side before crawling into the rig.

"Get out of my rig!" Cyrus cries, pushing himself up to go after them. But the man still on deck drops a right hook across his jaw so hard and fast, it sends Cyrus flat on his face. Which seems impossible with how big Cyrus is, but if these guys wanted strength, Freeman's has given it to them.

The man's glowing sneer lights up his blond hair till it's almost white. "Do you know how hard it is to build up a good supply of product in this wasteland without trucks?"

"Look, man," Cyrus begins. "I don't know what you—" The man points his weapon at Cyrus's head. The bulkier man scurries back. "Woah! Wait a second."

"And you shippers drive around on these things like you own the Grid," the dealer continues. "You own nothing now. Whole Grid's gonna belong to us. Ain't no room for you."

Bam! Bam!

My heart pounds against my ribs. My eyes squeeze shut. *I don't want to see this. I can't see this. Not again.* But when I look back up, Cyrus is still there, very much alive and yelling, "No! No!" The gunfire must have come from inside the cab. His passenger. My chest heaves. It won't be long before they murder Cyrus too, and then the rest of the crew after that.

I look down at my necklace and swallow the lump in my throat. I know what I've got to do. For Mac. For Cyrus. My hands shake. I swore I'd never do this again. I touch the necklace's smooth body against my lower lip and brace myself against the tires and the dirt. Horrified, I breathe the word that gives me nightmares over the pendant's black frame.

"Cry."

I pull the chain over my head. The black triangular pendant, once stationary and harmless, reacts to my call. It buzzes, clicks, and twists around itself in a violent dance. It scratches against my palm with the motion. I toss the thing toward Cyrus's rig, hoping the distance is close enough to the users but far enough from me. I know it's not. I'm too close. I cover my ears with my hands seconds before it discharges in a sonic slap of sound.

The noise is an instant trigger. My vision tunnels into black. Unwelcome memories resurface in my brain. Memories I'd long since buried. I wish I could stop it, or at least brace myself for what

I know is coming. But I don't just get to remember the past. No, I'm about to live it again in inescapable color.

My senses obey my pendant's song. The Grid's noises muffle and vanish, like I've jumped headfirst into a deep ocean. I dread the nightmare to come. All I can do is breathe. In, out. In, out.

Then, one by one, unnatural fluorescent beams flicker on in a line far above my head. I wince, getting accustomed to my past surroundings. The rounded room, with geometric cutouts in the walls that house my old bed, is adorned in murals of my childhood. Multicolored dragons, chartreuse sprites, and lifelike princesses are strewn across the wall. *An artistic prodigy,* my schoolteachers had once said. One that can change the world. Kind of a joke now. Can't believe my parents believed them.

I hold my tiny, six-year-old, paint-drenched hands to my eyes then will myself to drop them. To run. But I can never seem to move my tiny legs. Jagged blue rays pierce through my skin, lighting up the spaces between color smudges. Oh, no. It's *that* vision. I know what happens next—what always happens next.

My fingers trace the wings of the dragon. My older self fights my younger self's impulse to jump. But my childish body won't obey. *I can fly,* it tells me, and then moves to the window to release controls.

No, you can't! You can't! I scream, but my kid mind ignores me.

The closer I get to the window, more of the massive drop from the thirty-fifth floor comes into view. Fear and exhilaration spike my breathing. I push the button by the frame. The window mesh breaks away the upper half of the pane. I climb over the lower half and straddle one leg on each side.

My bedroom door whooshes as it slides open. The noise brings my attention to the back of the room. Dada bursts through, as tall and lanky as I remember. A brow creased with worry below his black-framed glasses as dark as the beard on his face and close-cut hair on his head. He rushes me. Mama follows, her blonde locks flowing behind her in breathtaking slow motion. A tear falls down my seventeen-year-old cheeks at the sight of them. But my six-year-old self couldn't care less, self-indulged and delusional.

"Watch me, Dada! I can fly." Arms spread like the dragon I imagine I am, I tilt to the side and topple out the window.

Gravity yanks me down. Wind, harsh and stinging, flops my limbs back like noodles. Windows and neon lights zoom past. My body tumbles, twists, and turns upside down, right side up, and back again.

I lose all orientation. That, or my eyes play tricks on me. The buildings blow apart into millions of blocked fragments. My mind rattles along with my body. The strange wreckage swirls about me, speeding up and turning white. Several shards collide with my skin. Their flaky touch freezes on impact then melts away. *What on earth?*

"Juniper?"

My shoulders shake.

"Juniper, c'mon, Princesa."

The ground below me returns. I blink awake, though somewhat still in the trance. White shards from the buildings whip around the silhouette of the guy bending over me.

"Hey there," he says. "You hurt?" He comes more into focus, the shards fluttering around him. Light from the rigs bounces off his glasses.

"Dax?"

He sighs out in relief. "Can you move?"

Wooziness ebbs and flows over me. I wait until my world stabilizes. I push my heels to the ground. They feel sturdy enough. "I think so."

He takes my hand and helps me to my feet. I'm a little wobbly on the way up. He notices and doesn't let me go. "Come on then," he says, "we've got to get moving." There's a crack in his voice. Like he's trying very hard to keep it together. Through the fog in my head, his anguish sounds off my own alarm.

"Mac," I cry, snapping back to reality. "Dax, we can't go. The users attacked him. I tried to stop the bleeding, but I—" The spot where I left Mac's body is empty, dusted over in a blood-tinged white covering. "Where is he? We've got to help him."

Dax tightens his grip on me. "He . . . he's on Slate's rig." I can't tell if that's a good thing. His words sound like a big pile of despair. He looks up at the falling debris, uneasy. "We can't stay."

I don't ask if Mac's alive before Dax guides me through an ocean of flaky white. My surroundings jar me. I can't see much past the light of the rigs. Everything illuminated by their beams moves about in the screaming wind. Even the rigs themselves wobble from the force. My brain tries to convince me the floating shards are still building fragments. Am I awake, or is this still part of the trance?

"Dax, what's going on? What is this stuff?"

"It's called snow." Looking back at me, he tugs up the cowl of his jacket till it covers his nose. "Get ready, city girl," he says over the wind. "You're in for a front row seat to a full-blown Weather Flux."

11

AS IS STANDARD REGULATION FOR
every city I've lived in, rain runs on a strict schedule. It can only
deviate under extreme circumstances or by city council vote.
Temperature is even more regulated. A constant seventy-five
degrees year-round. We are always notified. Always prepared.
Extreme weather is only mentioned in schoolrooms or story pads.
I've heard of snow, seen pictures of it, but never once actually
touched the stuff. The closest I've been to winter weather was an
indoor ice rink Tori dragged me to last fall.

Dax has every right to think I'm sheltered. City dwellers all
are, in the most literal sense of the word. As beautiful and new all
this swirling snow is, the words *Weather Flux* bring back years of
terrifying history lessons. I doubt any were exaggerated. I move as
close to Dax as possible, hoping we're getting in the trucks and out
of this storm fast.

Hunched over on the side of the road, several users twitch,
groan, and cry out in fear as we pass. Their wide eyes roll to white.
Freeman's blue pales as it drains from their skin. They must still
be under the trance of my pendant. A couple shippers tie the users
back-to-back. Others relieve them of their weapons.

It isn't long before I spot Cyrus. Huffing and enraged, he charges
the blond user who threatened him and shot his passenger. It takes
both Rook and another shipper to keep him from tearing the man's
head off. Though, from the user's gushing nose and ballooned out
eye, it looks like he's already been beaten to an inch of his life.

"No, Cy, no more," Rook grunts out from the impact of Cyrus
crashing against him.

"Out of my way, Rook."

"He ain't worth it." Rook shoves him back a step or two.

Before Cyrus can charge again, Dax lets me go and lodges himself between the men. Hands to Cyrus's chest, he somehow resists the larger man's force.

"You're done," he says. "Hear me? Killing this piece of trash won't bring Boone back."

"No, but it'll make me feel better." Cyrus pushes Dax a few feet back. But Dax is quick on his feet, rushing up to the larger man and grabbing him by the shirt.

"And we'd all feel better," Dax agrees. "But not with a storm on our doorstep and a crew that needs us. So, either stay here and end one lowlife or get back in your truck and save our crew. You decide." He straightens, his hands leaving Cyrus's chest. I cringe, expecting him to be bowled over by the much bulkier man. But instead, Cyrus yields, pauses, and storms off.

"The weather's fluxing," Dax announces to everyone. "Load up and drive out." As the crew rush to their rigs at his orders, he takes off down the road without me. I weave through the shippers, scrabbling to keep up. He's nearly at his truck by the time I reach him. It's still banged up, but at least it's now sporting a windshield.

"What about the users?" I call to him from the base of the rig's ladder. "We're going to leave them here?"

He climbs the ladder within seconds. From the top rung, he gives me a sideways glance. "I'm not taking them with us if that's what you're asking."

"No that's not what I'm—Dax, they tried to kill us. And some of us, they actually—" I choke on my words as I climb after him. "Is tying them up enough? What if they escape and another shipper crew comes through after we leave? They'll walk into a trap." I reach the top of the ladder to find him inspecting the outer parts of the cab.

"It'll have to be enough," he says. "If we don't leave now, *we'll* be the ones trapped."

As if on cue, a thunderous boom followed by mechanical clicks pierce through the storm. The sound startles me and my foot slips. I drop a few rungs but hug the ladder in time to keep on it. I pull myself upright, and the noise fades, swallowed by the blowing wind like it never happened. I risk a glance over my shoulder to see what's about to kill me now. But swirling snow and darkness blanket everything beyond a few feet from my face.

"What was that?" I ask, my voice competing with the howling wind.

When Dax doesn't reply, I look around to see him leaning over the edge of the rig's deck, staring out into the distance. His jet-black hair and dark clothes thrash over his statuesque frame. Another boom shakes the truck. He leans back and reaches down for me.

"Hurry."

I grab his hand. We're both up on the deck in no time, bolting to get in the cab. Another boom. Only this one doesn't fade like the last. Instead, the rumbling sound intensifies. Dax's movements are hectic, and he's in the cab before I even see him move. I'm right behind him. I strap myself in, mesmerized by the low drone and searching for its source. A few flipped switches later, the truck comes alive.

The communication screens flicker on. Pain sears my heart at the sight of Slate's tear-striped face on Mac's screen. Dax said Mac was on her rig, but I didn't think that meant his truck was now Slate's. What's worse is she's the medic, driving instead of tending to a dying man.

"Slate?" Dax asks, his face pinched tight.

She grasps her short, burgundy hair with both fists. Grimacing, she shakes her head no.

Air escapes Dax's lungs in a moan, like he's been punched in the gut by a Quell. His head drops and he wrings the wheel, over and over. I may hardly know the guy, but I expected him to lash out— throw something or yell obscenities over Mac's death. God knows it's what I want to do. Instead, Dax's quiet reaction overwhelms me more than an outburst ever could.

"Let's go," he utters, then wrangles the stick by his side. The truck jostles, bursting forward. We turn onto the only road out of this forsaken place. As the rig punches though the falling white, a brittle cracking sound spreads across the truck's surface. The new windshield seems to do its job. As does whatever they did to the engine. Those creeps who worked on this hunk of metal sure wanted a working truck to steal.

Through the blanketing snow, the station's towers shift and sway in the wind like they're alive. I lean forward, tilting my head to get a better view. *Wait a second.* It isn't the wind moving them at all. Giant metal extensions grind out from the tops of the towers, curving in on each other to form a protective dome. Each segment emerges with a boom, followed by the mechanical clicks and scrapes I heard earlier. They must be the station's Weather Flux shield. But when walls emerge from their sides, trapping us in with the smugglers, I understand Dax's urgency and dig my nails into the arm of my seat.

The rig accelerates with the rising rumble of its engine. We near the gates, once glistening and now monstrous. I can't help but glue my gaze onto the concrete walls closing in on us. Is this how shipper life is? Working under a constant threat of barriers crushing you to pieces? It hasn't even been twenty-four hours, and this is happening again. No wonder no one wants this stupid job.

As the lead truck, we make it past the gates first. But it doesn't seem like there's enough room for everyone to squeeze through. My eyes dart to the screens below. I don't have a great view of the trucks behind us, but I can watch relief pass over the face of each driver down the line.

Rig two. Rig three. The walls boom and grind. I turn to my side mirror. The station shrinks from view, and the space for escape disappears. Slate squeals out. Her voice startles my attention back to the screens up front. Leaning forward, she smacks the wheel then flops back. Rig four. Two more to go. The driver with the dreads heaves a heavy sigh. Rig five.

Only Cyrus remains. Tension tightens his mouth and forehead. I turn back to the mirror. The space is almost gone. The tower lights merge through the snowy haze.

"C'mon, c'mon," Dax urges, his head traveling back and forth from the storm in front to the screen below. My chest tightens when

Cyrus's screen flickers waves of static. All I can do is close my eyes and pray.

One more boom crashes through the violent storm around us, its meaning clear. The station is locked tight. Either Cyrus made it out or . . .

"All clear." Cyrus's voice floods me with relief. And when I look over at Dax and see the expression on his face, I know he feels the same. If not more. "Close, but clear." The large man's voice is dry, worn. Making it through a crushing gate is less exhilarating when you've lost your friend minutes before.

I can relate only slightly. Tori's not dead. Or, at least, I hope she's not. Fear for my friend bubbles inside me again. I try not to picture myself in Cyrus's position, watching Tori die before my eyes as I lie there helpless. But the images keep surfacing, and a waterfall threatens to burst from my eyes.

Determined not to wail like a baby in front of Dax, I stare out into the Flux. The raging wind pounds our truck back and forth. Dax struggles to keep the rig straight on the road. Freezing, I rub my arms and stick my feet close to whatever is blowing heat on my toes.

We drive in near silence for what feels like hours.

Or days.

Or years.

I don't know how much longer I can keep my eyes open. I chance a look at Dax. He rubs the bridge of his nose under his glasses. How long can he push the rig? Adrenaline only goes so far before heavy eyelids win out. My own lids feel the string of exhaustion pulling them tight.

Snow falls in buckets outside. A good hour or so ago, nothing stuck to the ground. Dax had mumbled something about the earth being too hot for the snow to pile up. I shake my head at the thought. I may be new to this whole blizzard business, but right now, nothing is hot. And although I can't see past the headlights, this stuff mounds up out there so fast it's—

"That's it," Dax blurts, giving me a start. "We're done." He's been so quiet, I almost forgot the sound of his voice. The tiny red light by the screens is on, flashing. He must have opened the communication between the rigs without my notice. "Can't see a blasted thing in this whiteout. One wrong turn and we'll be spending the night in the bottom of a ditch. Everyone slow 'em down." He cranks up on a pole by the wheel and turns the stick to kill the truck's movement. The mechanical blades over the new shield come to a halt. Fat flakes cover the glass, blotting out the outside world.

"What are we doing?" I ask through a yawn. Dax tightens his forehead in confusion, and I repeat myself. "What are we doing?"

"We're staying here for the night." He unstraps his waist and pushes down on his armrests to lift himself off his chair. After opening a hatch behind the seat and digging through, he tugs out a metallic silver coat. Wrinkled, it's puffed like the clouds swirling above us. He slides his arms in the holes. The coat swallows him.

I stretch my legs and search for the lever that drops my seat back. It won't be the most comfortable night's rest, but anything beats sleeping outside, or worse, at that station. Dax reaches for the cab door, and I sit forward.

"Where are you going?"

"Slate's rig," he answers, a hint of dread laces his voice. His intention is clear, and sorrow weighs on me. He's going to check on Mac. I wonder how well they knew each other. How hard is this for him? And then I remember what's in my pocket.

"Dax," I say as he cracks the door, howling wind and frosty air pouring in the cab. "Do you know who this is?" I pull out the picture of the tattooed girl from my pocket. My bloodstained fingerprints mark the top corners of the photograph. But the image of the girl remains untarnished.

Dax's face sours. He snatches the picture from my grasp.

"Where'd you get this?" he snaps.

Whatever civility we had vanishes. I should be used to his demanding barks by now, but I've only known this guy a day. A horrible disastrous day. Anyone snapping at me like that raises my defensive walls. I take a second to gather my thoughts and gate my words.

"On Mac. When I found him. Before I passed out." I tell him nothing of how I found Mac alive. Nothing of what he begged me to promise.

My response doesn't lighten Dax's mood. It does the opposite. His jaw sets. He throws open a drawer on the dash, digs in, and yanks out an orange plastic rod the size and width of my arm. His wrist snaps. The rod expands into a hollow pyramid. He cracks it along all three edges. It brightens the cab with each break. Then he slams it on the floor behind us.

"That'll keep you warm. Crack it if you get cold."

He turns and shoves open the door. Winter blasts through. He steps halfway through the doorway before fixing his wrathful glare on me.

"There's a pull-down cot in the back and a spare parka in one of the storage bins. And, Princesa," he says, tapping the image of the tattooed girl, "don't tell anyone about this." Stuffing the picture in his coat, he exits the cab, leaving me alone in the dim rig in the middle of nowhere.

I AWAKE WITH A JOLT TO LOUD BANGS

reverberating through the rig. I sit upright and clutch the heavy blankets of the tiny pull-down bed I tossed and turned in last night. Without leaving the cot behind the cab, I scan the empty confines of the truck for the source of the racket. But as morning light pours in from the cab's windows, I'm met with silence and the occasional hum of wind. Another nightmare.

I pull the coat tighter around my waist. I'm grateful Dax cracked open the fire pyramid. Doubt that's what it's called, but Dax didn't stick around long enough to tell me the warming triangle's name, so that's what I'm calling it. It worked enough that I didn't freeze, but I'm too used to city temps. Warmer than the surrounding snowstorm isn't near as warm as my bed back home. This place might as well be one giant ice generator. After digging through at least seven storage bins, I finally found a puffy tangerine coat. I assume it's what Dax meant by *parka*.

Whatever it is, it's the only thing that got me through the nightmares. I slept for a half an hour at a time before horrible dreams forced my eyes open. At first, they were the typical ones. Bloodstained streets, gurgling screams, a dome city ablaze. But as night dragged on, images of Tori's neck crushed in a Quell's grip startled me awake again and again.

So instead, I spent the night praying things would change. That the plan to rescue Plex would be called off. I didn't get an answer. Which I'm sure means a big fat no. Day couldn't come fast enough.

Stretching my legs, my calf Slate bandaged still stinging, I leave the cot. The socks on my feet slide a bit on the gray metal floor.

Maybe I'll catch sight of someone outside the cab windows, though I'm not in the mood to see Dax. That's for sure. I still don't know why showing him that photo made him so upset. Upset enough to leave me here by myself all night. I didn't want him sleeping in the same rig as me, but someone could have made sure I didn't die out here.

Bang, bang, bang!

I stumble, almost falling into the bed from fright. The sound wasn't a dream after all. Someone's outside beating on one of the cab doors. I duck behind the wall separating the back of the truck to the cab. Whoever it is, I doubt it's Dax, pounding on the door of his own truck. And I'm sure those smugglers didn't follow us, but still, I'm not about to open the door and find out.

When the banging dies down, I peek my head around the corner. Outside Dax's window, a figure in an orange coat like mine cuffs two black-mitted hands around a goggled face. When the figure moves from the glass, wavy, burgundy strands of hair flap about in the wind over a fur-lined hood. I know exactly who it is.

"Are you awake in there?" Slate's bright voice is a welcome sound. I climb into the cab and over Dax's chair to push open the door. Raging wind blows in. And I thought it was cold in here. It's far worse out there. I shift to let Slate's smaller frame inside the truck. Shutting the door behind her, she pulls off her hood. She pushes up the bug-like goggles off her angular eyes to rest on her forehead.

"Brrr." She shivers. "There might be no wind in here, but it's not much better than out there." She jabs a stick in the slot by the wheel, turns it, and then pushes a few buttons on the dash. Warm air embraces my legs. I rush my frigid fingers to the source of the heat and rub away the sting of cold.

"Thank you," I breathe out, warmth sliding over my shivering limbs.

"No problem. Sorry for the chilly sleeping conditions. We can't run the trucks all night if we want to make it to the farm."

I nod. Keeping the thing on would have been nice though. "It's okay. There are worse places to sleep." Like that fueling station.

I continue to rub my fingers to life while Slate watches me in silence. Examining me? I rack my brain to think of something to say to break the awkwardness, but she beats me to the punch.

"Oh, hey, I brought you these." She digs in her coat and pulls out three hand-sized packages from one pocket and a bottle of water from the other. "Most of the foods on this rig are Dax's weird concoctions. Doubt you'll want any of that. The guy eats like a pregnant woman."

I crack a smile. *Bet I'm not the only one who turned down Frankensandwich.* I break open the package closest to me. The sweet and tangy aroma of blueberries wafts out. My mouth waters at the muffin's golden-brown top. I tear off a part of the muffin and stuff it in my mouth. It's heaven. "Mmm, thank you," I manage through the food.

Slate continues to look at me, like I've got a head covered in synth upgrades gone wrong. I try to ignore her, finishing my muffin and moving on to the next. But the cab gets more uncomfortable by the second.

"I don't get it," she spits out finally. "Why did you do it?"

I look up from my muffin, midchew. "Do what?" I ask, mouth full of baked sugar and fruit.

"Why leave the city for this?" She waves her hand in the air then glares back at me. Her expression has gone from kind to distrustful. It's not hard to guess her meaning. "You can teleport anywhere you need to go. You have every convenience handed to you on an electronic platter. Even your weather is controlled. But you're here. I just . . . I don't get it."

I stop chewing and swallow the rest of my breakfast whole. This isn't a conversation I want to have so early in the morning. Especially not after the night I'd been through. I shrug with as much nonchalance as I can muster.

"What can I say? Those recruitment ads were convincing."

She smirks, but there's no humor in her eyes. "Shipper recruitment ads are crap. Aimed at rebels who watch the feed on the outer wall screens to attract the cause-minded ones. You don't strike me as someone shipping for a cause."

"I sure don't," I agree, a strong hint of drop-this-now in my voice. Wherever she wants to take this chat, I don't want to follow.

"Come to think of it," she goes on, ignoring my tone, "you and your friend are the first city dwellers I've seen on a shipper rig." After pulling out another muffin from her pocket, she opens it and takes a hearty bite. She narrows her russet eyes at me. "What's so bad with city life that it made you take on the toughest job in the Grid?"

Her voice cracks over the word *job*, and something in her eyes shifts from questioning to sadness. And then I get it. She's not here to interrogate me. Her friends died only hours ago. She's heartbroken. Maybe she thinks learning why a privileged city girl would choose this job might heal the hurt. But my true reason for leaving my aunt and uncle isn't an uplifting tale.

So instead, I deflect. "I guess I didn't know what I was getting myself into." I look out over the snow-covered wasteland. Bubblegum sunlight reflects off its swirling surface. "Right now, I want to make sure my friend is safe." There's a touch on my shoulder. I turn back to see sympathetic sorrow on Slate's face. "So, what about you?" I ask, itching to change the subject. "What made you want to be a shipper?"

She slowly leans back. "You have any brothers?" she asks at last.

I blink. "Um, no. It's just me."

"Well, I've got enough for both of us. And if I'm not shipping, then I'm stuck on the farm with them. Dealing with these guys is loads easier than anything my big brothers dish out."

I nod and take another bite. I've heard having siblings is rough, but sometimes I'd love to have someone to share life with. Someone who's been there since birth, who really knows me. Then again, things don't go well for anyone who sticks around me too long. I've known Tori for two years now, the longest friendship I've ever had, and look what that got her. Though I'm not responsible for Mac's death, my presence sure didn't help. The guy's dying wish was that

I find that girl in the photo. If I can't help Tori, I'll at least keep my word to Mac. Dax can get over himself.

"So," I try to find the right words, "did Mac have any family back on the farm too? A sister? Or a girlfriend?"

Her gaze lifts from her muffin to me, slow and wary, like I said something taboo. A knot twists in my stomach at the stiffening the air between us. I brought up her recently deceased friend too soon. Maybe Dax was right, and I should have kept my mouth shut.

But then she looks to the roof and sighs, wiping away sudden tears. "I can't believe we're talking about him in past tense." Her eyes glisten over and her voice hitches. "Yes. He did have some people on the farm. Most of us do. Which, by the way, we're only a few miles outside of it right now. But with all this snow piled up, we aren't going anywhere in these trucks. Most of the guys are staying here. Been shoveling us out since daybreak. We need a few people to head out on foot. The farm has plows that can make us a path. You want to go with us or shovel with the guys?"

A trip across the frozen wasteland after the night I had isn't how I hoped to spend the day. But I doubt I'd be any help shoveling out monster trucks with bodybuilders. "I'll go with you," I answer.

"Great. You'll want to wear something warmer than that gear you've got on. There are winter clothes in the bin next to the one where you found the parka. We leave in ten." She stuffs the rest of the muffin in her mouth, snaps the goggles back over her eyes, and ducks out into the cold.

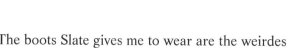

The boots Slate gives me to wear are the weirdest things I've ever had on my feet. Strapped into two flat, oblong squash rackets, they give me a wide stance as I flop in and out of the snow. Slate insisted I wear them to widen the surface area beneath me, otherwise I'd sink into the snow. I assume it's deep, seeing as the white stuff has buried the rigs up to the headlights in the unshoveled parts. I also wear a pack full of gear on my back and tinted goggles pressed to my face. Holding two long, skinny poles in each hand, I test every step I make. Apparently tops of short trees and other debris could mess me up if I knock into one.

Slate corrects me as I struggle uphill. It doesn't matter how far she gets from me. Her "no, not like that" or "be more deliberate, test where you're stepping" is impossible to ignore. It'd be easier to follow her direction if I didn't have to match Dax's super-fast pace.

He didn't look thrilled at my presence. I've no idea how Slate convinced him to let me come along, but he sure wasn't happy about it. Instead of, "Hey, Juna, how was your freezing cold sleep last night?" all I got was a bag tossed at me and, "We walk in a single line to the farm, stay behind me the whole way." He may not have tacked on "Princesa" at the end, but he sure said it with the tilt of his head. And now he's far ahead, while the three of us fight to keep up. Or only I fight. I'll bet Rook and Slate could keep up easily if I weren't dragging them back.

I push on, packing the snow as fast as I can while my legs burn. I might be the weak link here, but I'm sure going to be the strongest weak link I can be. Head down and poles out, I press up the hill, one foot after the other. But when I near the top, I almost collide into Dax's still form. I lose my footing and topple backward.

Gravity pulls me into the snow. Powdery flakes cloud up when my shoulder hits, and the icy stuff covers half my face. I expect to sink deeper, but something catches my coat, keeping me from falling all the way. I shake away the flecks from my goggles to see Dax standing over me, yanking me upright.

"You okay?" he asks and brushes snow from my coat.

I'm a little shocked by his sudden concern for my well-being, but manage, "Yeah, I'm fine. Why did you stop?"

He points down the hill. "We're here."

Down below, a half mile or so away, sits a snow-capped building. As wide as a skyscraper is tall. Its off-white metal exterior blends into its surroundings. If the snow weren't so stark, I wouldn't be able to see it at all. From this distance, its ridged frame appears void of any windows. It holds one gigantic hole in the center of its wall. The hole extends from the ground to the building's jagged top and is for sure bigger up close.

"Let's get down there," Dax commands. From within his fur-lined hood, he nods toward the farm and descends the hill. Slate and Rook have already started.

I lean back as I make the descent with as much caution as possible to avoid a face-first tumble into the snow. We reach the bottom of the hill, and the road flattens. The only reason I can tell we're on the road is from the wooden poles spaced along either side. Otherwise, everything is an empty canvas of white.

After a strenuous trek over the terrain, we arrive at the hole in the wall. It's much, *much* bigger than I guessed. Six rigs could pass side by side through it easy. And now that I'm this close, I wouldn't call it a hole, as much as a massive metal gateway. There's nothing lighting the interior of the gate besides the high sun. And even its rays only extend a few feet past the opening. Shadow swallows Dax as he steps further in. Sunlight has burned my vision, and when I step into the dark, I can't see anything but the green outline of Dax's back.

Great. A black tunnel of nothingness. What I always wanted. Breath catches in my chest. Muscles in my arm twitch, and my coat constricts around my throat.

But soon my eyes adjust, and the anxiety fades when my surroundings come into view. There's light in here after all. Sure, the bulbs are forty feet up and recessed in the crevasses of this archway, but they're better than nothing. And by the time I catch sight of Dax, he's pounding away on a metal wall about twenty feet ahead.

Making way for Slate or Rook, I move toward the dead end. Dax's poundings reverberate through the cold, empty space. A flapping sound draws my attention to the dim ceiling. Pale creatures with pointed wings abandon their nests, startled by Dax's noise. In a group, they fly out the exit into the wasteland. I'm not sure what they were. Birds? Bats? A mix of the two? When I look back, a glowing white screen swirls over half the wall exactly like a holo-ad. I stumble a step away. It's high-tech. *Super* high-tech.

When I turn to Slate for answers, she's already nodding her head like she can read my thoughts. "Farms aren't part of the Grid," she says, pulling the goggles from her eyes. "In the Grid, yes, but definitely not *part* of it."

"State your name and business, Gridder." A scraggly kid with sepia skin and short coiled hair appears on the screen. I'm guessing he's a couple years younger than me, from the crack in his voice. Dressed in a solid gray uniform, he hardly looks at us while he fidgets with some papers in his hands.

Dax removes his hood. The strap of his goggles is still wrapped across the back of his head. "We're not Gridders, Milo. Open the gate."

The boy stops his shuffling to face us head-on. He scooches closer to the screen. "Dax! Oh, hey. Didn't recognize you without the big guys." With clenched fists, he pretends to turn a rig wheel made of air, miming what he means by *big guys*. "And there's Slate. And Rook. Red hair, red neck! Am I right? And some girl with ratty blue hair." I self-consciously run my fingers through the strands that escaped my bun. Yeah, it's knotty and windblown, but—ratty?

"No trucks though," the boy observes. "Where's the rest of your crew? You guys walk here or something? Pretty terrible conditions to be doing that. With the Flux and all. We expected you yesterday, but you show up now? That's some wild timing with all the—"

"Milo," Dax interrupts the boy, jaw tight. "Open the gate."

"Yeah, yeah. Of course, of course." He moves like he's about to comply but stops and leans into the screen. "Oh, wait, sorry, can't. Farm's been on lockdown since the Flux rolled in. That's what I was about to say. Only Hatcher can open the gate now. But she's with the Quell that showed up and initiated the lockdown."

My heart skips a beat. The Quell. Did they keep their word? Maybe Tori is all right, waiting for me on the other side of this metal wall.

"She said I can only disturb her if I see shipper trucks," Milo goes on. "So, are they behind you, or something?"

"Our trucks got stuck out in the Flux last night," Dax informs him, irritation growing with each word. "They're a few miles back, covered in snow. We need plows to dig them out. That's why we're here on foot."

Milo scratches the back of his head. "Well, I'm sorry. I mean, if you don't have any trucks then I can't—"

"Milo, you lily-livered piece of buzzard bait." Rook pushes past me and rips off his goggles. His eyes are slits of green fire. "How are we supposed to bring you our trucks if you ain't gonna let us get the plows? March them toothpick legs of yours over to Hatcher and get her to open this gate."

Unfazed by Rook's insults, Milo breaks into a toothy laugh. "Nice to see you too, Rook. But really, have you met Hatcher? She'll have my head if I pull her away with zero trucks to show for it. So, hang tight. I'll get the outer heat generators on so you don't freeze while you wait." He stands and flicks some switches around him.

"Tell her I've got something she's going to want to see," Dax says quickly, stopping the boy before he cuts the feed.

Milo stills. With narrowing eyes, he sits and leans over his control desk. "What are you talking about?"

Dax doesn't answer. Instead, he looks halfway over his shoulder, at me or Slate, I'm not sure. Then he digs into the pocket of his parka and pulls out something buried in his gloved fist. He raises his fist to the screen then uncurls some of his fingers. At first, I've got no idea what he's holding. Whatever it is, it impresses Milo, his eyes widening at the sight. But then a gust of wind blows through the tunnel, and a piece of Dax's possession flies up from his grip where I can see it.

A wave of icy dread threads through me. My fingers fly to the zipper of my parka. I pull it down and frantically search. I hope I'll find what I always find there. Instead, I meet bare skin. It's gone. I look back up at Dax. I don't have to see exactly what he's got in that dumb hand of his. The familiar gold chain dangling against his arm is enough. I have no idea when he snatched it off the ground, but that jerk stole my necklace and is using it as a bargaining chip.

THIS IS A JOKE. MY PRAYERS ARE
being answered with a joke.

For a solid minute, I stand inside the frigid gate open-mouthed and flustered. My heart urges me to rip my necklace out of Dax's thieving grip. My brain begs me not to. Since I tossed the pendant toward Cyrus's rig before Dax found me, I'm not sure if he knows it's mine. Or how he knows it's worth anything. Or this Hatcher lady.

Mac's dying words rush through my mind. *Tell her there is a cure. The users know. She has to find it before them.*

Did he mean a cure for Freeman's? Was he talking about my pendant? If the tattooed girl knows it can neutralize the drug, what else does she know? Does that have anything to do with why Dax got so angry when I showed him the photo? I'm holding zero cards and have no clue what game we're playing.

So, I don't lash out. I shut my mouth and wait to see how this plays out. One thing's for sure, as long as Dax has that pendant, I'm sticking to him like glue.

"Okay, I'll get her," Milo says. "But you'd better be right, Dax, or you're taking Hatcher's heat." He cuts the screen's signal, and we're left looking up at a blank wall.

Dax stuffs my necklace back into his parka pocket before he turns to face us. I flatten my expressions to neutral, squashing any hint I'm on to him. He glances around, more at Slate and Rook than me, his face neutral. Either he doesn't suspect me, or he's bluffing, seeing if I'll weed myself out.

"Maybe our luck is turnin'," says Rook.

Before I ask him what he means, the ground shakes. There's

a low boom and the circular farm gate opens into a half crescent
of white light. Dax, Rook, and Slate bend down to take off their
snowshoes. I follow their lead. By the time I unlatch one boot, the
others already walk through the door. I unlatch the other boot, pick
up both shoes, and run after them.

The second we're inside, I'm met with a gush of wind from air
jets in the entrance frame. I pull my hood over my head to keep my
mouth free of hair. Soon, the jets are replaced with a rush of heat
that rivals the Grid. Well, before the snow Flux. I can't get my coat
off fast enough. The others remove their coats and collapse their
poles, stuffing them both in their packs. They leave them on a shelf
in a recess, and I copy the action.

We trail a group of middle-aged men through a wide room
as white as the world outside. Unlike the shippers' station, this
place is sleek and modern. The walls are lit with long stretches
of rectangular lighting. Several screens sit embedded in their
geometric protrusions. What's spread across the screens is
motionless data—no rolling ads, no city flare. This place is all
business. Even the men display zero individuality. Dressed in plain
ivory jumpsuits, they blend in with their stark surroundings. It's
like following floating hands and heads of male-pattern baldness
through an empty science lab.

At the other end of the room, there's an alcove where the phrase
L19 is painted black on the wall from floor to ceiling. I guess it
stands for Level 19, but that would be a weird thing to label the
first floor.

From one side of the alcove, which seems to be a hallway, a
woman strides around the corner. Her ankle-length, white kimono
jacket flaps behind her like a cape. Beneath it, a pair of simple black
dress pants swooshes when she walks. Everything, from her deep
brown complexion to her bald head reminds me of Cyrus. That
and her sharp body language makes me think she's as much on the
warpath as Cyrus was when he went after the users who murdered
his friend.

She's older than me by fifteen years or so. The small wrinkles beside her mouth and eyes would look like laughter lines if it not for the heavy scowl she aims at us. A thin scar runs from the top of her shaved head, over her left eye, to end right above her lips painted raisin black.

Behind her, Milo trails close, holding a stack of loose papers against his chest.

"You're late," the woman says, directing her sharp accusation straight at Dax. A woman of many words, she stops in front of him and says no more. Though they are about the same height, the lady, who I'm sure is Hatcher, seems to loom over him. Her posture is such as one who owns the place, everyone in it, and all the shippers too.

Dax nods. "Ran into a *storm*." From the way he stresses the word storm, I've no idea if he's referring to the snow Flux or a chaos storm. I worry it's both.

"That so?" Hatcher says after a stretch of uncomfortable silence. "Care to explain?"

Dax tilts his head to look around her, and I follow his gaze. There, in the far corner, is a hardsuit talking to one of the lab workers. Covered from head to toe in dark metal, they blend in with the floor-to-ceiling black screen so well. I would have missed Quell presence without Dax pointing it out.

"Heard you have visitors," he says, avoiding her question, or answering it. I've a feeling they're saying paragraphs for every single word they utter.

Just like Uncle Trek and Aunt Marna. Many times, when we were in public, I'd stare at the two of them making no sense to anyone but themselves. After a few years, I learned the cues, picked up the code words. If Dax is half as cautious as my aunt and uncle, I'm sure he doesn't want to tell the details of our trip within Quell earshot.

Hatcher's eyes flicker, taking a second to ponder his words, then she gives a quick nod to the hall behind her. "The farm's popular right now. Come on. Let's find you a place to put your things."

On the surface, her words are sweet, welcoming. But as she

twists away, her jacket snapping behind her, I'll bet she's saving her chastisement for less prying ears.

We follow Hatcher down a hall and into another lab that's full of more than data screens. Thousands of hand-sized plants hang through ivory trays. They're stacked on vertical towers that stretch up to a ceiling of fluorescent light. An onslaught of spicy scents rush over me. They remind me of a sandwich Uncle Trek let me taste one time his boss gave him a natural food ticket. Arugula, he called it, and basil. Definitely basil. In the center of the lab, an enormous glass tube houses a full-grown tree. Men and women, dressed in white coveralls, inspect it and its surrounding plants. They push buttons on a circular display at the tree's base. Some lean over scaffolding beside the towers. Others adjust misters below the trays at their plants' exposed roots.

I try not to stare. It's so odd and beautiful. Like nothing I've seen in the cities. We have small rooftop gardens and a few aisles of natural produce—if you can afford to eat beyond your city-allotted limit or get your hands on a synth allergy food permit—but not this. If this is only the tip of the farm iceberg, how big is the rest?

"And this is just one of the synth food rooms," Slate says beside me, waking me from my daze by reading my mind. Or reading the wonder on my face.

"Synth food?" I ask. My awe shifts to confusion. I knew synth food was made in labs, but even with all the tech around me, I didn't picture it would be in anything so natural looking.

She indicates the stacks of plants. "Doesn't taste as good as the stuff grown in the dirt, but it's consistent. We can grow tons of it year-round. Cities can't get enough. Mix it with a bunch of chemicals to get an insta-meal, or condense it into a pill to swallow and boom, no one's got to cook. Not how I'd want to eat, but hey, nutritious, cheap food for everyone, right?" She quotes the Synth Food Market's slogan in such a way that makes it obvious she's got problems with big synth food companies.

I bite my lip to keep from answering. Digesting synthetic food in the form of a pill or out of processed just-add-water packages isn't how I like eating either. But when it's cheap and the only option, I'd choose eating over starving any day. The fact that the cities are trying to get nutrients into our food actually makes me feel better about the stuff. Not worse.

At the back of the lab, a couple of metal elevator doors slide open. A group of workers exits, pushing out dollies of fruit-filled crates. Hatcher, and soon the rest of us, file into the new empty space. No one turns to face the way we came in as there's a door on the elevator's opposite side. Unlike the elevator at the shipper station, this one has an operating touch screen. Beyond that, there are no other screens, and we ride in silence.

When the elevator opens, we step into a hall that's straight out of a ritzy eco restaurant ad. The convex, mirrored walls reflect oval skylights. Clean and minimal, this place is a stark contrast to the treetops filling the corridor's long window. Feeling brave, I walk close to the window. At first, I see nothing but treetops and my reflection. Milo was right. It is a rat's nest. Running my fingers through my hair does little to help my messy knot. I try to fix a few loose strands when we pass the trees, then stop. The vastness of the farm opens like the mouth of that terra cetus.

It's massive. Thousands of crops are patched out in a green and yellow quilt that covers an entire city. A city that's dug deep, really deep, into a pit. *L19.* We were nineteen floors up. And now, I'm here well over thirty stories high staring down at a valley so low its workers move around like specks. My world spins, swirling into grayness. I stumble back, brushing against Dax.

"Woah," he says, catching me by the elbow. "You all right?"

His scent is a mixture of metal, musk, and spicy soap. I take a second to collect myself. "Sorry, I—I'm fine." I don't know why my old fear of depths picked right then to act up. The way he looks at me with a brow raised above his frames tells me he doesn't believe me. When I don't offer any explanation, we pick up our walk down the hall.

He glances over to figure out what scared the new girl. "Looks like they're getting ready to harvest."

"Oh, really?" I ask, lacing my response with as much disinterest as possible. I refuse to turn and see what he's talking about. Instead, I fix my messy hair, braiding and unbraiding.

"You don't have to worry," he says. I startle. Did he guess my phobia? Am I that obvious? I drop my hands from my hair, and he goes on. "They can't get in here. All those guys are the same farmers I saw last month."

I work up a grateful smile and nod. I didn't even think about the Freeman's pushers infiltrating the farm. But if he wants to think that's the reason for my freak out, I let him. And then, because it's the nicest he's been to me all morning, I chance the question that kept me up last night.

"You checked on Mac last night," I start, shaky. "Is he . . . ?"

Dax breathes long and deep through his nose. He gives a small, quick headshake, and my heart sinks. Dead. Mac's dead, and I could do nothing to help him. Why did he have to give me his dying wish? Someone else would have understood. But no one else was there. I close my eyes, trying to remember the girl he wanted me to seek out. Warm terra-cotta skin. Tats. Straight black hair, or it might have had some wave. I think her nose was small, or long. If only I hadn't shown her picture to Dax last night, I'd still have that photo.

That's two things I've got to get back from this guy.

It's not long before we reach the end of the hall. Hatcher stops outside a closed door and turns to us. Putting her hands in her jacket pockets, she looks at Milo.

"The apple harvest needs more hands. Take the rest of the shippers with you. I'll call when we're done." She moves slightly to address us. "Daxal will join you later."

Milo's face falls. "The harvest? I thought—" he says, but with one fierce look from Hatcher, he swallows whatever he was about to say. Probably for his own safety. I doubt this lady takes the word "no" well.

"All right, this way." Milo slouches down the hall we came from like a kid grounded for a week from the virt-net.

Instead of following him, I bend down to unlace and relace my bootstraps. I'm staying as close to that necklace for long as I can.

Oblivious to my spying, Hatcher flattens her hand on a screen I hadn't noticed by the door—a palm scanner. Not any palm scanner, one of the scanners Aunt Marna had me practice hacking years ago. A Biometrics 2714. One that took me two weeks to crack. The scanner accepts her print and the door slides open.

"You coming?" Slate asks, halfway down the hall.

I don't budge. My feet are nailed to the floor as I watch Hatcher and Dax with my necklace disappear behind a sliding door. Every fiber of my being wants to rush after them—to salvage the last physical tie to my parents. But what can I do? If they know it's mine, I've no idea what they'll do to me. Slate snaps her fingers. I force myself instead to follow her into that farming hole. And hatch a plan along the way.

THE FUNNELING FARM ISN'T AS

terrifying on the ground as it looked from high above. It helps that the place is lit up like a synth with glow skin. I can see exactly how far down it goes. No surprises. If we steer clear of the sharp drop-offs to the lower levels, I can pretend we're all on one plane. There's no pit. We aren't sinking into oblivion. I'm fine.

I grab on to one of the fruit tree trunks to steady myself when Milo stops. Behind him stretches row after row of these trees, plump with crimson bulbs of fruit.

"It's a lot, I know." His voice dips in and out from high-pitched little boy to baritone. Hands on his hips, he surveys the orchard. "Wouldn't be so bad if we had the harvesters up and running. But with the parts still sitting on your rigs, that ain't happening till we dig y'all out. And who knows how long that'll be. Well, I'd know if I was in there with Hatcher, but nope. Out here with you guys, picking apples. With my hands. It's not like we just had the biggest find since ever or anything. Can't believe she didn't let me stay. *Apples.* You've got to be kidding me. Like I'm some snot brat who doesn't get to—"

"Shut up, Milo." Rook waves him off. "If we wanted to hear bellyachin' we'd be helping Rudy at the hog stalls. Now, where's Nova?"

Milo opens his mouth to defend himself but stops. His forehead wrinkles in confusion. "Nova?" He looks down the row of trees then points to someone I can't see at this angle. "Right there, with the others. Why?"

Rook doesn't answer. Instead, his attention is bent on Slate. She stands hugging herself, with her eyes fixed ahead.

"You ready?" he asks.

"No one's ever ready," she manages in a shaky voice. "Not for this."

"Well, let's do it anyway." Rook gently takes her hand, and together they pass Milo.

"Wait, I didn't give you your—" Milo starts, but the two shippers don't respond to his words and are out of earshot in seconds. "Baskets," he finishes with a sigh to no one. Rubbing his neck, he turns to me. "Welp, I guess it's just you and me. What's your name, newbie?"

I bristle at the word newbie. Not sure I've ever taken orders from a guy who looks young enough to babysit. But here we are.

"Juniper," I say, trying to see the girl Rook and Slate are now talking to. Looks like a girl. It's nearly impossible to tell around the walking wall that is Rook.

"Juniper. Like the tree?" Milo asks.

I nod. I've never seen the evergreen tree in real life, but I remember how fond my mom was of them. *Like blue-berried Christmas trees*, she'd say before kissing the top of my head at night. *And you, sweet girl, are my little blue Christmas.* My heart and bare neck ache at the memory.

"That'll be easy to remember," Milo says. "Got a few of them growing right outside my place. And your hair matches the berries. Well, they're a little paler, but close. Mind if I call you Berries?"

I try not to wince. Not another nickname. "Yeah, a little."

He laughs. "I'm Milo. I work in the control room most days. Me and my brother Jengo. He's older, but I'm the handsome one. Don't worry about the manual labor. I've had my fair share of farm duty. I'll show you how it's done. All you have to do—"

He keeps jabbering, but I tune him out the second the girl I assume is Nova collapses to her knees. I get a full view of her face. Tears stream down her rosy cheeks. My breath catches. I've seen her before.

In Mac's photo.

I may not have had the bloodstained paper long, but I know it's her. Same straight black hair. Same narrow nose and heart-shaped face. Only, when she puts both hands to her mouth, I note one undeniable difference. No tattoos. Her red flannel sleeves are pulled up to her elbows, and not a single drop of ink stains her pale forearms. I blink. Maybe they were fake tattoos in the photo? But who would cover themselves that heavily in fake artwork? Maybe she had them removed. This place might be higher tech than the Grid, but I doubt they offer tattoo removal services. Then why does she look so much like the girl in that picture?

"Is she okay?" I ask, interrupting Milo's monologue.

He turns around. Rook, Slate, and a few other workers guide the hysterical girl through the trees and out of sight.

"I don't–" Milo stops and spreads out his hands. "Come on. We're going to handpick with less than half of us now?" He looks around for someone to acknowledge him, but no one does. Not surprising when his audience is a crew of five farmers who don't look like they can hear him over whatever's pumping through their earbuds, and me.

"Maybe we should get started," I offer, hoping he'll move us closer to where the girl disappeared. I want to get a better look or eavesdrop or something. Plus, they might say something about my pendant.

"Good idea, Berries," he says, slapping me on the back. "Like that can-do attitude."

I don't hide my cringe this time, partly wishing back Dax's princesa title.

He moves us into the orchard. Once we near the place where the group went, there's nothing there but trunks, leaves, and dirt. I glance around, hoping to catch sight of them.

"They'll come back later," Milo calls to me, far down the row.

I jog to catch up with him. "Who was that girl?"

He frowns. "What girl?" His face clears. "You mean Nova? Surprised you don't know about her. Her being a shipper once and all. You really are new, aren't you?"

I'm not sure the question is rhetorical. He leaves a silence for me to answer, but he also starts to pick fruit like he couldn't care less if I do. *Snap, snap, snap.* He plucks apples and drops them into the basket. I guess he's done talking about Mac's girlfriend. But I'm not.

I watch him for a few picks, then copy his technique as best I can on the tree beside him. I pluck and drop apple after apple into the basket between us. "Is that typical?" I ask. "For shippers to leave the trucks and work the farm?"

"Here and there." He shrugs. "Happens more with the girls. Grid's a hard place to work, you know. Some people ship only to say they've done it. Nova did it longer than most. Probably because of her sister."

My ears perk. "Sister?"

He grins, like he enjoys knowing something more than someone older than him. "Astrid. Didn't matter how hard it got, she refused to leave the shippers. Crushes will do that to you."

And here we are, exactly where I hoped the conversation would drift. "She had a crush on a shipper?"

Milo stops his picking and becomes a bit too animated. "Huge crush. Most people don't know this, but once she became the guy's girlfriend, her brother got mad and sent her to—*oof*—aw, man!"

While he spoke, he bumped into a basket and knocked the whole thing over. Apples roll this way and that, through his lanky legs and down the hill. We fumble about to pick them up. A few fruits interfere with the other farmers. They give him annoyed looks before tossing them to Milo, who already has his hands full.

"Thanks, guys," he says, trying to catch them without losing his collection. "Okay, I got it. Ow! Watch it, Knox, I know where you sleep." His threat only makes the farmers laugh.

A burly, balding man in a checkered shirt calls from down the row. "If y'all are done messing around, we've got two loads ready for processing."

Milo brightens. "Yes!" With his arms full, he dashes to the basket and tosses the apples in. "We'll take them! C'mon, Berries." Before

I register what's got him so excited, he runs behind me, ushering me forward.

At the edge of the trees, he stops in front of two stacks of brown boxes piled high on a hover cart. Twice my height and three times my width, the stacks are filled with red and green fruit. They must be the loads that need processing. Whatever that means.

"Nothing to it." He kicks the release brake pad on the hover cart. There's a whoosh of air then the cart jerks forward. Milo reaches out and catches it with his hand. He swerves the stack to show how easy it is to move when it's hovering four inches above the ground. We use hover carts to move sofas and fridges every time Uncle Trek gets the urge to upend us again, so I'm not new to them. But I smile anyway when he turns to address the farmers. "Don't wait on us. Gotta teach our newbie the ropes."

He pushes his stack back toward the main building. Behind him, the farmers snicker and shake their heads. We soon step off farm soil and onto slick floors. Cool air brushes my skin from the fans pulsating above, and the hum of electricity surges around us. It's near impossible to hear Milo's insistent chatting. Which would be nice if I weren't trying to follow him through the unknown with a huge pile of boxes blocking my view. I stop several times to peer around my stack. Each time he's farther and farther ahead. The guy either doesn't care that I've never been here and have no idea where I'm going, or he's that oblivious. I ram the stack into white wall after white wall. It's like we're in an overgrown rat maze. There's a loud clang and the apples rattle, but I don't damage the walls, so it's not that bad. Until I run into a person. Apples tumble from the cart and papers burst in the air, falling like the snow outside.

"Hey!" a man cries out. "Watch it."

I look around the stack. "Sorry. Are you okay?"

The middle-aged man in a lab coat rubs his nose and picks up the scattered papers. I leave the stack and help him. By the time we've got the apples in the cart and papers in his arms, he gives me a curt nod then turns to leave.

"You're welcome," I mutter, picking up one of the apples I missed and sticking it in my pocket. The empty hall forks in three directions with zero sign of Milo. Great. I peek down each hall. There's no moving pile of boxes in any of them. Only repeating rows of skinny lights and a few wall screens. Maybe one of them has a map or a "Processing Center This Way" sign with an arrow. *Eeny, meeny, miney . . . that one.*

I take the far-left hall and head straight to the first screen. I swipe my hand over it, and it flashes to life—right to a password screen. I mutter and push the stack to the end of the hallway. Which seems to take forever before it opens into a courtyard.

I hope this is the processing area. Walls with open balconies and greenery hanging down encircle the space. They extend several stories to end at a ceiling of artificial light so bright, it rivals the fake sun of the cities. In the middle of the courtyard sits a rectangular fountain surrounded by a stone bench. There are people everywhere, moving around like they've all got somewhere else to be. Some wear calf-high boots and sweat-stained shirts, pushing hover carts filled with tools. Others, in lab coats, cluster together, eyes glued on holo-pads. None of them are Milo. I try to stop a few people, hoping they can give me directions, but can't get anyone to look up from what they're doing. After a few attempts, I manage to get the attention of a girl with long blonde braids dressed in gray overalls.

"Hi," I say when she stops. "Do you know where the processing center is?"

She peers around the brown sacks in her skinny arms to look me up and down. "'Course I do. Got to put these down first. Hang out here for a sec, and I'll show you, okay?"

Thankful, I nod. When she heads off to wherever she was going, I sit down on the stone bench and wait. Seconds turn to minutes. Two, then three, then ten. I assume the girl forgot about me when I hear voices coming from the other side of the stack.

"It's already passed the primary vote," says a hushed male voice. He must be sitting right against the other side of the stack. "I'm telling you, that's why we're crawling with hardsuits."

"C'mon," says another man, incredulously. "They ain't here cause of the Plex and their laws. It's a routine check. We get one every year."

"We do," the first man agrees, "but in November. I'm telling you, once Orange Pipe convinces those idiots to make that stuff legal there, the rest of the state will pump every farm, city, and square inch full of hardsuits. Loads of Quell will be the only way to keep that junk out of places it ain't legal. They might've been plugging leaky holes before, but the whole dam is about to break. If you don't get your brother and his family out of the Plex now, you ain't gettin' another chance."

Their voices drop into mumbles so low, I can't make out any more of their conversation. But what I did hear rings in my ears. The Plex. Orange Pipe. Those morons must have passed a primary vote to make Freeman's legal inside their dome. Stupid, stupid people.

I lean back on the fountain bench and glance around at the courtyard walls and farmers rushing about. At least these people don't have their synthetic heads filled with—

A flash of light bursts from one of the balconies. It shines out a window a few stories up in the building to my right. The flare is bright but quick, over before I can shield my eyes. I rub my lids with the palms of my hands and bat away the green dot forming when I close them. It's like I stared at the sun. What could have—I look back up at the rounded windows and almost fall into the fountain.

Standing beside the floor-to-ceiling window, Hatcher is holding up my necklace by the chain. She dangles it within her thin fingers and ogles over it with Dax. His arms are crossed over his chest, and he nods at her every word. But the person standing next to him has me squinting. No, it can't be. Tall and lanky, with buzzed, blond hair. And in no way supposed to be here without my best friend.

Zane.

He slaps Dax on the back and grins so wide I can practically count all his pearly whites. My fists clench. Pearly whites I'll gladly knock out one by one if something has happened to Tori. Forget the stack, forget Milo. I jump to my feet and run.

AS FAR AS I KNOW, THE BEST WAY TO

Zane is straight ahead and up. I thought the courtyard was crowded before. Now it swarms with farmers. It's like they all dropped what they were doing to wander about in front of me. I swerve around a couple of men carrying trays of plants and through a line of kids following a woman.

I rush through the open doors of the building ahead. The place is familiar—same marble pillars, same small trees in square boxes. I must be in that lobby Milo led us through on the way to the orchard. Good thing I made a mental note of everything from here to Hatcher's office.

No one stops me in the elevators or down stale hall after stale hall. It's not long before I'm outside Hatcher's office, staring at the solid white door keeping me out. I eye the palm scanner. I know I could crack it in under three minutes. But then I'd get a whole lot more questions than answers. And all I care about right now are answers. Where's my best friend kind of answers. So, I opt for the safe route, and knock. And wait. And knock. And wait.

Either they can't hear me, or they don't want me in there. I look to the palm scanner again, tracing its edges with my fingers. I step closer to the door and hear voices from the other side. They're muffled so thick, they come across as low mumbles at first. I press my ear to the metal and make out Dax's words.

". . . about it, but I don't know," he is saying. "I just met the girl. Figured I'd ask in a week or two, once I got to know her better. See if she can handle it. But from what I've seen so far, we might as well have a full-blown synth on our crew. Can't open a manual door without help."

My cheeks burn at his bluntness. So that's what he thinks of me, a useless girl holding him back? Never mind that I saved him and his entire crew at that fueling station. I tighten my grip on the palm scanner. Fine, guess I'll add giving him a piece of my mind to the list of things I'll say once I get through this door.

"I wouldn't underestimate her," says another male voice I'm pretty sure is Zane's. "Her friend had a lot of stories. If even half of them are true, she can help us."

I press my ear forward until it's flat on the door. I can't think of what Tori would have said that would interest them. Sure, she knows me better than anyone. But I've never told her the secret things Aunt Marna and Uncle Trek taught me. Nothing of the self-defense training or the hacking. So, what did she tell him? That I can draw him a pretty picture or make risky life choices?

"*Can* help us, or *will* help us?" This time it's Hatcher's voice, moving from one side of the door to the other like she's circling the room.

"If she wants a paycheck, she will," says Dax. "Otherwise, we don't need her. One of the crew can stay back. Take her to Austin and we'll figure something else out."

A lump forms in my throat so thick it takes two swallows to get it down. Take me back to Austin? Back to my aunt and uncle and then the Plex?

"There's no time to figure anything else out, Daxal," says Hatcher. "The window to get her in there is almost gone. It's bad enough the Quell have her friend. We were lucky to get two low-grades. Now all we have is one. We'll have to—"

I stop listening and fall to my knees. My chest spasms. The Quell still have Tori? I should've been more forceful. Refused to let her come. What am I going to do now? I've got to find her somehow. I've got—

A series of hydraulic wooshes and clanks sound at my right. I scramble to my feet. At first, I see no one, the wall protrudes out, blocking my view. I poke my head around to catch sight of a crimson metal suit disappearing around the corner. A hardsuit. A Quell. EVOLEN-6.

My heart starts to race. She'll know what happened to Tori. The back of my head still stings from where she slapped me. So, I doubt she'd tell me anything, but I've got to try. I round the corner, bumping into a potted fern or two. When I look down the hall, the hardsuit is gone.

But I can still hear her. *Whoosh. Clank, clank. Clank, clank. Whoosh.* To the left. I rush to follow. Through a hall and down some stairs. *Whoosh. Clank, clank. Clank, clank. Whoosh.* I hear her to my right. I swerve. This hall is empty like the last. The overhead lights flicker, and there's a strange burning scent swirling in the air. The Quell's banging sounds vanish, but at the end of the hall, a door slowly closes.

I dash to catch it. Seconds before it clicks shut, my fingers slide in. I bend forward to catch my breath. When I finally steady my breathing, I slip into the room. Into the ink-black unknown.

I tense, but then press on, carefully letting go of the door and allowing the darkness to swallow me up. Not even a sliver of light spills in from the crack under the door. I can't see a thing. Not walls, not floor, not my hand in front of my face. Why aren't the lights on the Quell's suit brightening this place? They should be on. I should be able to see in here. This was a bad idea. I turn back, run my hands over the door till I find the handle, and jerk down.

It's locked.

No, it can't be. I shake the cold metal handle vigorously. It rattles but doesn't budge. Panic, anxiety, and everything I can't handle in this dark trap of emptiness sizzles through me. Tori. I have to think of Tori. What does she always say to me when it's like this?

Pretend you're not there. You're somewhere flat, bright, and you can see it all.

Okay, I can do that. *Flat, bright, and I can see it all.* I repeat the words as I close my eyes and breathe through nausea. *Flat, bright, and I can see it all.* I remember one of my elementary field trips to the city park. No ink-black tunnels. No deep pits. Just an open field and the artificial sun warming me. The thought soothes me. My breathing evens, and I'm able to move on—to feel what's around me instead of imagining it.

I shuffle forward until my boot collides against something hard. A desk? I run my fingers along its surface—cold, smooth, covered in boxes and bags of I don't know what. Pebbles? Rice? Something rattles several feet ahead. I freeze. It shuffles and twitches. Like it's digging through papers or piles of garbage. Maybe it's the Quell, but I can't tell. A Quell should sound more like a mechanized war machine—with heavy footfalls and loud clanks of metal. And I should be able to see the thing. Whatever's in here with me, it's more like a mini cleaning bot on the fritz. Only, I haven't seen any cleaning bots since I got here.

I edge forward. Whatever it is, I hope it's got a light screen on it. I'm only a couple of feet closer when it stills. I don't hear anything for a few seconds. Then it expels a string of odd noises straight out of a trippy video game. Shrills and clicks bounce off the walls. I can't tell if there's only one of these things in here or dozens. The faint burning smell intensifies into the hot stench of a full-blown bonfire.

And then I see it.

At first, it's only four blue dots. Whatever sensors it has have picked up on my presence and flicked to life. But then the glowing dots blink. I step back. It clicks and coos. The feathers covering its two faces and snake-like necks spark from electric blue to neon orange, red, and fuchsia. The colors descend in a bright flash all the way down to its lengthy, sharp wings and tail.

A grid beast.

I'm in here with a grid beast. And not just any beast. One with firecrackers for feathers and two heads. The bizarre bird, about the length of my arm and as tall as my calf, inches closer to me. Its heads snap with quick twitches to watch me with all four ice-blue eyes. Heat radiates off its feathers like they're actually on fire.

I scramble back, knocking into a bag of something and landing on my side. I yelp. The firebird follows me and hops onto the overturned bag. At least in its glow, I can see my surroundings. Stuffed silver bags fill almost every inch of this place. Besides that, it's just me and Two-Heads in this storage closet. No EVOLEN-6 and no way out.

I scoot closer to the locked door. The grid beast goes ridged at my motion. Its glacial eyes lock onto my every move. I reach for the handle above my head, but stop when the bird scrapes the metallic bag with its razor talons. The screech of claws against metal sends a chill across my skin. We stay frozen, eyeing each other for so long my legs go numb.

I try again for the handle. It puffs out its chest, throws its heads back, and lets out a piercing crow. Panicked, I scream. My cry doesn't deter the bird. It crows from each head, one after the other. It's like someone took my holo-cuff's alarm tone, remixed it with trills and clicks, and stuck it down this bird's throats.

I lower my fingers from the handle. Satisfied, the bird shuts up. Instead of screaming till my ears bleed, it hops off the bag and comes at me. I press against the door as far as I can go. Two-Heads hops right beside my hip, leans over, and pecks my pocket. I bat at it, but it keeps coming back. When I finally shoo it away long enough, I reach in my pocket to pull out the apple I stuffed there.

"Is this what you want?" I ask.

It chirps when I show it the shiny red orb. I roll its snack to the other side of the room, and the bird follows. Thankfully, Two-Heads prefers fruit to flesh. I hope that's either the most filling apple known to man, or the grid beast is a slow eater.

With the creature distracted, I go for the door handle again. But this time, when I reach for it, the thing turns on its own. I scoot back seconds before it opens. Standing in a light that seems brighter than the sun are Dax and Zane.

Confusion wrinkles Dax's forehead as he looks down at me. "What are you doing in here?"

I cough, stand up, and catch myself on the doorframe before my numb legs give way. "I was trying to find Milo. Or wherever it was he wanted me to put that apple stack. Which now I've also lost."

"And you thought you'd find him in a storage closet?"

I try to shrug nonchalantly. "I can't find him anywhere else. But then the door locked on me, so it wasn't like I could search the rest of the building."

Zane stares past Dax. "That what I think it is?"

I don't follow his wide eyes. The only thing interesting in the storage closet is the fiery red grid beast. Instead, I cross my arms and block the entrance. Zane has a ton of explaining to do, and I'm determined to make him spill every word.

"It's a bird," I say, then shift further to block him. "What are you doing here?"

He stretches his neck this way and that, trying to find an opening. He wants a look at Two-Heads but doesn't want to knock me over to do it.

"We heard you scream," he says. "Feed room door jams all the time. It's why they leave it propped open."

I sigh. While I'm glad they came along to free me, I want to know why he's here at the farm in the first place. And not with my best friend.

"No," I start to spell it out for them. "I mean—" Before I can say anything else, Two-Heads peeks out from between my legs.

Zane utters an exclamation and jumps back. "It *is* one!"

Dax cuts loose a string of Spanish with such vitriol, I don't want to know the translation.

"What?" I ask. The bird that seemed ready to bite me or set me on fire seconds ago rubs both heads on my calf like a house cat. "What is it? What's wrong?"

Dax has joined Zane. The two of them are up against the wall on the other side of the corridor. Both their faces have gone ashen.

"Mala suerte," Dax says under his breath. "It's a mala suerte."

"A mala-what?" I ask, now wary of the creature. "Is it going to hurt me or something?"

"You?" Dax answers sharply. "Not at all."

I take a step forward and the bird follows, still rubbing my leg and cooing. "Then what's the problem? It's like you guys have never seen a bird before. I admit it's a weird little bird but feed him an apple and he's my best friend, I guess."

"*Your* best friend," Zane stresses. "No one else's."

Proving his point, the grid bird swivels around my leg and rushes the two of them, hissing like a glitching holo-projection. To their credit, neither of the guys yelp, but they do flinch.

"Then why don't you feed it an apple too?" I suggest. It's not like the farm doesn't have plenty of them. I'm sure they can keep their own animals fed. Or maybe that's why Two-Heads was in the closet in the first place.

"Because I like keeping my hands," Zane answers.

Two-Heads snaps at him then hops back to my side.

"Okay, fine," I say, "He's grumpy and only likes me. Tell me where his keepers are, and I'll take him to them."

Zane laughs and Dax shakes his head. I can't tell if they think I'm plain dumb or the greenest shipper known to man. Probably both.

"No one keeps a mala suerte," Dax informs me like his little statement is common knowledge.

"Unless you want the luck of a pile of waste on burning day," Zane adds, earning himself a sharp glare from Dax.

"So, what?" I say. "He just snuck in here?"

Dax lifts a shoulder. "Something like that. Mala suerte birds are strange things. They show up whenever they want and attach themselves to whomever they want."

"Not that you'd ever want that friendship," mutters Zane, then looks at me expectantly.

I close my eyes for a moment. I've no idea why he can't tell me what he's going on about. But fine. I'll bite. I open my eyes. "Why not?"

"Because it's a bad omen."

"An omen?"

Dax sighs in exasperation. "A stupid omen and a stupid superstition. The only real bad thing about it is it's a nasty bird that's hard to get rid of."

"More like impossible," Zane corrects him. "Until it thinks its mark doesn't need it anymore, those birds will stick to the unlucky guy like metal on a Quell unit."

I frown, unsure if he's pranking me or warning me of something unfun in my future. He drops his voice to whisper to Dax. But he's not very quiet, and I catch every other word or so.

"Unlucky . . . can't . . . never . . . her . . . bad idea."

It's then that Mac's explanation of a chaos storm replays in my head.

If he's really unlucky, we maroon him. That's that.

My nails dig into my palms. They aren't seriously going to maroon me because a weird little bird didn't try to bite me? It's beyond stupid. And what are they going to do now that I'm at the farm? Leave me here?

Dax lifts his hand to cut off Zane's word stream. Unlike his loud buddy, he keeps their private conversation going so low I'm forced to guess what he's saying. Something in my favor, I hope. But probably something more like what he finished telling Hatcher.

If she can't do the job, we don't need her . . . send her back . . .

Over my twitching corpse.

"Look," I say, interrupting their little pretend-the-girl-we're-talking-about-isn't-right-in-front-of-us time. "I don't care what you do with the bird, or where it came from, or what omen you think it means." I point at Zane. "All I care about is why you're here and Tori's not."

Zane slumps against the corridor wall. Dax watches him, as if wanting to know the same thing.

"That's fair." Zane rubs his hand over his buzzed, blond hair before saying any more. "They shouldn't have taken us in the first place. The Quell think they know everything. Can pick up on any high-tech in the Grid. So instead of listening to me when I said we had nothing, they held us up in a tiny room with two bunks. All while they dismantled my rig. To find, guess what, nothing.

"Your friend's a tough one. Put up with all the Quell junk during the interrogations." He shakes his head. "They shouldn't have put her through any of it."

Interrogations. My imagination runs wild. I picture my best friend enduring all kinds of tortures because of me.

"Why isn't she here, Zane?" I demand a bit loudly to drown out my imaginings.

He shakes himself from whatever funk he was in before answering. "Don't know. Right before the Quell let me go, they said someone was coming for her. Whoever it was, she seemed relieved."

Someone was coming for her? That couldn't be right. Sure, her stepdad and mom would do anything for her. But unless Tori sent a text before Dax confiscated our tech, they wouldn't know she was in the Outer Grid at all. Let alone stuck in a Quell holding station. So how would they know where to go get her? Unless she did sneak some kind of device into the rig. Though how she hid anything from a bunch of tech-detecting hardsuits is beyond me.

Zane must notice the confusion on my face. "They told us both to write down contact info when we arrived. Quell must've contacted her people. Told them where she was. I wanted to stay till I knew she was safe, but they forced me out the second my rig was put together."

His gaze is on the floor, and I can tell leaving Tori behind is eating at him. But for me, it's like one of the weights on my shoulders fills with helium and floats off. Tori must have contacted her parents. Which means she's out of the Grid and home safe.

"There's something else we need to talk about," says Dax. Unlike Zane's downcast demeanor, his chrome shades focus right on me with no qualms.

Yet again, his talk with Hatcher races through my mind. I've no idea what they want me to do. Why did they let me come on this trip in the first place? I have a feeling I'm not going to like the answer. Especially since it comes with the real chance he'll send me packing if I fail.

Right as I gather enough courage to ask him what he wants,

Rook barrels down the hall. He scans both directions at the fork. When he spots us, he closes the distance to Dax in two breaths.

"Retrieving trucks are ready to go," he reports. "If we head out now, we should have the crew here before sunup."

Dax's posture instantly eases. "Best news I've heard all day. All right, gear up. Let's go get our boys."

Both Rook and Zane obey his orders, marching down the hall without as much as a glance at me or the weird bird. But Dax doesn't go with them. Instead, he moves closer to me, his voice just above a whisper.

"The mala suerte is a complication, Juna," he says, using my nickname I mentioned on his rig. I'm surprised he remembered it. "We're lucky it was hiding from Rook."

Hiding? I look down and sure enough, Two-Heads is behind the door, picking on leftover apple bits.

"I can convince Zane to keep his mouth shut," he says. "But Rook's a whole different matter. I'll get Glowen to set you up a sleeping pod while we're gone. And we'll talk when I get back. In the meantime, do whatever you can to keep that bird out of the shipper's sight. I don't believe in marooning someone based on a mythical bad luck bird, but you'd better believe my crew does."

THE GIRL WHO OFFERED TO HELP ME

in the courtyard is the same girl Dax asked to find me a room for. Glowen works in the farm's grid beast research sector, so he said she shouldn't be freaked out by my new pet. We travel through the near-abandoned back halls he insisted we use. She tugs on her two blonde braids while keeping a good six feet space between herself and Two-Heads. If this girl is his definition of composure, I'd hate to see someone terrified of the bird.

"It's not that I haven't seen one before," says Glowen, owning up to her aversion. Her huge brown eyes lock onto Two-Heads. It's a good thing the hall is void of furniture or obstructions. Otherwise, she'd crash into it all. She stumbles over her own feet as if to prove my point.

"It's just, well . . ." Her mousy voice trails off. I couldn't hear her very well in the first place. Her breathy tone can't compete with the machines working the fields outside the hallway. One of the gigantic orange vehicles flies near the long strip of window to my right. It's a sleek ship, like the skycabs people use in the cities. But it flies so close to the ground, its underbelly grazes the wheat field below. Attached to its shiny nose is a wide bar of spinning blades, chopping the field up into a dense yellow cloud. While I'm grateful the cloud blocks my view of the farmers, I'm not sure how well it blocks their view of me. Or at least their view of me with this bird. So, I pick up the pace, hoping the girl will catch the hint.

"It's just," she says again panting, running to get in front of me, "the only one I've seen was in a textbook. Much smaller. Much less, well, alive."

"You have somewhere to put him, right?" I ask. I hope she doesn't want to stick him in the same place she's putting me. Because I'm not bunking with a wild animal, let alone one that gives everyone here the creeps.

"Sure. Somewhere," Glowen says without conviction.

I look down. She's a tiny thing. Smaller than Tori and a couple years younger than both of us. Her skin is so ghostly pale, I can't tell if she stays out of direct sunlight, or if the bird has her spooked. With her size and aversion to Two-Heads, I don't know if she'd be much help getting the bird to wherever "somewhere" is.

The hall dead-ends to a white door with a palm scanner. She flattens her hand against it and the door slides open with a whoosh.

"Welcome to the grid beast sector," she says.

We step out of the stale white hall into a thick forest. It's every big-budget jungle experience hologram playing at once. Solid, wide-leafed plants in hunter and jade fill a sector that's got to be twice the size of the orchard. While the hall blasted us with the cool seventy-degree AC I'm used to, this place feels more like the Grid. Hot, sticky, and air so thick it's like breathing in soup. It makes me glad I'm still in the temp-controlled shipper gear. I'd swear we actually were outside if I couldn't see the geometric beams above us, closing us in like a city dome. I squint. White snowflakes fall onto the glass, or plastic, or whatever it is up there.

"Is that—"

"Yep." Glowen nods before I can finish. "This is the only place where you can see the Grid from inside. It was supposed to be an observational outpost sector. But we found the grid beasts we recuperate like it here. So now it's their home too. Until we can get them back in the wild, of course."

That's new. I had no idea anyone cared about mutated animals anymore. I wrote a freshman history paper on a group of animal activists who tried to do something for the beasts. They said it was humanity's duty to restore what we've destroyed through our chemical negligence. A few years after the chem clouds subsided, the activists followed a colony of three-eyed rats back to their dens.

They hoped to find out more about the creatures that burrowed under the domes. What they found instead was a plague that shut the Plex down for a full year and killed thousands. Since then, no city dweller does anything to help the grid beasts. Other than that one story, I've never heard of anyone post-Weather Collapse giving a second thought to the altered animals out here.

So why do these farmers keep a sector like this? What could they gain from rehabilitating these mutant creatures?

More questions fill my mind while we walk the narrow catwalk through the trees. But the further we walk, the less Glowen talks, and I start to fill the silence with worry. Will the shippers really get rid of me because of a bird? Did Tori make it back to Austin okay? Will Aunt Marna and Uncle Trek find me out here and drag me to the Plex?

Anxiety builds. Like my head is in a food packet cooker, ready to blow with any more pressure. I've got to distract myself, strike up some sort of conversation.

"Have you been working in this sector long?" I ask.

She scrunches her face in thought. "Longer than most, I guess. Not as long as my parents. They've been at it forever. And their parents before them. One Pickering after the other. Since the beginning of the outlying farms, I suppose."

My eyes widen. That long? Outlying farms have been a part of Texas for hundreds of years. Or at least since the early days of the Collapse.

"So, it's a family thing?"

"You could say that," Glowen says. "My sixteen sisters would agree with you."

I have to grab the catwalk's rails to keep me upright.

"Sixteen?" I squeak. It's rare for a city family to have more than two kids. Unheard of to have any over four. But this girl has *sixteen* sisters?

"How can you have sixteen siblings? Why haven't your parents been . . . um . . . you know . . ." I look around as if a population official might overhear me. Which is dumb. I don't have my cuff, so they can't listen in. We're hundreds of miles from the city. And if anyone cared to throw her parents in a detention cell for birth overages, they'd have done so by now.

She smiles at me like having double-digit sisters is the most normal thing in the world. "Actually," she remarks. "I've got nineteen. But my three brothers drive rigs." She laughs at my gaping expression. "You really are city-sheltered, aren't you? No one limits births on the farms. It ain't like anyone in the city's going to drop their cushy life to tough it in the Grid. If we want any new farmhands, we've got to make them ourselves. It's typical for whole sectors to be run by one family."

"Wow," I say, because I'm not sure what else to say. What it would be like to have that many siblings? Or any siblings at all. The lonely nights might have been easier to bear with someone close going through the same thing. It'd be nice to have someone understand why I can never go back to the Plex.

"Glowworm!" cries a girl's voice, rousing me from my thoughts.

Glowen moans. "And there's one of my sisters now."

Below the catwalk is a girl who looks like Glowen might in a couple years gazing up at us. Her blonde hair is in a high, tight bun. She's about two sizes too lanky for the tan overalls that end way above her ankles. In her hands are two silver buckets the size of my head. On her freckled cheeks is a grin of superiority aimed right at her younger sister.

"Thought you'd wiggle out of vorgle duty, huh?" She drops the two buckets to the dirt. Gray liquid splashes out of each. Either I'm imagining it, or something moves in the dark water.

"Wouldn't dream of it, Orla," Glowen answers. "You'd hunt me down if I did."

The other girl shrugs in agreement. "Someone's got to make sure you keep your promises. We wouldn't want little Milo to know about your crush on him, or anyone else to find out about what you two do when—"

"Okay, okay!" Glowen shouts, her face burning a fiery shade of red. "I'm coming down. Shut your blabbing trap, will ya?"

Orla shows her teeth, then trots away into the trees.

I want to tell Glowen it doesn't matter her sister spilled her secret. I hardly know her and only met Milo hours ago. If she wants to crush on the little guy, go for it. But she avoids eye contact with anything other than the plank we're walking on. So, instead, I choose a different topic.

"What's a vorgle?"

She picks up both buckets and hands me one. "Come on, I'll show you."

Bizarre creatures flutter, scamper, and creep around us. I bet it takes us twice as long to reach the vorgle enclosure as it would if Glowen went by herself. I keep stopping to ask questions. "What's that green furball?" "Is that a scaled monkey?" "What's that thing with pink-flowered legs, plant or animal?"

Glowen answers without a hint of annoyance. "That's a horseltoad," she says. "It's called a morwamp." And, "Yes, but don't touch it or you'll be stuck in bed for weeks."

I keep both hands in my uniform's pockets the rest of the way. Soon, the plants become so thick above us I can't see a speck of dome roof. Our clear path dead-ends ahead. Glowen takes a big step off the pavement and onto the dirt and grass. She motions for me to follow. I move forward a little but am not sure where else to go. The only thing ahead is dense brush and massive, broad-leafed plants. Glowen flattens her hand on a leaf the size of her head before looking back at me.

"It takes a second to get used to," she says. "Don't worry, your eyes will adjust."

Before I ask what she's talking about, she pushes the leaf down and bright light bursts out. I shield my eyes, which are burning behind their lids. I rub them a couple times until the pain subsides enough to open them again. And what I see once the blur dies has me gasping in awe.

I've played my share of high fantasy virt-games both at home and in the reality rooms of several clubs. So, it's not like I haven't seen trippy, oversaturated scenery before. But no fake forest of wonder comes close to what is in front of us. Mushrooms the size of my legs, and some as tall as the trees we passed earlier, grow in a rainbow array around a large pool. Light explodes from beneath their polka dot caps in pinks, whites, and tangerines. I guard my face from the glare with my arm as I move deeper into the strange garden.

The teal grass below me grows well past my shins. A few of the trees, the ones closest to the pond, are tinted blue, wide as my waist, and somewhat translucent. On their branches, clear perfect spheres bubble out almost like a bizarre disease. Each bubble is half filled with a fizzing indigo liquid I can't place. It almost looks like one of the battery charger drinks I've seen enhanced synths guzzle down. Whatever it is, the pond in front of us teams with the stuff. I hesitate to move closer, but Glowen doesn't miss a beat. She hauls her bucket right to the bank and kneels.

Beside her is a white wooden sign with black letters that reads:

VORGLE POND
DO NOT ENTER!
FEED AT OWN RISK.

Glowen notices me staring at it. "I know," she says, "it sounds scary. It's a weird creature, sometimes cranky, but as long as we pay attention and stay out of the water, we'll be fine. Vorgle's been in the pond longer than I've been alive, and there hasn't been an incident in at least twenty years. The research we get from what grows here alone is worth it.

"The glow-mushrooms," she explains, nodding to the nearest fungus, "they keep lit ten hours longer than anything you'll find in a city. And vorgle burls," she says, pointing to the see-through bulbs on the blue trees, "Those things'll give you a day or two of oxygen by sucking on them. Don't ask how they found that out. Anyway, Hatcher likes our data, so we get to keep it."

She reaches into her bucket, picks up a writhing fish by its back fins, then tosses it into the pond with a splash. I expect a monster to snap its jaws at it from under the water. After a minute or two, nothing does. Glowen moves from her knees to sit beside the bucket, looking like this might take a while.

She throws another fish, followed by the same outcome. I sit down on the other side of the bucket. Two-Heads scratches the blue-flecked dirt near my feet. He kicks the stuff between his feathers before laying on his belly. It sure seems like everyone's freaked out for no reason. So far, he's only been a friendly little bird.

After several minutes, Glowen is still throwing fish into the multicolored pond. I figure it is as good a time as any to get a few questions in.

"So, this Hatcher person," I begin. "She's the boss around here?"

With her eyes still glued to her task, Glowen nods. "You could say that. Her family was one of the ancients who started this branch, so it makes sense she and her brothers run the place."

"Brothers?"

"Jengo and Milo. Team Hatcher." She throws in another fish. "At least that's what they called themselves when we were kids. Always pretending to run the place. We all thought one of them would one day. But that was before their dad passed away. Before Amara came back and took on the Hatcher title."

"Milo and Hatcher are siblings? I wouldn't have guessed that." There must be a huge age difference then. While she doesn't look old enough to be my mom, she definitely looks like she could be his.

Glowen nods, her cheeks pinkening. "Did you . . . meet him?"

There is a hitch in her voice. I'm not sure if Milo flusters her in general, or if she's still embarrassed by her sister. Either way, she's wearing her heart for the gangly boy all over her red face.

"I met him when we first got here," I say, and then an idea hits me. Maybe I can get something out of her about my necklace. Like why the Hatchers and Dax know anything about it at all. "He didn't want to open the door," I go on, "because of the lockdown. But then Dax showed him some piece of jewelry, and he let us in."

As I'd hoped, Glowen reacts at the mention of jewelry. Her eyes open wide, and she drops a fish into the bucket with a plop. She knows something.

But within seconds, she's recovered and is back tossing fish. "Jewelry? That's weird. What did it look like?"

I scrunch my brows, pretending to think about it before answering. "It seems like it was a pendant on a gold chain. Triangle. Black and glossy. Like a stone."

"A triangle? And Milo let you in during a lockdown because of it?" I answer with an affirmative, but she seems distracted and doesn't acknowledge me. She picks up a fish without thinking and dangles it over the bucket, her gaze darting around aimlessly like she is trying to piece together a puzzle.

I start to ask another question when something moves in the water. Something bigger than the little fish she tossed in. I only catch a glimpse of the thing—a dark blob on my left, near the shore. But as fast as it came, it disappears, leaving the five gray fish to swim alone. Wait a second. I squint. One, two, three, no, there are only four. Four fish. I could have sworn there were five.

And then the blob appears again. A dark spot surrounding one of the fish. I blink. Maybe it's my eyes playing tricks on me, but the water on the shore pulls in, like the blob is a mass of water gathering in one place. Impossible. But that's what it looks like—a heap of water piling in on itself, becoming something else. A monster creature.

Cones of water solidify around the fish. They circle it in rows, sharp and deadly. Teeth. I gasp as a fish is sucked into the water creature's mouth in a swelling black cloud. Then another. And another.

"Glowen?" I look over at her as I back away from the shore.

She doesn't react, still lost in thought. I reach over to tug at her shirt, but right then, Two-Heads jumps between us and flaps his wings wildly. Orange and red feathers smack against my cheek. The bird screams—one head and then the other, like an ear-splitting warning siren. I toss up my arms to guard against him when there is crashing splash and I'm soaked.

I shove the bird away and quickly look back. Where Glowen sat, all that's there is a turned over bucket and an empty shore. My eyes snap to the pond. Glowen is scrambling to swim then crawl out of the forbidden pool, but she keeps slipping.

"Help," she cries, "help me."

I reach out to grab her. The second our fingers touch, the water piles into a massive heap behind her. What I'm sure is the vorgle locks onto her ankle, yanks her back, and pulls her into its army of spiked teeth.

THE SHRIEK THAT EXPLODES FROM

Glowen half deafens me and half dies in watery gurgles. I'm not sure if the vorgle bit her or not, but it sure tries to drown her. The sloshing purple pond clouds with black smoke around her body. Her blonde braids dip under the surface.

For a millisecond, I remember the sign beside me. It begs me to listen to reason. *Do not enter! Feed at own risk!* Whatever monster pulls Glowen down will only pull me down with her. Down, down, so far down. But my body ignores my thoughts and fears. Before I know what I'm doing, my shoes are off and I'm in the pond.

A few steps in and I'm waist-deep. I brace for a freezing entry. I'm met with the exact opposite. Gross, clammy water slides over my skin as I storm further in. It's like hurling myself into someone else's murky bathwater. Or maybe I'm already inside the creature's body. That thought sends my gag reflex into overdrive. I push down the urge to heave and dive headfirst into the spot I saw Glowen disappear.

It's near impossible to see anything down here—a far cry from the well-lit pools of the city. And the creature's black ink only makes it darker. A forest of water plants, dead leaves, and sticks swirl in front of me. My strokes alternate from swimming to shoveling debris out of my path and back again. I spy Glowen's silhouette, blurred and thrashing, but it plunges away faster than I can make up ground. I was able to take a good breath at the surface, but if I don't get to her soon, I might run out of air. I might drown.

I block the thought before it takes root. I kick harder and tell my phobia to go away. She won't drown. I won't drown. I'm almost there. The muck thickens around me, pressing in on all sides. My arms struggle with each stroke. It's like they're caught in a mess of seaweed. I glance down at my right arm to see what's roped me. There's nothing there. No plants, and hardly any pond gunk. Nothing. Except when I move my arm again, there's even more resistance. The water beast is prying me away. *Turn back*, its invisible hands warn. *Let me have my snack, or you're next.*

To which I answer, *Not a chance.* I fix my eyes on Glowen, pour every second of Uncle Trek's rigorous swim lessons into fighting the monster's grip. My lungs burn for air. I'm making progress, but the task is exhausting. My chest tightens. My muscles weaken as I stretch and stretch and . . .

And then I have her.

Her bony wrist is in my grasp. With every tired muscle I have, I swing my body around. I kick like this is the last time I'll ever use my legs. She doesn't do anything to help. Not that I expect her to. I'm almost to the surface when the vorgle lets loose a cry. The scream screeches through the water like unconstrained speaker feedback. I thrust against the creature's grasp on my limbs. It must have a better hold on Glowen. She is harder and harder to pull along the closer I get to escaping this horrible pond.

And then I'm in shallow water. My knee rubs against the dirt below me. I break surface, take a breath, then yank Glowen up. A second later, I fall back down. With both hands, I shove her head out of the water. I can't tell if she's breathing or not. I keep holding her head up while I try to rescue us both. We near the shoreline when she moves.

She's not dead. I'm not dead. *Thank you!*

After pushing her ahead of me, I crawl to the shore. She is on her hands and knees, coughing. As I collapse, I can't help my own hacking. I take deep, shuddering breaths. We did it. We got out of that horrible place and—something grabs my calf.

I try to crawl forward, but it tugs me back. I fall flat on my face. "No!" Glowen's voice rasps.

A rush of water engulfs me as I slide back. Gravel stuffs my mouth and shoves up my nose. I try to spit out the grainy sludge and gasp for air. But the monster pulls me back too fast. I scramble for any ground to grab hold of—a rock, a weed, anything.

And then I see him.

Two-Heads stands a few feet from me on shore, feathers ablaze. The pond itself somehow rolls away from him. Rolls away from me. I cough out dirt the second air hits my face. Behind me, the vorgle screeches and recoils.

I lift myself up on my elbows and stare, unable to come to grips with what's going on. This bird can't push back a pond by lighting itself on fire, can it? Yet, there he is, overpowering the sour pond stench with the pungent scent of smoke. Every ounce of water flees in a perfect circle away from its talons. Then again, maybe it's the very creature itself fleeing.

I'm unsure if moving toward a flaming bird that scares human-eating monsters is the best idea. But I do know I don't want to drown. So I stand to head toward him. I make it a good three steps before the pain in my injured calf flares and knocks me down. It's the same calf that was cut up back in the rig. I crawl forward, but I'm not fast enough. The water splashes at my feet. But I don't have to struggle for long. Glowen is by my side, and with her are some girls I don't know. They reach under my arms, lift me up, and pull me to dry land.

They take me to a spot far away from the pond where they set me down on an enormous mushroom. I sink into its cushy pink top and try to get my overworking lungs under control. Once I can breathe again, I thank them, but none of them look at me. I count four, all dressed in similar brown-and-tan linens I saw the Pickering sisters wear. They either fuss over Glowen or fume at her. One of them I recognize. Orla glowers over a drenched Glowen who is flopped down on a giant blue mushroom across from me. The older sister's face is tomato red.

"The vorgle, Glow?" Orla points back to the pond. "You seriously went into the vorgle pond without a revolter? Have you lost your mind? I can't believe you went near that thing without one let alone into it."

"I didn't forget my revolter," says Glowen. Her airy voice isn't as soft as before. She's still choking up water, but she's not near as quiet as she was before. "It dropped out of my pocket when I fell in."

Her answer doesn't ebb her sister's anger. Orla begins pacing and flailing her arms around. "So, I've got to take you off this one too? Bad enough you ain't helping with the south-end. And you think the Grid will treat you better? If you can't handle yourself in the farm, you sure can't handle yourself out there. I don't care what delusions you and that Hatcher boy have. Saving endangered grid beasts out there means nothing if you get eaten by a vorgle in here. We need every hand on deck to farm this place. To farm it! And farming comes with rules. Wear pants with pockets that hold your stupid revolter next time." She pulls a flat rectangular device out of her pocket, chucks it at Glowen's chest, then storms into the jungle.

The other girls stop to check on Glowen. I bet they're her sisters too. All of them are blonde. Each is clothed neck to knees with layered linen in shades of wheat and brown. Sister after sister hugs Glowen and pats her on the back. Then a couple of them do the same with me, thanking me for saving their youngest sibling. I don't mind the thanks, but hugs from strangers when I'm sopping wet isn't my favorite. They squeeze a little too tight for a little too long. It's awkward and weird and reminds me of how much I miss Tori.

Just when I peg them as the nice siblings to Orla's evil sister act, they brush off Glowen's injuries. One by one, they tell her to take care of the mala suerte bird by herself. None of them offers to help. None of them gives her a break. Glowen's semi-smile fades the longer they rattle on. Each of them lists off the chores they've got to do instead of staying with her, then trot into the brush behind Orla.

I'm no longer jealous of Glowen's siblings.

"Well," I say once they've all left, "if you have any other weird and cranky creature to show me, can it wait till tomorrow?"

Glowen gives a small smile. "Yes, kind of all creatured out myself." She stands then tugs at the hem of her huge linen shirt. "Wish I could pretend this is all just water." With both hands she wrings out at least a pint of water, or maybe vorgle guts, onto the dirt. Without looking up, she adds, "Thanks for coming after me. I owe you."

"Don't mention it," I say then follow her lead and ring out monster juices from my own clothing. She looks like she might say more about the rescue, so I cut her off.

"Guess he's bad luck after all." I nod to Two-Heads who sits on a rock, hoping it will change the subject. My Aunt Marna would be over every moon in the solar system if she knew I saved this girl. I don't think she'd let me live it down for weeks. Maybe a subconscious Marna voice egged me to jump in the pool in the first place. Into that dark, deep, monster-infested pool. I shiver. Better we never mention it again.

"Can't say I enjoyed being scared into a vorgle pool by a two-headed bird," says Glowen. She steps closer to the stone where Two-Heads sits, but not close enough to touch him. "What do you think spooked him?"

Right now, it looks like nothing spooks him. With all four eyes closed, he careens his necks back to prune one burnt-orange feather at a time.

"I have no idea," I say. Though I wish I did. One minute he's calmly watching Glowen feed the wildlife, and the next he's trying to make her the main course. I'm beginning to see why Zane was so opposed to this bird.

Or maybe that wasn't it. Maybe he saw the vorgle and wanted to warn us. He did save my life at the end, after all.

I move beside Glowen and we both watch the bird. "Did you know he could do that?" I ask. "The thing with the fire feathers?"

She doesn't answer at first, then says, "The what?"

"The feathers," I repeat. "It looked like they were on fire when he stepped in the pond and dried it up. The whole bird was on fire."

There is puzzlement on her face. "Juniper, the bird didn't dry up the pond. It was a revolter." Reaching into her pocket, she pulls out the black device Orla threw at her. "My sister tossed one in when you went down. It's what we use to scare aggressive grid beasts."

She holds the device out to me. It's about the length of her hand and a little wider than her thumb. She snakes her finger around to press the circular button in its center. Moving back to the bank, she drops it in the water. The pond retreats in on itself like before, leaving a few feet of dry land. Only this time, there's no bird.

"Don't ask me how it works," says Glowen as she picks up the revolter from the pool then quickly steps back. "I have no idea. Something with sound waves effecting the Grid-mutation. But if we need to, we push that button, and the beasts move back. We keep one on us at all times in this sector. Here." She tosses me the device.

Not expecting it, I fumble before catching the thing. "Wait, don't you need it?"

She gives a rueful smile. "More than I thought, I guess. But there's a whole wall of them in the storage room. I can pick another one up later. You can have this one. You can't take it out in the Grid, but it will help you if you run into anything else in this sector."

I rub the device with my finger. I wonder what shippers could do with something like this in the Grid if there was no high-tech ban. Images of the terra cetus busting through the earth to send concrete at my face surfaces in my mind. I doubt a flimsy rectangle the size of my thumb would do anything against that thing. But then again, I've watched my necklace knock out full-grown men in seconds.

"Thanks," I say then unsuction my uniform pocket to drop the piece of tech in.

Two-Heads sees the motion as a cue to hop off his stone and trot toward me. His feathers brush my skin as he circles around my feet. They tickle a little but none of them burn.

"Are you sure you didn't see him turn into a ball of fire?" I ask again.

Glowen shakes her head. "But that doesn't mean you didn't see it." She pauses as she looks at Two-Heads. "And until we can get it back out in the Grid, I think I know the best place to keep it."

It wasn't hard to get Two-Heads to follow us to his new enclosure. Anywhere I walk, he follows. It also wasn't hard to get him to stay. The area Glowen suggested for his pen is tucked away in the far corner of the sanctuary. While most of the sector is covered in jungle, the part closest to the back wall is dry and barren. A stark contrast to the blizzard raging outside. Two-Head's pen is a patch of the arid wasteland matching the Grid days ago. He loves it in there. He instantly found himself a mound of red clay to flop down on and bathe himself. Add a couple apples, and he'll never leave.

So much for this bird following me everywhere.

Even if he is the bad luck bird of everyone's nightmares, Glowen assured me he can't escape his pen. They used the same enclosure to contain some combusting goats last summer. Since the chain fence and metal net kept those escape artists in, she's sure it'll do the trick on one bird.

With one less thing to worry about, I eat dinner with a few of the scientists in peace. None of them said "hi" or sat near me, but we are all in the same chrome-plated mess hall together, so I guess I wasn't alone. The food is fantastic. However, the grilled onion soup and potatoes remind me of the meal Aunt Marna makes on the anniversary of my parent's death. I can't eat more than half before heading to my sleeping pod.

I'm sure I remember the way there. Straight down the white corridor until I reach the hall filled with condensed bedrooms. I don't have any idea what time it is, but since fewer and fewer people are walking the halls, it must be late. Soon the walls turn black and are honeycombed with the familiar windows of sleeping pods. Most of the pods' lights are off and accordion curtains are pulled tight. But at the far end, one square is still lit.

It's not long before I reach my pod at the end of the hall. Each room houses a single twin bed and a nightstand. Though my aching body would love my pod to be on the bottom row, my room is one ladder length up on row two. I climb almost all the way up, when something catches my eye and I freeze.

Built into the end wall of the sleeping corridor is a Biometrics 2714.

I must have missed it before since Glowen led me through here the opposite way. But there it is. Right beside my bed. I don't have to wait for an opportunity to break into the one by Hatcher's office. All Biometrics connect to a single network. If I can register my palm as an approved read on this scanner, it will work on Hatcher's scanner. No one's here to watch me. I can do it now. I can get my necklace back.

Antsy jitters run through my fingers, but Uncle Trek's training slows me before I make a hasty dash to the unit. Cameras. Where are the cameras? Right corner, left corner, nothing. Good. Cameras that close would be the hardest to trick. Back right would be the easiest. I check, nothing. That leaves back left. And there it is at the far-left corner of the corridor, a tiny blinking red dot. Which will make this hard, but doable.

All right. Let's make this as real as possible. I climb up one more rung, stretch into my pod like I'm reaching for something, then hook my left foot around the ladder's side. I make a show of the rung holding me back then bend over in the most believable pretzel position I can manage. I pretend to free my foot with my left hand. My arched back, and I hope my long hair, cover what I'm doing with my right. The scanner's interface is exactly as I remember it. I restart the system with a few forced reboots, making the shutdown look like a centralized power surge. Then I navigate through a backdoor in the startup program. I breeze through the first five lines of code in the reprogramming protocol. I'm about to place my palm on the scanner and enter my vein authentication into their database when a whoosh sounds behind me.

My pulse skyrockets. I swipe the screen to black as quick as I can. I'm not sure if it was fast enough for whoever stands behind me. I try to look over my shoulder, but have to blow the hair from my face, and almost lose my footing. Gaining my balance, I about die when I see who's below me.

"You know, Princesa," Dax says, a giant smile on his face, "if you want to do gymnastics before bed, there's a gym here for that."

"YOU-YOU'RE BACK."

Thankfully, my leg is wrapped around the sleeping pod ladder
to keep me upright. I'm not sure how much hacking Dax saw me do
on the palm scanner—if any. But he scared me enough that my body
seems to have contorted at the sight of him. I try to straighten myself
but fail. My arm is stuck. *Why are these rungs so close together?*

"Sure am," he agrees cheerfully. "Right on time too." He's
getting sick pleasure out of this. Here I am, twisted in an impossible
position, getting a charley horse in the process. And he's down
there grinning till his dimples form craters, doing zip to help. He
still wears those dumb sunglasses too. Inside. In the dark.

"What's that supposed to mean?"

"Well, I always wondered how city kids climbed ladders that
aren't automatic. Now I've got my answer."

I glare at him. "You saw me climb plenty of ladders on the rig. I
slipped then got stuck trying to free myself. That's all."

He crosses his arms and cocks his head. Okay, fine, he's not buying
it. Well then, I'll have to sell it better. Helps that I'm actually stuck. I
yank on my arm, but it doesn't budge. Each pull feels like I'm ripping
my muscles apart. That and the uniform which clings uncomfortably
to my skin, still damp from the vorgle incident. Miserable all around.

I grunt and pull one more time when a firm hand on my back
stops me. Dax is on the ladder below me. I'm so conscious of the
palm scanner behind me it hurts.

I shut it off. I think I shut it off. I had better have shut it off.

I ache to look at the screen and make sure, but I know he's
watching me. So, I keep my eyes focused on my arm.

"Here." He reaches under the ladder rungs where my arm is stuck, lifts the top rung, and pushes down on the bottom. I twist my arm and pull free.

"Thanks," I say, rubbing my elbow.

"De nada."

I expect him to climb down, say goodnight, and let me go to bed. But neither of us moves. He's one rung below, so close his side presses against my leg. He smells stronger than he did by Hatcher's office—of mint and basil and sweat. My heart hammers at his nearness. I'm not sure what his game is. Get all up in my space till I crack and spill my secrets? *Well, it's not happening.* I bite down on my lips, refusing to say anything, or even move until he does. I don't know if he catches the hint, but after a few seconds he shifts.

"Looks like you've handled your mala suerte problem," he says.

I nod. "One hundred percent bird of bad luck free. Guess all he needed was a place to stay and an apple or two."

"Oh, yeah?" He surveys the space, looking behind the ladder and down the hall, unconvinced. "That all it took?"

"Yeah," I say. "That is all it took. I'm no wild animal expert, but I know a look of contentment when I see it. That bird's staying penned in that sanctuary till both his heads stop breathing."

He grins, pushes off the rungs, and steps down. "If you say so, Princesa. Then we'll see each other bright and early tomorrow. We start in the mess hall at five sharp. Don't be late."

I wait until he turns the corner at the end of the hall to stretch out the cramp in my thigh. Perfect ending to another messed up day in the Grid. I woke to an empty truck in the middle of a snowstorm, lost my mother's necklace, was almost drowned by a water monster, and got caught committing a crime by my boss.

Yep, every new day is better than the last.

I climb into the pod and pull the accordion door shut. On the nightstand, there's a plain pair of white pajamas someone laid out for me. I change into them and throw my soiled uniform next to what looks like tomorrow's clothes. The pj's are a little snug, but

I don't care. They cover everything they need to, and they're not drenched in vorgle innards.

I flop down on the bed—which is more comfortable than anything I've laid on in days. The tension of the day seeps from my limbs. I itch to hack the scanner again. Dax is long gone. There's no one out there. But if my pretzel move didn't fool the camera before, it won't fool it now. So instead, I let my heavy eyelids win and pray five a.m. doesn't hit me like a shipper truck.

I wake to a strange noise coming from the end of my bed. Scratch, scratch, rip, twill. There's an alarm screen sitting on my nightstand. Unless I set it wrong, it should be waking me up for Dax's call time. But I didn't expect its alarm to sound so weird. Or smell so weird. Like burnt toast or a fried holo-pad or—

Something's on fire!

I shoot upright and yank my sheet off. I reach for the lamp on the stand. The room is dark, so at least flames aren't licking my walls. When the light clicks on, I see the source of both the smell and the sound. It's not a fire, but I wish it were.

Sitting on my floor with no possible way to be in here, Two-Heads scratches and rips my uniform to shreds.

"No, *no*, you stupid bird!" I wave my arms and lunge at him.

His wings flap in a wild, orange display. He caws from both beaks but backs off my clothing. I pick up the charcoal fabric to assess the damage. What was once a weather-resistant shirt and a solid pair of pants are now strips of useless rags. I drop the scraps to my sides and turn on bad luck bird.

"How did you even get in here?"

Two-Heads answers with a couple squawks. He circles a spot by the door then drops to the ground. He's not at all upset that he destroyed my uniform. Little creep tilts his heads around to preen his feathers in oblivious bliss.

I slump against a pod wall. I hate that Dax was right.

This bird is impossible to get rid of. How can you ditch an animal that not only escapes his pen but can walk through walls? My door is shut tight, there's not even a—I look down at the sliver of light under the accordion frame. Okay, so there's a little space under the door, but not enough for a bird that big to squeeze through. And how did it find me? My scent? I sniff myself. A couple days in the Grid with no shower and a dip with a vorgle, and I might as well have bathed in garbage.

I check the time. Four-thirty in the morning. I remember where the showers are, so I have time for one. But I can't get a new uniform and this bird back in his pen before five.

Two-Heads stands and squawks, pacing at the entryway.

"Shush," I chastise him. "You might wake someone." I know he can't understand me, but I also knew yesterday he couldn't open a shut door, yet here we are.

If he does understand what I'm saying, he doesn't care. He keeps on squawking. Any second now he'll wake whoever else is in this sleeping hall. And if any of them are superstitious shippers who see me with bad luck fowl, I might as well say hello to my new life stranded in the Grid.

"All right, fine," I say through clenched teeth. "We'll take you back to your pen before I have my shower. But don't think I'm going to feed you any apples after what you did to my uniform."

Two-Heads responds by chirping after I lift the door. If he's so content to go back to his pen, then why in the world did he escape in the first place? It's like he wanted to ruin my day. If that's the case, then Zane was wrong. Mala suerte birds are bad luck for everyone, especially people they stick to like a virus.

I find another pair of white pj's in the drawer of the nightstand. Glowen shows up outside my pod a few minutes after Two-Heads appeared. Seems she's been up through the night researching mala suerte birds and couldn't wait to tell me what she found.

"If you take them to a high enough spot," she says, "they get comfortable and forget their mark." She scrolls through the holopad in her hands and bounces on her toes. It's like it isn't the crack of dawn and she hasn't shown up out of the blue.

After Glowen helps me get Two-Heads back in his pen, I find the showers. I take a quick rinse and dress in the cleaner pj's. Even if these clothes are for sleeping, at least I'm in something.

I tie my hair up in a wet ponytail with the band I have around my wrist and head down the hall. I know I'm going to look dumb wearing these pj's, but I'll have to ask the shippers for a new uniform, and they're all in the mess hall. Or I hope they're still in the mess hall. The clock on the wall screen says five-oh-two.

Okay, so the shower took longer than I thought.

I pick up the pace and walk straight into the now crowded courtyard. Great. Sure, it was crowded the first time I was here, but it was almost empty last night. I didn't think about a massive people traffic jam slowing me down. Farmers and scientists stand in groups looking at graphs or pushing hover carts heaped with veggies. They slow my gait to a grinding halt. I check the time. Five-ten. I don't want to think about what Dax will say when I show up this late.

I maneuver around the swarm of people as best I can. It's five-fifteen by the time I exit the courtyard. I run the rest of the way to the mess hall, nudging past a few people on the way. When I step into the metallic cafeteria, I see the same scientists and staff I saw last night. But no shippers.

Maybe they're somewhere in the back. I jog down the steps then survey the room. A few people sit on the balcony level. A couple of empty tables are near the back door. And a slew of people stand in line for what smells like pancakes and bacon. None of them wear the black or gray shipper gear.

"Danish?" To my left, a short woman offers me a square pastry out of the basket in her arms. I almost decline but remember how many times I've been hungry the past few days, so I free the Danish from her tongs.

"Thank you," I say when she hands me two more red, fruit-filled pastries along with a small carton of milk. "You haven't seen a group of shippers around here, have you?"

"I have," she answers. "They left a little bit ago. Hungry bunch. Had to refill my baskets twice to keep up with the big ones."

That doesn't surprise me. Not with shippers the size of Rook or Cyrus.

"Do you know which way they went?"

She nods, the black coils around her face bouncing when she does. "Half of them said they were going up to level twelve, and the other half went straight down that hall there." She points to the door at the back by the empty tables.

I have no idea which half I should meet up with. But since I'm this late, down the hall sounds much quicker than up twelve levels. I thank the woman then dash out the back.

At first, I'm not sure I'll be able to tell which way the shippers went. But when the hall dead-ends to only one doorway, I know I've found them. I step close to the slick metal frame, hoping it's not locked. I trip the motion sensor, and it swooshes open, right into the largest gymnasium I've ever laid eyes on.

There, a few steps down from where I stand, ten or so shippers tackle an obstacle course of Uncle Trek's dreams. They've got parallel log climbs, floating monkey ladders, a spinning balance bridge. Cargo nets extend at least thirty feet up, and a rock climb modeled after the side of a scraper looms in the back.

If this is what these guys do in their off time, no wonder they're ripped. Well, I guess most of them are guys. Slate's holding her own on the quadruple step. Behind her is another girl I can't make out at this angle. And there's Rook, flipping over a giant tire, and Zane spidering up a cargo net. And a few other shippers I recognize from the monitors on Dax's rig. Which makes me wonder, if they're all here—

"Decided to join us after all, eh, Princesa?" Dax comes off the rock wall rubbing his wrists and heading my way. He's still in the charcoal shipper gear I always see him in, but this time there's no jacket. Sweat glistens off his toned, bare arms.

"Here I am," I say, trying to keep my eyes on his face. "But I thought we were meeting in the mess hall."

"We did. At five o'clock." He twists his arm so his watch faces upward. "It's five-thirty. Well past time to be out of your nighties. Don't you think?"

I wish my cheeks weren't as red as they look reflected off his glasses. The fire in my face says they're probably brighter.

"I ran into some trouble," I say, my voice a whisper. I resist the urge to cover myself with my arms. My clothes aren't see-through, but I never thought I'd show up for a job in my pj's in front of my teenage boss in a gym. *I'm in a nightmare. A weird, trippy nightmare. Going to wake up any minute now.*

"Let me guess," Dax says, matching my undertone, "feathered trouble."

It's not a question or even a guess. He knows.

I don't bother to deny it. I already look stupid enough in this getup, why add a lie he'd see through to the mix? But I'm not going to announce my bad luck problem to the room either. I still keep my voice low. "He got out and tracked me down. Glowen saw where he chewed through the fencing. She and her sisters are fixing it now. He won't be a problem."

"Looks like he's already been a problem," he points out. "You're late. You aren't wearing your gear. And you're down here with the recovery team when you should be on twelve getting produce ready to load."

Twelve? I feel the blood drain from my face. *Stupid. Should've gone upstairs after all.* At least there I could do my job and I wouldn't have to stand here getting chewed out.

I'm about to head to the elevators when the girl next to Slate flips her black hair from her face and I get a clear look at her. Her eyes are puffy red, but there's no mistaking who she is. Nova. The sister of the girl in Mac's photo. But isn't she a farmer? Why is she in shipper gear?

I turn to ask Dax, but when I do, he's already followed my gaze and put two and two together. He saw me with that photo. He knows I got it from Mac.

"Nova's helping with this run," he says.

I blink but don't say anything. I watched the girl burst into tears over Mac yesterday, but she's going on a run today?

"What's the recovery team?" I ask.

"We split into two groups for the San Antonio run," Dax says. "One group delivers to the warehouse inside the dome. The other searches the Scar to recover any parts we can use for rigs."

"The Scar?" I repeat because I'm sure I heard him wrong.

He can't mean the San Antonio Scar. What used to be a stretch of highway, the Scar was destroyed by earthquake and storms a year before they sealed in the city. People fled to the dome in droves to escape the Fluxes. Some made it. Most were either flung around in their cars or buried alive by the storm. It carved out a canyon so massive it can be seen from space. Sitting outside city maintenance, the safety hazard remains untouched. Or so I thought. As far as I knew, no one went there. But I guess shippers don't let little things like falling into a canyon stop them.

Dax nods as if he read my line of thought. "The Scar isn't a place for newbies. If you head up to twelve now, I'm sure Fledge will have a spot where—"

I stop listening to him and look back at Nova. I've pretty much screwed up everything I've tried to do in the past few days. But if I go on this recovery mission, I'll get a chance to talk to her. Find out where her sister is and fulfill Mac's last wish.

"I want to go to the Scar," I say, interrupting him.

"—you could stack melons and—Wait, what?"

"I can help on the recovery team," I clarify.

"You can, can you? That's real cute, Princesa, but I—"

"Hang on," Zane says, coming up behind him, running a towel over his hands. "She's going with us to the Scar?"

Dax holds up a hand. "I never said—"

"Oh, good." Zane breathes in relief. "No offense, Juna, but a place like that is dangerous for someone new, let alone for someone with the . . . you know." He makes not-so-subtle bird flaps, then mouths the word "omen."

Something in Dax's expression shifts from mild irritation at me to utter frustration with Zane. "Tell you what," he says, looking at Zane. "Just to show you this has nothing to do with luck and everything to do with experience, if she can complete the course in less than five minutes, she can come."

I don't know if this pacifies Zane, but it lights a fire under me. He must think the course will either scare me off or embarrass me so badly that when I fail, I'll give up and go upstairs. But he has no idea about my background. I stifle my grin and stick out my hand.

"You're on."

19

"IF YOU'RE GOING TO CLIMB THE NET

like that, you'd better be prepared for a rough go and a lousy time."
Uncle Trek leaned against one of the structural poles that held up the
cargo net obstacle in his gym. He looked down. Bright red numbers
ticked away on the holo-cuff projection across his forearm.

"Who cares . . . how fast . . . I can climb a net?" I asked, trying to
hold on to the swaying ropes without both legs slipping through the
holes. My winded sides burned, and my vision blurred with sweat.
Uncle Trek had me run every other obstacle in his new gym eight
times before we attempted the net. I didn't know why he thought I'd
be perfect at climbing a ten-foot net on my first go. He'd already seen
how much I'd stunk at everything else before it.

"We live in . . . a city of . . . synths and scrapers," I went on. "This
is probably . . . the only cargo net . . . still in existence."

Uncle Trek smiled at my remark. His thick, auburn beard had
grown since we'd moved to Austin. I'd gotten used to the beard, and
even to Aunt Marna saying how handsome it made him. But I wasn't
used to him dragging me to the gym he opened a couple of weeks
earlier, insisting I learn "life lessons." I had no idea how running over
logs or climbing nets would teach me lessons in life.

"Tell you what," said Uncle Trek, "if you make it to the top in
under thirty seconds, I'll let you go home early. Even take you to
Mazo's for a scoop of natural ice cream. If you go over time though,
you tell me exactly why you threw the Peterson Scholarship."

My eyes went from the rope to his face. He knew. But how? The
full-ride art scholarship was never a for-sure thing. Anyone could

have beat me out of it. So, when I came home in the best fake tears of my life at the end of the semester, I was sure I'd covered my tracks.

"What do you mean?" I asked. "I was beat by a better artist."

Uncle Trek raised a single bushy brow. I didn't fool him before, I wasn't fooling him then. Don't kid the king of kidders.

"All right," I said, realizing my only way out of this conversation was up, "start the timer."

He pushed a button on his arm, and I flew up the net. I wobbled the entire way, but I was sure I reached the top in record time.

Only I didn't.

Uncle Trek didn't tell me my time. Instead, he dropped into the nearest chair in front of the net and sat with his chin in his palms ready to hear my story. After huffing and puffing at the top, I took my time climbing down to meet him.

"It was to the Plex," I said when my feet touched the ground. "The Peterson Scholarship was to UTP only. They didn't say anything about that on the application or on their site. I overheard my teacher tell a synth kid she shouldn't apply if she wanted to go to an in-dome school. So, I asked one of the admins, and not only is the scholarship for UTP, but the winner can't transfer to any other university. Have you seen where UTP is? What street it's near? I know I said studying art is my dream, but I can't go to that school. I can't. So, I changed my submission last minute. I . . . I'm sorry. The synths are right. I'm a worthless basic after all."

This time, real tears wetted my cheeks.

Uncle Trek rubbed the back of his shaved head, sitting in silence and watching his gym members run the courses. Then he stood and put a hand on my shoulder.

"Dreams and goals are nice to have, June Bug," he said, his voice deep and tender. "But they don't define you. Not all of us achieve our goals. Sometimes that's because of fear, and other times, we lay down what we want to pick up something better. Don't listen to bullies. Either way, win or lose, every person still has value."

I wiped my tears with the back of my hand. "How do you know the difference?"

"Between what?" he asked.

"Between when you're giving up your goals because of fear and when you're doing it for something better?"

"The short answer—love," he said. "The long answer comes from putting love in practice. Easier said than done. Sometimes it takes a lifetime to master. But when the situation comes to put someone else before your wants, you'll know. Now come on, I'll show you how to climb this thing for real. After that, we'll go get that ice cream anyway."

The obstacle course in the farm's gymnasium is different from any of Uncle Trek's gyms, however. This place can house both of his locations in the Austin and Houston domes with room to spare. But there's one similarity that has me smiling as I stand on the starting platform. It's bright in here. Lit up like a holo-screen's brightness cranked to max. Not a single nerve shakes my limbs. I can see the whole flat, sturdy ground. And though I've never attempted this course, everything is familiar. I've run each obstacle ahead with Uncle Trek in his gym until I either beat his best female patron's time or passed out.

Dax clears the rest of the shippers off the course with a double finger whistle. Grumbling, they move to the steps on the other side of the gym and sit, wiping sweat from their brows.

"All right, Princesa," Dax says, walking around the course on ground level. His voice booms for all to hear. "If you're going with us to the Scar, you've got to run the whole course. From the blue platform to the red. You don't make it in under five minutes, you're out. You skip or cheat any obstacle, you're out. You might as well pretend the floor is hot lava, because you touch it once, you guessed it, you're out."

I bite back a smile. "Got it," I say.

He moves in closer to the platform and looks up at me. Crossing his arms, he surveys the course then me. When he speaks again, his voice is quiet. "You don't have to do this if you don't want to. The rest of San Antonio is just as interesting as the Scar. And I'll make sure Zane shuts his trap about the bird."

I look away then bend my knee to starting position. This isn't about sightseeing or proving I'm not bad luck. This is about fulfilling a dying man's wish . . . and getting my pendant back.

"I'm good," I say. "Let's go."

Dax shrugs. He hustles away from the platform. He's not even halfway to the steps when Zane stops him.

"Hang on," Zane says, loud enough for everyone to hear. "A dry run isn't close to what it's like on the Scar."

Dax huffs a sigh. "What are you getting at?"

"You want to see if she can cut it? Turn on the virt-course."

A virt-course? They have a virt-course? I scan the gym again. Behind the steps, a waist-high black box sits flush against the wall. Its surface is covered by rows of black metallic spheres. How did I miss it? Virt-projectors. Zane hops over to the box and scoops up four or five spheres. He twirls them through his fingers as he trots back to the course.

Unease turns my gut at the sight. Even though I've been through virt-courses before, I usually know what I'm getting into before the mayhem begins. I have no clue what's programmed into those projectors, but I already agreed to run this.

Dax frowns. "Come on, that's not gonna—"

"Don't worry," Zane interrupts, "these are high-quality virt-projectors. They're not . . . cheap." He emphasizes the last word with a wink. I know what he's insinuating, the bribe dripping off his bad pun.

Dax's brows raise over his glasses. The joke isn't lost on him either. If Dax doesn't use the virt-course, Zane will spill the secret of the mala suerte bird to the crew. And if what Dax said about his superstitious crew is true, I'm in for the marooning of a lifetime.

Dax looks at me. "What do you say, Princesa?"

So it's on me now. "Do I get to know what's on them?" I ask.

Zane glances at the spheres then shakes his head. "They're Russian roulette issue. Never know what's coming up next till we turn it on. Keeps us on our toes against the Flux." He turns to the rest of the crew. "Anyone used one since we got here?"

"I used one yesterday," says Rook. "Killer bees in a rockslide. What a stupid scenario. Angry hunks of junk stung me with them electric stingers till I 'bout had a heart attack." He twists to lift his olive uniform shirt. Several green and purple welts dot his freckled, muscular side. "Don't know who programed them suckers. But if they ever come near me, they're gonna wish their mama birthed them on the left side of never."

"There you go," Zane says, grinning. "Killer bee rockslide is out."

I stare at him in annoyance. If these projectors simulate scenarios with enough immersion dedication to sting with electric shocks, I should say no to all of them. The next scenario is always worse than the last. But I've got no choice. Dax won't let me join them unless I beat the course.

I lock my eyes on the course. If I memorize the obstacle order, focus on what I know over what I see, hear, or feel, I can still do this.

Angled ramp first then the quad steps and spinning bridge. I've got to speed through those obstacles to save time for the second half. Next are the swinging ropes then the hanging doors and the cargo net. I shake my arms loose at the thought of those upper-body killers. Last is a huge leap from the top of the cargo net's base to the red platform. Easy.

"Okay," I say. "Turn it on."

Dax mumbles something about my funeral, then jogs off the course floor, nodding to Zane. I turn from the two of them, ready myself, and breathe. There's a low buzz in my right ear. It stretches up to a high electronic whistle as Zane flips the virt-projector on one by one. I don't see them take off from his hands. But soon the flying spheres are in position, hovering in all corners of the course.

Since I'm standing on the starting platform, one of the spheres glides a few inches from my face. It takes a quick scan then flies off. I'm its target for the next five minutes. The rest of the spheres shine lights from their centers in my direction, locking in on my face. The shippers on the steps will see some of the scene they create, but I'll get the full show. A few of the spheres in the upper corners gush gas from the open plates on their surface. I hold my breath. I've only seen virt-projectors use gas in scenarios once, as a hallucinogen. That might not be what they're doing. I don't have time to object, though. The spheres flash and buzz, then disappear altogether. Their projection replaces the real world with an artificial one.

I blow out my pent-up breath as the world shifts. The platform is gone. The obstacles are gone. I stand on something hard and gray. *Concrete? Stone?* Everything around me is buried in a swirling storm of beige. I can hardly see my hands in front of my face. Tiny bits of gravel pelt me from all sides. Some of it gets into my mouth. I wince then spit. It's like I ate a handful of dirt. My loose hair whips up in a torrent of thrashing blue strands in the howling wind. I try to tug them behind my ears, but the gusts are too strong.

I give up and look back at the course. The angled ramp has to be here somewhere. I squint and see it. It's not smooth or metallic like it was seconds ago. Now, a jagged rock curves out from the left of the platform in the ramp's place. Everything past the rock disappears into a wall of rust-colored dust. But at least I can see the rock. I know what comes after it so—

The room plummets into darkness.

I widen my eyes in shock. The move is a mistake. Gravel, still blasting through the gym, attacks me with a few grains to my right eye. I squeeze my lid shut. It burns like fire on a stick to the face. I rub my eye with my shirtsleeve. I knock the grain loose, but it still burns. I can't see in here. I can't run the course in pitch black.

"Light it up!" I hear someone yell below. Dax maybe?

At his command, a row of lights cuts across the rock's surface in an unnatural line. It's the ramp. More lights pop up in the distance, blurred, but there. The obstacle course lights slice through the projector's illusion. At least somewhat. The room has flipped from utter black to blazing red.

I'm on another planet. Somehow, these shippers ported me to Mars.

"Ready?" Dax calls.

I don't have time to ponder my new surroundings. I clench my right eye and get in position.

"Ready," I answer.

Dax whistles. I push off the platform.

My feet slam against the angled ramp. Gravity yanks my body down to the right. I run hard and fast, defying its pull. In seconds, I clear the ramp, push off, and land with one foot on the quad steps. Except they're not steps. They're boulders. On instinct, I jump to the next boulder. Then the next, then the next, until I reach the small, grassy spot before the spinning bridge.

I dig my feet into the ground to stop my forward momentum. Ahead, the grassy spot is cut off by a wild river, churning and violent under the red clouds. I know it's an illusion. Even if the cold drops of water sprinkle my cheeks, there's no river here. But I can't see a bridge. Not a speck of it. Just rushing waves and a whirlwind of gravel pounding my face. Frantic, I search. Nothing, nothing, nothing. Panic quickens my heart rate. I've got to get through this, or I'll have no time to rest my arms later.

And then I see it. A sliver of wood peeks out beneath a wave. I lock onto its position before it disappears again. Okay, I know where the bridge is, but I have no idea what part I saw. The left edge? The middle? The right edge? It might have been the right edge. If I'm wrong, I'll slip off for sure. There's no time to second-guess myself.

I outstretch both arms to balance and run. The bridge, now a log, rolls right. I compensate, running to the left. The fake river smashes against my ankles. I don't know how the projectors make me feel it—wind mechanisms I guess—but the waves are brutal to push through. I'm halfway to the other side when I reach the end of the log.

And slip off.

I throw my body to the right. Fake water pounds against my back. It's cold, wet, and doesn't feel fake at all. I reach out to grab anything. My forearms graze the log. I pull it in tight. My legs dangle, but they don't touch the ground. I'm not out yet. I pull both legs in to wrap around the log.

Speed is out. I can't run this thing anymore. I'll have to punch through the rest of the course. Hugging the log, I shimmy to the other side, climb around, and pull up on the platform.

Once I'm out of the water, I bend over, grab my knees, and breathe. I've got zero time to recoup, but I can't move an inch without air. When I look up, rows of vines flail before me in the relentless torrent. They seem connected to nothing but the red dust above. Below, they're tied to rocks the size of my head.

The rope swings.

I reach for the rope closest to me. It swings back in the wind. I wait. It swings forward. I reach again. It moves again. Frustrated, I retreat to the back half of the platform to focus. I'll have to time it right and jump. I sway my body with the rope till I'm in synch with its rhythm. It's not perfect, but close enough.

When I grip the vine, I expect a smooth plant slickened by the river's spray. What I'm met with are rough braids that burn my skin and don't match the illusion I'm promised. It's jarring. I'm glad I won't be on them for long. I lean into the swing, moving forward and back until I gain enough momentum to jump to the next rope. And then the next. I jump as high up on each vine as I can—give myself space to recover. At first, it's easy. But near the end, my arm strength starts to wane. I jump, then slide so far down, I'm crouched on the rock, inches from the ground and elimination. Afraid I'll fall if I dismount too early at this weird angle, I let the vine swing one more time. Then I leap and land.

It's not a pretty landing. I don't roll or twist or look like I meant to do anything on purpose. No, I flop down right on my injured calf and cry out. Gravel invades my open mouth again, shutting me up. It's worse than before. Some of the granules grind in the back of my teeth when I clench my jaw. Gross, but not like I can stop to brush. So, I spit and move on.

What was next? The cargo net?

I scan the thick fog for anything resembling a thirty-foot net.

What I find is so strange, I bet that projector used hallucinogens after all.

Surrounded by an angry storm of red, a figure emerges from the dust. The body shifts from a silhouette of burgundy to a person with form and features. She's a girl. A girl with a slight limp, one open eye, and electric blue hair. I move my arm. She moves hers. I step forward. She steps forward.

I'm staring at myself.

I look terrible. The illusionary dust has dyed my white pj's a dirty orange. My hair is caked with a solid layer of gravel. The wound on my calf has split open and dotted my pants in blood. *Am I really bleeding?* These projectors' attention to detail is surreal. I can't tell what's real and what's not.

Either the girl ahead is a clone or there's a mirror blocking my way. Assuming the latter, I reach out to touch the mirror. My fingers slide along smooth glass. I put both hands flat on the surface and push. The mirror moves back at the bottom but not at the top, like it's hanging from something.

Hanging? Oh, right, the hanging boards.

I run my hands along the glass until I find the edges. Sure enough, the mirror extends no further than arm's length on each side. It's the hanging boards. I shake my arms then feel around the right side for a place to grip. I can barely get my hand around the mirror's width. This thing's going to be a beast on my grip strength.

I grasp the right side with both hands, then wiggle my fingers until I have a firm enough hold. With a deep breath in, I jump, wrapping my legs around the lower side and my feet hugging the bottom edge. The board moves with me, but I hold on.

I don't waste any time and stretch for the next board. But when I reach out, there's nothing but air. *What the . . .* I swore the boards were only a few feet apart. The dust still makes it near impossible to see through. And with my eye shut, it's even harder to locate the next board.

Slowly, I crack open my watering right eye. I blink a few times before I can see through the sting and blur. When I do, I don't see a mirror image of me hanging onto the transformed board. Instead, an aerial shot of the shippers sitting on the steps is projected across this board's surface. So, it's not a mirror, but a screen. Still struggling to hold on, I turn to see if the image matches reality. If it does, I can't tell through the dense clouds of red dirt.

I'm not sure why the projector is showing me the shippers, but at least I can see an outline of a board now. I reach out again and grab the next board's side. I switch both legs and pinch the board with my feet before I move my other arm over. My muscles strain, but I breathe through it.

Adjusting, I glance at the next board's screen. It still shows a feed of the shippers. Only now, half of them are on their feet. Tearing through the steps is a swirling cone of red dirt. I assume it's an illusion until the shippers scream behind me—male and female, loud and violent.

I lose my grip on my left arm and almost my right, but I pull back in and grab tight.

It's not real, I remind myself. *None of it is real.*

I shut my eyes and focus on what I know. There's only one more board. I'm almost done. I stretch out the same distance as before and find the next board. Once I grab it, I open my eyes, avoid looking at anything on the screen, and pull myself fully to the final board. The board shakes, making it hard to dismount. But after a few swings, I jump off and land.

The cargo net is easy to spot. It hangs from a massive cliff in the shape it should be. I can't reach it from the grassy platform. There's a trampoline here somewhere. I take slow steps forward, pushing down with my feet. I stop when the grass sinks unnaturally then springs back as I lift my foot. I lock my gaze on the spot then move backward as far as I can to get a running start.

My arms are jelly. I loosen them with a quick shake before I run forward, jump on the trampoline, and fly. Arms and legs out, I snag the net and climb. Each pull higher weakens me. My climb slows whenever the net sways.

I'm halfway up when a curdling scream startles me. It sounds like it came from one person. A girl. I look down mid-climb. From this vantage point, I see through the dust to where the shippers should be. Except they're gone. No Rook, no Zane, no Dax, no one.

The sight grinds me to a halt. Something bad happened. The entire crew left?

Or this stupid virt-course is jacking with me. If they're still there, they'll turn it off when I finish. If they're not, I'll climb down and find the virt-controls myself. Renewed energy pumps through my limbs. I climb faster. Up and up until I'm at the top.

I collapse on my knees. My chest heaves. I made it. One jump to go. I give myself only a second to breathe before standing. Since the virt-projectors are still going, so is my time. I look around. The platform's edge isn't far. I move to the cliffside then stop.

What is this?

There's no red platform.

There's nothing that resembles a platform. There's nothing but a dark, never-ending pit. I can't jump into a pit. I can't even look at it.

A scream wails behind me. I turn. At the bottom of the course, one of the shippers races for the cargo net.

Nova.

She leaps for the net and misses. She's too short. She tries again. When she misses again, I see what's chasing her. A silver body, slick, scaley, and as wide as two grown men, arches out of the gravel-covered ground. I catch the monster's face once. It's eyeless, consisting of a giant mouth filled with bloodied teeth. Nova's screams pierce my ears. No one's there to save her.

No one but me.

Panicked, I spin toward the pit. It's stomach-turning dark. If I jump blind and somehow land on the platform, Zane will turn the whole thing off. But if he's not there, even if I win, the projectors will keep going till I climb down and find the virt-box. There won't be enough time to rescue Nova.

Sometimes we lay down what we want to pick up something better.

Mind made up, I run for the cargo net.

20

"HELP! ANYBODY, PLEASE!" NOVA'S cries disappear beneath the roars of the snake-like monster behind her. Her black locks cake against her warm skin. Any loose stands whip about in the dirt storm raging through the blood-red virt-course.

I slide to the edge of the platform. Uncle Trek's quick descent techniques come to me on instinct. With both hands, I grip two horizontal rungs, lean forward, and flip my body over, landing face out. The wind jerks the net, but my grip is solid. At this angle, I find each step with ease. I speed down the rest of the net. In seconds I'm at the bottom.

Nova gazes up at me. Relief floods her eyes.

"Come on," I cry, holding down a hand, "jump!"

She looks back for a brief second before bending to leap for me. Her feet leave the ground. The snake monster emerges below her, open-mouthed. Her hand is inches from mine. Close, so close.

Then she passes right through me.

My eyes go wide at the same time an awful buzzer blares through the course. Nova disappears. The snake monster disappears. The whole terrible red storm course disappears. I'm left hanging on a cargo net in the middle of a brightly lit gymnasium.

All the shippers sit on or stand near the stairs. No one is hurt, and no one is missing. The whole thing was an illusion. Even Nova, the real Nova, sits in one piece—not a slick black hair out of place. Some shippers stare open-mouthed and a few clap. I don't know why.

I lost. Seconds from the end, and I lost.

Dax stands exactly where I saw him last, frowning. Of all the people here, I thought he'd be the most excited at my failure. Now he doesn't have to take the new girl in pj's to the Scar.

I drop from the rope and bend over my knees to catch my breath.

"Whew, Juna," says Zane. He catches the virt-projectors as they zoom toward the receiver bracelet on his wrist. "For a newbie, that was a good run."

"Better than a good run," says Rook. He slaps Zane hard on the back, causing him to fumble with the projectors. "What was *your* first time on this course? Without them projectors?"

Zane's grin disappears. He scratches his buzzed head then mumbles something under his breath.

"Sorry," says Slate, coming up behind him. "What was that?"

"Five-twenty-five," Zane says again, begrudgingly. "In my defense, I still hold the second fastest time in the virt."

"Who holds the fastest?" I ask.

None of them says anything, but they all look back at the steps where Dax moves toward us. Face stern, he makes a beeline for me. I'm not sure what I did to make him so mad, but if I don't move soon, he'll lay me out flat.

I take a step back as he stops right in front of me. I know whatever he's about to say, I'm not going to like it.

"You're in."

I blink. "What?"

"I said you're in," he repeats, then turns to address his crew. "Slate, get her whatever uniform you can find in the resource room. She's an eight. There might be some left over from a few years ago on one of the lower shelves. I'm not taking someone in pajamas to the Scar."

I stare at him dumbfounded, unsure which shocks me more— that he's taking me to the Scar when I lost, or that he remembers my clothing size.

"Hang on," protests Zane. "You can't be serious. It was a good run, but she was over five. You said—"

Dax cuts him off with a lifted hand. "I know what I said, and

I know what I'm doing. In case you've forgotten, there's more to surviving the Scar than a pocket of parkour moves. If we don't have each other's backs out there, we might as well pet a terra cetus in the mouth. I don't take people who don't put shipper lives first. Juna rescued one of us right when it cost her. So yeah, I'm serious."

He shifts as if to go back to the stairs, but stops for a brief second. He moves his head to look at me, and when he does, his mouth lifts at one corner. It's so slight, I'm not sure if he's happy with me or not. Or if I'm caught in an illusion because when he speaks again, his voice isn't angered. It's melted, and raw, and thick like caramel sauce.

"Well done, Princesa."

He tilts his head like maybe he winked behind the frames then leaves.

I don't know how long I stand there staring after him. Long enough for my eyes to burn. Or my gut to burn. I don't know, but something is burning.

"Come on." Slate's voice wakes me from my weird stupor. "Let's get you dressed."

"I look like a skycab."

Slate surveys me and tries to bite back her laugh. "What do you mean? No, you don't."

I give her a look, hold up my arms, and spin. From neck to toe, I'm covered in bright yellow fabric. Normally, I like yellow—it's one of my favorite colors—but this is overkill. There are strips of black here and there to break up the banana explosion. But the way the black bands lay, along with the shine off the hard plating on my shoulders, knees, shins, and elbows, I'm a skycab personified. I squint into the floor-length mirror outside the resource room.

It's easy to imagine myself zooming across scrapers, picking up commuters.

"Yes, I do," I argue with the girl kneeling beside me. "Might as well pick up some customers downtown."

This time, she does laugh and finishes buckling up some straps by my knees. "There. Now you look like you're supposed to in the TR-18 uniform."

"Like a skycab?"

"No," she says. "Like a mutated bumblebee."

Now I laugh. She's right. The horizontal stripes across my legs and waist have turned me into a giant bug. I've seen bees in old movies and in a nature museum by my parent's apartment when I was a kid. It's an old memory, but one I remember vividly. Chasing the bees through the protected enclosure, the smell of flowers, and the one piece of honey toast my mother bought for me after I begged for it. I try to remember the taste.

"I shouldn't have let him go." Slate's voice is no longer lighthearted. She sits on a bench nearby. "He always loved the TR-18. Said they cheered him up. When they discontinued the yellow suits, he collected as many as he could find. This one's from his collection."

I hesitate. "I'm sorry," I finally ask, "who are we talking about?"

"He said he'd be right back," she goes on as if I didn't speak. "Just wanted to go check on a weird noise outside the unit. So, I thought . . ." She takes a breath. "I should have told him to wait. Cy and Boone had it covered. But he insisted. I let him go. It was my fault."

I close my eyes. Mac. We're talking about Mac.

Silence stews between us. After a while, I glance down at her. Tears roll over her cheeks. Her breathing shakes on the inhale and she sniffs, staring at the blank wall.

"I know that feeling," I say at last. I move from the mirror to sit on the bench beside her. It doesn't seem like she notices, so I lean back and continue on, almost talking to myself. "When you can't stop seeing what you should have done. Hearing every word you should have said. Playing out every move you should have made. The more those should-haves play in your mind, the more they trick you into thinking you can change what happened.

That if you figure out what went wrong, you can somehow make it right. But . . . but you can't. Because you don't have a time machine. And it wasn't your fault they died in the first place. Because no matter what it was you could have done to stop them from doing whatever, you can't see into the future either. And if the constant replay would stop for just one minute, it would be nice."

Lost in my own words, my eyes drift over to see Slate staring at me.

I clear my throat, then straighten. "Look, all I know is you didn't kill Mac. Users did. They're to blame, not you."

She sniffs then wipes her eyes with her uniform sleeves. "I know. It's just so raw, if you know what I mean. Boone was in a different rig, so I didn't know him very well. But I shipped with Mac for years. He was a good guy. Always looked out for others. Especially his—"

Her voice trails off when something catches her eye. I follow her gaze to find Nova standing in the doorway. Her hands are stuffed in her pockets and her eyes gloss with tears. Slate rises immediately to comfort her. Nova shakes her head.

"It's okay," Nova says, her voice soft and lyrical. "Rook said he needs you to go over some things with him before we leave."

Slate gives the girl a quick hug before looking back at me and exiting the room.

"Juniper, right?" Nova moves away from the doorframe.

"That's me." I stand. "Nova?"

She nods and gives a small smile. "This is so weird. It's not every day I introduce myself to someone I watched save my life. Or my fake life, I suppose. But thank you."

"Don't worry about it," I tell her. I can finally talk to this girl, and I have no idea what to say. All that comes out is, "Anyone would have done it."

"Some of them," she amends. "Others, I don't think so. Depends on how ominous the situation looked."

More luck-based decision-making. "Are all shippers obsessed with luck and omens?"

"It's in the training manual," she says dryly. "Lift heavy stuff, watch out for Fluxes, and fear anything unlucky. Page seventy-two."

I smile. "I take it you're not superstitious?"

She shakes her head. "One of the few. Chaos storms are stupid. Yeah, horrible stuff happens. But I wouldn't leave some poor guy behind because of it."

"Have you ever seen them maroon someone?" I ask.

"Not on any of my runs," she says. "It's been a while since I went, but no, it never got bad enough for that. Shippers like to threaten it though. Which"—she looks at me—"is why you should come with me on my rig to the Scar."

Her eyes are hopeful. I feel like I won the lottery.

"That would be great," I tell her.

I might not know how to bring up Mac's words or my necklace right now, but I'm sure I can think of something on the way. She could tell me where to find her sister or—

"She's already got a spot."

We turn to the voice at the door. Dax leans against the frame. I didn't hear him come in. I wonder how long he's been standing there.

"We're taking three rigs to the Scar," he says to Nova. "You'll be with Rook and Slate."

Nova's jaw drops. "What? You're not letting me drive?"

"You're in no condition to—"

"*I'm* in no condition?" she snaps. "We lost two of our guys out there, Dax. *Two* guys who were a part of our crew day in and day out. I might be going just because you need someone to break the news to Astrid, but I can drive a truck. I know how to keep it together. If you're going to bench me, you should bench Cyrus too."

She doesn't wait for his response and shoves past him. Dax rubs his shoulder but doesn't go after her. I fight the urge to punch him.

One step closer to my necklace and two steps back again thanks to Glasses Guy.

"She has a point," I say once she's gone. "Cyrus was pretty upset about Boone."

"He was," he agrees. He straightens from the doorway and looks right at me. "But there's one difference. Cyrus isn't my little sister. Come on. You're riding with me."

THE LAST TIME I RODE IN A GIANT

truck alone with Dax, I remember having more breathing room. The air tasted crisper, less stifling than it does now. Though this is the same truck I slept in during the Flux, I swear it shrank. Each time Dax leans over to push a button on the screens, his hand comes within inches of brushing mine. It sends whole flocks of geese across my skin. I'm not sure why though. I spent the entire trip this close to him no problem before. Why is it bothering me now?

Maybe it's because I can't stop thinking about how Nova is his little sister. Which also means Astrid is his sister. And if Milo's right, then it was Dax who sent her away when she started dating Mac. All of which are curious, but don't make my belly do these weird flips like it does when he opens his mouth to talk to the crew.

Or I'm hungry and his lunch sits there on the dash, taunting me. It permeates the cab with the smell of honey, fried cheese, and toasted bread. Not as bizarre as Frankensandwich. But the banana slices and elbow noodles hanging out the sides sill stretch the sandwich label.

"Do you ever eat anything normal?" I ask.

The frown he's worn since we left the farm changes to a half grin. "You want a bite?"

I keep my mouth shut because the pastries from this morning aren't cutting it, and I do want a bite, but the thing is super weird. I'm worried it might make me gag.

"Go on," he insists. "Normal food is overrated."

"I'm okay." I shake my head then look out the window.

The snow from the Flux is still lumped across the wasteland in dirty white patches. Evaporation rises off the mounds, painting the landscape in ethereal wonder. Dax said it's hot out there. I'm sure he's right seeing how fast the blankets of snow are melting. I'll bet he's right about other things. Like that sandwich. That warm, inviting, satisfy-my-hunger sandwich.

"Okay, maybe just one bite." I grab the sandwich with both hands, lean over, and take a huge mouthful. The strangest thing happens—it's not bad. Not in the slightest. An explosion of contrasting flavors bursts inside my mouth. The powdered sugar dances against lightly salted toast. Soft banana texture pairs with the cheese-filled noodles in ways that stun me. I know one thing for sure. I was wrong about Dax.

"This is amazing," I say, my mouth stuffed with honeyed goodness.

His half grin stretches into an all-out smile.

"You can have the rest if you want."

I swallow then look at him bug-eyed. "Really? But what will you eat?"

His lips twitch. "I've got more in the back."

"All right. Thanks." I take the rest of the sandwich and pull it to my side of the dash. I try to take every bite slow—to savor each splendid morsel. Like a master painter blending the right amount of paint to make works of art, I'm convinced Dax portioned this sandwich with a great amount of thought. I want to give it the relishing it deserves. But I can't help but stuff my face faster and faster.

"Wow," I say again once I'm finished. "Tell me everyone loves that sandwich."

"So far, you're the only one who's tried it."

"Are you kidding? Is this the first time you've made it?"

He laughs and I can't help but stare at his dimples. "No, actually. You're the first shipper to try _any_ of my sandwiches."

I can't believe my ears. Well, I can a little. His sandwiches are odd. But the shippers seem adventurous. He must be exaggerating. Someone had to have tasted one along the way.

"Not even your sisters?" I say this without thinking, but it doesn't seem to bother him.

"Nope. Nova's been a vegan since she found out what went into sausage links at her fifth birthday party. And Astrid won't eat anything that doesn't pass her picky meter—the blander the better. Other than mi madre and a few people growing up, you're it." His cheeks tint a little.

This is the first I've heard him talk about his family. "What does your mom think?"

He twists in his seat. "She's my biggest fan. Loves everything I make . . . when I get to see her that is." His words fade into nothing, and I'm sure the last few weren't meant for me.

I want to ask what he means, but he's not smiling now. He's focused on the road ahead, nothing else. It's clear he misses her. It hasn't struck me before, with the chaos and everything, but, for the most part, these shippers spend long periods of time away from their families. Dax is only nineteen, and he's been gone from his parents for how long? Days? Weeks? Months? The land is harsh, there's no thanks, and you have to make major family sacrifices to stay employed. I may not want to go to the Plex, but I don't want to abandon my aunt and uncle forever either.

Whatever happens, please don't let them stay in that horrid place. Once they realize it's not worth saving, please show them they should give up, so I won't have to ship long-term. I don't want to miss them forever.

The more we sit in silence, the more my thoughts bug me.

"What's that thing in the back?" I ask, switching the topic.

"You noticed it, huh?"

This guy's favorite pastime is teasing me. Of course I noticed it. The rigs going to the Scar are kept almost empty so there'll be room to fit whatever is salvaged. That antique, one-person vehicle is the only thing back there.

"Hard to miss," I remark when he offers no explanation.

His grin returns. "*That* is a 2083 rat snake buggy. The best all-terrain, diesel kart of its kind. Lasted decades past similar models.

One of the few ground vehicles still functioning without heavy alterations. And the joy of mi abuelo's collection."

The pride in his tone is palpable.

I stretch around in my seat to look in the back. Golden light from the midday sun spills in from the cab's windows. It bathes the buggy's black body in a warm glow. Most—if not all—vehicles I've seen are encased in a solid frame. This kart looks like it would struggle to keep people from falling out the sides. Dirty metal bars slope from back to front, encasing three crimson seats. There's a row of headlights across its top and a couple of long antennas popping out its back. For the most part, the thing looks unfinished. Like whoever built the insides didn't care to cover it up with any outsides.

It's familiar in a weird way. I've never seen anything like it, and yet . . .

"It's a whaler kart," I finally realize, making the connection to the Grid nomads.

Dax laughs. "They wish! But yes, it's supposed to look like one of theirs."

"Why?"

He taps the wheel with his thumbs. "We're going to make a pit stop on the way. It won't be long, but it's something we need to do." He pauses. "How much do you know about Rebels Against the Dome?"

I search his face to see any hint of a joke. They call themselves RAD? I want to laugh, but I'm not sure if he's about to confess his membership. So instead, I answer, "Not much. I saw them on some newsfeeds bombing city outposts."

"They do that," he acknowledges. "The worst ones succeed sometimes. Not that it ever does any good. It makes the city tighten up security. Nothing changes. But they hate the synths and the domed cities, and most of them are kids of the purged ones. So they grew up with a chip on their shoulder."

"The who?"

He clicks his tongue. "City didn't tell you about the purged ones? Huh. Well, guess it's not fun to talk about how paradise was really made. After the purification storms, the Plex—and later every other dome—decided the Grid was a nice place to dispose of criminals. Called it population control. Said there weren't enough resources to go around, so some people had to go."

I have to interrupt him. "But there *aren't* enough resources. That's why we have natural food allotments and synth foods."

"Right. Because *that's* true. You've seen the farm and what we can grow there. So much that we fill entire cities' requests with a surplus every harvest. If they'd request more, we'd supply more. No, what we really need are more shippers, more rigs, and Quell to protect us in transit. The city could provide that if they wanted to. But they don't. They want control. And anyone who speaks up against them gets labeled a criminal. Once you're a criminal, you get pushed out here. All city-tech is ripped off your body or dismantled so you can never return. They purge you. Purged ones make some disgruntled rebels. And most of RAD hates shippers."

"Why would they hate you? You're not exiling them or removing their tech."

"No, but we work with the city and keep the domes alive. If they get rid of us, the city goes under. We always make sure we're not infiltrated by loyalists when an ex-rebel joins the crew. Even then, they don't get informed on all our operations. Otherwise, a traitor could sell us out, and we'd find a bomb under a truck."

The idea of a bomb strapped under my feet sends jitters through me. I shift in my seat. Since most of the shippers come from either the farm or ex-rebel groups, I can see why they have trust issues.

"And that's why we need you." His words throw me. I thought we were talking about rebels and pit stops. What could he need me for?

"Me? For what, to check for bombs under the rig?"

I meant it as an absurdity. But his answer is serious. "No, that's Rook's job. Guy's honest and loud. Makes a great bomb inspector, but not right for this particular job." He taps again on the wheel. "You though, you're a low-grade from the dome with about as few city upgrades as a basic."

I squirm in my seat–the chair ten times more uncomfortable than it was a second ago.

"Not only would no one at the rebel base recognize you," he continues, "but without body tech, you could pass for a whaler instead of a city girl."

I look at him like he's lost his mind. Then I catch his meaning. "Wait, are you saying you want me to infiltrate a rebel base for you?"

"I wouldn't say infiltrate," he says. "More like go between. See, if we don't know what's going on with the rebels, we won't know when we're driving into a dome free and clear or when we're heading straight for a trap. We've got to keep eyes on them. Best way to do that is to have our people in with their people. Since there's no city-tech in the Grid, we can only debrief our informant face-to-face. And rebels keep track of all our faces."

"But they don't know mine," I finish for him.

Things start to make sense. Like why the shippers were all on board with hiring Tori and me on a minute's notice. Why Dax put up with my Grid ignorance. The weird conversation he had with Hatcher back in her office. I'm here for this reason and this reason alone.

"What were you going to do if I wasn't here?" I ask. "If the rebels know your faces, how did you debrief your spy before I came along?"

"We used to use actual whalers. A few of them didn't mind helping us for trade. Lately, we lost contact with them, so it's been a while since anyone's spoken to our mole." He sits a little straighter in his chair and rolls his shoulders back. "And you're right here. Now we don't have to worry about what if. Plus, if you help us, I might change my mind–"

He arches his long body back against his seat and reaches in his pocket. After digging around in the fabric, he pulls something out and plunks it down on the dash with a clank. When he lifts his hand, my body drains of blood. My heart squeezes whatever's left to throb in my ears as I stare at the triangular black pendant in front of me.

"And you can have your necklace back."

PART OF ME KNOWS I SHOULD DENY

any attachment—pretend I have no idea whom the necklace belongs to. That the only reason Dax slapped it on the dash was to gauge my reaction. To confirm his suspicions of my connection.

The other part of me lunges for it.

Dax is faster. He snatches the pendant up, and its gold chain whips against my wrist. My empty fingers jam against the metal console. Dax slides my necklace into his shirt pocket before I can react to the pain.

"That proves *that* theory," he says. So, it was a test. A test I failed before I could blink.

"What theory?"

"The theory that you're more than you let on. Tell me, Princesa, how did a city girl like you get a hold of something the entire Grid's searching for, waltz right out here, and no one notices?"

Anger burns my face. "Give it back."

"See, I'd love to, but there's this little matter of a stop we've got to make and—"

"I'll do it."

To his credit, Dax doesn't grin as wide as I'm sure he wants to. He starts to say something, when one of the drivers opens the channel between rigs.

"Now or never," says Rook. I watch him adjust something on his dash on Rig Two's screen. "We headin' for the Scar or making a pit?"

Dax flips off the screens for the trucks going to the dome. He looks at me then pats his pocket before answering. "Get everyone ready. We're making the stop."

By get everyone ready, Dax meant get *me* ready. I didn't have any say on the weird outfit they put me in. I'm glad I'm not wearing the bee suit anymore, but this getup is tight, and I don't look like myself at all. Not that I can see the full effect. There aren't any mirrors out here, and my reflection is so wonky in the truck beside me, I might as well be in a fun house.

Looking down at myself, I doubt if even Tori would recognize me. The gray cotton shirt, cut along the ribs, exposes skin on my sides. It's weird, but at least it lets in a breeze. Without the shipper gear to cool me down, the triple digits hits me worse than before. The black bolero jacket they have me in isn't helping. I'm tempted to rip it off. But the metal spikes on its protruding shoulder pads have me afraid to touch it at all. I've got to be careful not to tilt my head too far either way. Death by fashion impalement isn't the way I want to go.

Strangest of all are my hair and face paint. My scalp hurts from how tight Slate pulled the braids on the sides. She jammed yellow feathers in wherever she found a spot. Then she smudged black paint around my eyes, cheeks, and forehead. I have no idea what they expect me to do at this base, but it might be to start a war.

Everyone else stays in their shipper gear except Dax. He dons a dusty-beige poncho over his uniform. Crouched inside the buggy they rolled onto the dirt, he inspects and tightens its parts. When it looks like it's just the two of us, Nova walks out from the back of Rook's opened rig dressed in the same beige poncho. Her inky hair is pulled in a severe high ponytail, and she hugs a book close to her chest. In her other hand, she holds a small gray bird. It doesn't wiggle, but its white, beady eyes bug out. Something white is strapped to one of its legs.

I bend to ask Dax if we're taking her feathered friend too when Nova throws the bird in the air. Its wings snap open. Flapping hard, the little creature darts away, disappearing into a speck in the distance. "I guess we're not taking the bird?" I ask without expecting an answer.

"No," Dax says, still focused on his tinkering. "It's a homing pigeon. Before we get to the base, that guy will let our informant know we're coming. So, you know, they don't shoot you."

I fight the urge to throw off my jacket and march back in his rig. I can't believe I'm contemplating infiltrating a rebel base, let alone already dressed and ready to go. I wish Tori were here convincing me not to do this.

Where's my best friend when I need her?

"Shoot me, huh? How much of this will I be doing by myself?"

Dax pushes off the bar he was tightening to look up. "Only a tiny part." My confusion must be obvious because he follows up with, "All you have to do is show up and show our informant the signal." He runs both thumbs across his jaw from ears to chin—the signal shippers give to say they can be trusted. "If anyone asks, you say you were scouting new hunting grounds when your ride ran out of fuel. Then wait for our mole's return signal."

Oh, sure, yeah. Super easy. "What signal?"

Dax doesn't answer. He just looks at Nova who now stands beside me.

"Ready?" he asks.

She climbs into the kart and sits in the back seat. After buckling in, she whips out a pen and jots something in her notebook.

"Enough," she says. "I still have to tell her what happened this morning. But we can go whenever you're ready."

I have no idea who they're talking about, but neither offers an explanation. Instead, Dax hops into the driver's seat and turns the buggy on. It rumbles to life, almost as loud as a rig and twice as shaky.

"You coming, Princesa?"

I wish I could say no. But he pats his pocket with my necklace in it. I resign to my fate and strap in beside him.

Every time we pass a dilapidated building in this wasteland, I'm convinced it'll be the rebel base. I'm sure Dax will stop at this one, or that one, or at the one with the broken yellow "M" on its roof. But Dax pays no attention to any of them.

Soon we turn off the larger road in favor of a winding dirt path to nowhere. The buildings grow sparse. The trees grow sparse. Anything that grows at all grows sparse. There's plenty of dust, though. The kart's wheels kick up thick, flaxen clouds of the stuff. Tiny grains pelt me in the face harder than anything in the virt-course. I tug up the torn scarf around my neck till it covers my nose. For the first time in days, Dax's glasses make sense. I narrow my eyes and wish he'd let me borrow a pair.

"So," says Dax, breaking the silence. "How long have you had that necklace?"

I twist to face him then turn back to Nova. She doesn't flinch at his revelation, just scribbles in her notebook. Exactly how many shippers know of my connection to that necklace?

"Long enough." I don't give him anything more. I'm not interested in a detailed discussion of my past right now. Not while he's bribing me to infiltrate a rebel base.

"Long enough for it to mean something to you?"

"You could say that," I reply, understating the truth. It means something to me, all right? I don't care how many people in the Grid are looking for it, that necklace means more to me than it does to all of them combined. But I'm not sure I want *him* to know that.

"I assume you know what it does."

I don't say anything. We both know I know.

"I've never seen a user hyped up on Freeman's get shut down like that," he remarks. "Like a switch. Seems to work on some people not hyped up too." He glances at me for a brief second, but his implication is clear. He knows why I was passed out at the station.

Or at least he thinks he does. My pendant works on anyone who took the nano drug even once. If I use it on anybody else, it does its job on me too. He might be figuring that out, but I don't want to help him along by confirming his suspicion. So, I stay quiet.

"And it doesn't have any city-tech trackers on it," he says. "Imagine what we could do to stop the drug trade out here. Quell won't know we have it. We might even make a dent in what they're doing to the Plex. Get people off it so they can recover. Maybe it'll lead us to the guys behind the trade and we could—"

"I do this job, you give me my necklace back." I stop him flat. My mind hasn't changed from when I first got into this mess. I'm shipping solely to avoid the Plex. Those people murdered my parents. They can rot in the graves they dug for themselves for all I care.

He rubs the back of his neck and looks me over a few times, his lips tight. "If that's the way you want to play it, Princesa, that's the way we'll play it."

He doesn't talk to me for a long time after that. I know I should be happy, but the longer we sit in silence, the more unease slithers over me. Like I said the wrong thing or should apologize for something. But I didn't misspeak. There's no way I'm saying sorry when he offered to help the people I despise the most by using my stolen necklace.

After an hour or so driving in a landscape of charred wasteland, Dax pulls over and kills the engine.

"What's going on?" I ask. "Why'd we stop?"

He unstraps, pushes himself out of the driver's seat, then moves around the kart to the back. "This is as far as we go. The rest you'll have to go on foot."

"What?" I scan the scenery. There's nothing but hills, rocks, and unforgivable wilderness for miles. "Go *where* on foot?"

"The base isn't far." The answer comes from Nova. This is the first time since we left that she's looked up from that notebook. I'm surprised she wrote in it at all through the kart's constant jostling. Pen in hand, she points to the massive rocks sitting at the bottom of the hill on my left. "Should only take about twenty minutes to reach the front gate."

"Front gate to what? I don't see any buildings around here."

"Neither do Quell ships," says Dax while he pulls things out of the back of the kart. "But it's down there. Look again."

I turn and look more closely. Rocks, rocks, more rocks. But it's all landscape. No houses, shacks, or buildings of any—wait. The haze lifts and there it is. One of the rocks is not only more rectangular than the others, it is also speckled with tiny windows. Around its front are stones placed in a semicircle with a large gap between them in the middle. I guess that's the gate.

"So, I just walk in there?"

"Only if you want to be sliced into pieces." Dax comes around to the front of the kart with a few metal boxes in his hands. "You can't see them from here, and you won't be able to see them up close, but there are tiny wires between both sides of the gate. They'll cut up anything that goes through. You'll have to wait for our informant to lower the gate. Here."

He sets the boxes down beside him except for a smaller one with a lid like a bottle top. He hands it to me. Liquid sloshes within it.

"Drink that if you get thirsty."

He doesn't tell me anything else, like how long this mission of his is supposed to take or what's in the bottle he gave me. I want to ask, but he's bent over the boxes now, so focused on pulling out pieces of metal I don't think he'd answer me. Nova isn't any help. Ever since Dax started speaking, she's been scrubbing her arms with a rag, ignoring us.

I watch Dax empty the boxes and piece together the contents. I blink. "Is that a gun?"

He stops constructing to look at me. "It's a just-in-case."

A BLANKET OF HEAT PRESSES DOWN

on my skin as I walk across the desert. Lifting the water bottle to my lips, I try not to think of the people with bombs ahead of me or the guy aiming a gun behind me.

I can't.

Will they see through my act? Is Dax a good shot? Will he shoot me on accident? Will he shoot me on purpose? Whatever the answers are, I'm afraid I'll find out soon enough.

Sweat slides down my forehead in streams. I hope I don't look less like a whaler and more like a drowned circus clown. Wind whips over me, harsh and hot. And there's a strange chirp-buzz sound in the distance. It reminds me the dangers aren't only ahead or behind, but in all directions.

I move on the path, toward the stone gate. At least the danger ahead comes with the hope of my necklace. When I come alongside the gate, I realize how off my depth perception was. The stone I thought would only reach my shoulders goes well over my head by several feet. Its surface appeared jagged from the kart, but it's been smoothed out and painted to look rough. There's no way anyone could get a foothold on it. If Dax's informant doesn't show to open the gate, scaling the wall is out.

Then it hits me. I never asked who the informant was. Not a name, not what they look like, nothing. All I know is whoever they are, they'll show up to open the gate. But what if someone else comes instead? How am I supposed to know who to give the trust signal to? If I give it to the wrong person, it'll blow my cover story. I should have asked—but I was too worried about my necklace to think straight. I need to go back. Dax might lose it if I do, with me costing him time and all, but I'd rather make us late than get myself killed. Then again, a rebel could have already spotted me. They might shoot me in the back if I leave now.

I lean into the wide space between the gate's walls to check around. At first, I see nothing and no one. Just a building cut from rock and dirt. Then a glimmer of light reflects off one of the wires Dax warned me about.

Wind catches one of the tiny braids on my left side. It flies up in front of my nose and hits a wire I didn't see. The wire slices it on the ends right above the band holding it in. Blue strands explode in a wild puff. A putrid burning smell attacks my senses, and I jerk back.

I cover my face and retreat further. No one's getting through that thing with those wires up. Gate about took my nose off.

"Well, you're a brave one." A female voice sounds from the other side of the gate. I lower my hands and search for the source. No one's around. "Or blind," she adds.

"Who—who's there?"

The girl laughs. "Option two then."

I raise a hand to my eyes to shade myself from the blazing sunlight. For a second, I don't see her. Beige dirt and rocks blend into one out here. Then a darker tan cloth flaps up with the wind, revealing her silhouette, and I feel like an idiot.

She stands right in front of me, albeit six or seven feet past the wires. A mask that matches the cloak obscures her face. Her hair is either pixie short or pulled back in a tight pony, then stuffed into her hood. It's like I'm back on my aunt and uncle's couch, binging ninja movies on their holo-screen at the sight of her. Knife sheaths rest strapped to her sides, and she's covered head to toe in tight beige cloth save slits for her eyes. I've seen guys like that drop dozens of trained men into pools of blood with nothing more than their fists and skill. If this girl can do half of what they can, I'm in serious trouble.

"I'm not blind, I didn't know how close I—" I stop. I need to say what Dax prepped me on, not defend myself. "My ride broke down nearby, *y necesito conseguir gasolina*."

I hope my Spanish didn't sound as dumb as it does to my ears. It's been a year since I took it in school. Dax had me repeat the phrase at least thirty times on the way here, but my words never came out as smooth as his. I'm not sure why I even need to say them.

Then the girl removes her hood and mask, and I know exactly why.

Her slick black hair spills from the high ponytail on her head. Wind blows its strands across her tattooed neck. She has the same heart-shaped face I saw a half an hour ago on the girl back up the hill with their brother.

Astrid.

For a second, I stand there, shocked. Then I remember myself and run both thumbs across my jawline. Her face slackens in recognition of the signal.

"So, my siblings didn't abandon me after all. My lucky day."

I'm not sure how to take that. Her words don't match her flat tone or annoyed face. I get a queasy feeling that she's not going to cooperate.

"Look," she says before I can worry much further. "Why don't you go back to your boss and tell him RAD isn't interested in the Scar right now. Dax can salvage till his heart's content. The rebels have bigger fish to slice than the shippers."

She throws her hood over her head, spins around, and leaves.

That's it. I have the info Dax wanted. I'm done. I can get my necklace back now. I should be ecstatic. So why does the queasy feeling only grow? It's like she's not telling me everything, and I need to stop her.

A picture of Mac's bloody body flashes in my mind. The desperation in his eyes begs me to find this girl–trusting me as he breathes his last breath. This is my only chance to make Mac's faith in me count for anything.

"He said there's a cure!"

She stops cold at my shout. We stand like that for a minute or so—me not knowing what else to say and her completely frozen. Then she turns, the motion slow and hesitant.

"What did you say?"

"Mac, he said there's a cure, and the Freeman's pushers know it." I leave off the part where Mac probably died at the station. There's a reason Dax brought Nova to break that news. I have no idea how unhinged this girl will get if she hears gut-wrenching news from a total stranger.

"A cure?" Her tone is guarded, skeptical. "He mention a specific group of pushers, or all of them in general?"

"A specific group."

She folds her arms. "Well, that's helpful, I suppose. He give you any names?"

I don't know where this line of questioning is going, but I answer anyway. "No, I only saw their faces."

"You *saw* them?" she asks in surprise. "Where?"

"At the fueling station outside South Austin."

Fresh anger flashes in her coal-black eyes. She narrows those eyes and tilts her head, sizing me up. "What's your name?"

I hesitate. I don't owe this girl any more answers. And yet, it still seems like she's hiding something. Something the shippers need to know. The shippers who housed me. The shippers who bandaged my wounds. The shippers who haven't looked down on me because I'm a basic or marooned me even though I'm the unluckiest girl in the universe.

I can do this one thing for them.

"It's Juniper."

"Okay, Juniper . . ." She steps toward the stone wall, leans in, and pushes something till it clicks. There's a crunching metal sound and a dirt cloud billows out in a line between the gate walls. "Let's put your memory to the test."

She swipes her hand in the space between us, unharmed. The gate is down. I know I shouldn't. I should turn around and forget I said anything. But I take one quick look behind me and step through the gate.

I have no idea what I thought a rebel base would look like, but this isn't it. From what I saw on the daily newsreels, I assumed these disjointed people lived in separate hovels scattered throughout the Grid. Never on a unified base. Back in Austin, I would watch rebels dart across the screen, fire ancient weapons at armored guards, and get taken down in seconds. All of them wore rags, none seemed to have a solid plan when faced with the Quell. So, as I trail Astrid through a sand-colored rock door, I'm surprised by what I see.

The tall entryway is low-tech. Static metal covers portions of the stone walls without a screen in sight. The main light source in here is the sun, pouring in beams through the slit windows above. It illuminates dirty copper piping, rusty crates, and frayed banners. And there's a strange chemical scent permeating the dry air. It's all sort of rundown and what I expected.

It's the people that surprise me. Several men rush about with boxes in hand or climb ladders to higher levels with energy and purpose. In the center of the room, a group of rebels cheer a man giving a speech. The black-bearded man spits curses and obscenities about the "dome scum." His crowd, young and old, cheer with each jab. These rebels aren't separate or disjointed. They're definitely unified, and they aren't living in separate hovels. They're here on a mission.

I don't look much different from them, dressed in my gritty whaler gear. Maybe that's why they don't pay me much attention when Astrid and I walk nearby.

The man's vitriolic words shift from insults on domes in general to hatred of specific cities. One city really. The Plex. I slow to listen.

"If we don't stand up and do something now, no one will. Orange Pipe, and all the other biotech corporate slugs destroying the Plex, are coming for us. They won't stop till the whole Grid looks like their personal garbage pit."

"You coming?" Astrid stands beside me, hands on her hips.

"Yes," I say, reluctantly leaving the crowd. I want to hear RAD's plans. Not that I care what happens to the Plex. I just don't want my aunt and uncle caught in the cross fire. Though I'm sure the rebels aren't going to do more than hurl insults and throw sticks at the dome like they always do.

Astrid leads me down a dim corridor that opens to a barren outdoor courtyard. At first I'm not sure what this place is. An aviary? An aviary without trees . . . or birds. There are some bird sounds though, chirping, cooing, and wings flapping. And there's a large shed set up flush against the courtyard wall. Most of it is made of ridged tin except for the front missing wall that's screened in with metal wiring. The closer we get, the more I see gray and white birds flying about inside.

There's a table filled with papers and a stone bench beside the shed. Astrid makes for the table, swipes a tiny paper from its top, then turns to me.

"Going to the Scar," she reads. "Need to talk to you about something big. Will have to switch places for a week or two." She looks at me over the paper like she wants me to respond. I give her a blank stare. "A cure is big," she says to me, "but I'm not switching. Not now."

"Switching?"

She raises her brows. "Figures they didn't tell you. Leave me in the middle of nowhere for months then show up without warning the first time I get an actual lead. What makes me think they'd tell the decoy about the switch?"

She folds the paper in half then sticks it in the back pocket of her torn pants.

"Okay, listen," she says. "Dax and Nova may not have prepped you for an informant update or a switch. But if you want to leave this place alive, you'll do what I say. Don't talk to anyone. Don't wander the base. Stay put wherever I leave you and wait for me to bring you out. Got it?"

Not everything she said makes sense, but I still nod.

"Good." She makes for the open door on the opposite side of

the courtyard, gesturing me to her. "Come on. My siblings can handle a little wait."

We walk through dim halls filled with closed doors and up a few stairwells. I mentally note each turn in case I need to find my way out. It's not till the third level when we're standing on a balcony overlooking the main entrance that she stops.

"Stay here," she orders, then heads for the other side of the balcony and down a dark hall, leaving me alone inside a rebel base.

Below, the man I heard earlier continues his speech in fever pitch.

"Plex already shoves pushers down our throats. Hyped up on the same drug those hardsuits are supposed to keep out of the Grid. They come in and murder us in our beds. I say, no longer! *Now* is the time. Now, while they think we're weak, we show them how strong we've become. We strike them in *their* beds! We won't stop until the great dome city crumbles up in piles of ash and ruin. Smoke will rise from—"

A flash of sunlight reflects off someone moving through the crowd. I advert my attention to a puff of blonde hair. A familiar puff of blonde hair. I've got to be seeing things. I rub my eyes. When I look again, it's worse than before. The girl snaking through the crowd has a pale blonde afro and umber skin. I swear she's the same girl I saved from the synth at the substation.

She's supposed to be at the Plex, visiting her sick grandma. How is she here?

"We're ready." I turn to see Astrid standing at the hall's entrance. Once she catches my attention, she veers around to where she came.

I quickly turn back to the crowd and lean over the rail. The girl is gone. I look and look. She's not anywhere. I knead my temples. I've got to get more rest. This job is making me hallucinate.

"Ready for what?" I mumble belatedly to myself, then trail after Astrid.

She stops in front of a closed door. Putting her hand on the knob, she waits for me to catch up.

"There are a couple people in here I trust. Everyone else is gone, but they'll be back in less than ten. You'll have to hurry." I still have no clue what she's briefing me on. If she means I have less than ten minutes to do whatever she's asking me to do, I doubt she's going to go over any details. I hope it's self-explanatory.

"Oh!" she says suddenly after opening the door a crack. "If they do this . . ." She releases the doorknob then raises her right hand, palm out. Then, with a quick sweep of her arm, she curves her hand down to touch her heart with her fingertips. "Do it backward. It's how whalers say hello."

Okay, so whoever is in here doesn't know I'm with the shippers. Noted.

She opens the door and nudges me in. A foreboding sensation presses in on me as I enter the dim room. It's a small space the size of an average scraper's sleeping quarters. I could cross to the other side in just a few strides. Not that I want to stay in here any longer than my allotted ten-whatever. It smells of lemon cleaning solution and body odor. Like someone took time to scrub every surface—which would take no time with the minimal décor in here—but forgot to bathe themself. There's a little table with some teacups on it, a painting, and an elegant golden chandelier. That's it.

Except for the only piece of furniture in here beside the table, which is a rectangular, white sofa sitting in the middle of the room. It's pristine—not a stich out of place. It's completely different than the rest of the worn, dirty base I've seen so far. The couch faces the wall with the painting. On the couch sit two people, both boys. Astrid shuts the door, and they turn.

One boy rises when he sees me. The other stays slumped on the couch, raising a brow at Astrid. Their features are so similar—medium, ice-blond hair, pale skin, angular eyes, and lanky limbs. I can't tell if they're older than me, but I'm positive they're brothers.

The brother who stood raises his hand like Astrid predicted. I do it backward, starting with my fingers over my heart. He grins—toothy and a little relieved.

"Been a while since I've seen another whaler. I'm Cadoc. My brother Sulien and I are from the tribe of—"

"No time for that, Cadoc," Astrid cuts him off. "Kazi will be back any minute."

"You sure about this, Ris?" asks the other boy from the couch, rubbing his neck.

I try to hide my bewilderment at the nickname. *Rid* would fit Astrid's name better, but I guess that's a weird thing to call her.

"I'm sure. Open it up."

Sulien rolls his eyes then drags himself from the couch. "Fine. But if you tell anyone I told you about this, I'll deny it. And so will Cadoc."

"Who am I going to tell? Hurry up."

The brothers share a silent conversation with sudden head jerks and nods. After a few seconds, Sulien shrugs and moves to one side of the painting, Cadoc to the other.

The intricate oil painting features an ancient ship caught in a storm. Rain and wind beat against torn sails and wooden frame. Men, painted with quick strokes, hurl crates into the crashing waves while a bolt of white lightning strikes the ship's mast. The painting takes up most of the wall. Its sheer size and attention to light and negative space make the scene even more striking. But I have no clue why the brothers stand there, messing with the bottom of its frame.

And then something clicks on both sides. In the middle of the lightning bolt, the painting splits in two. Both brothers pull their side away from the center. A gap opens wider and wider. Light spills up and out of the space. Soon, the painting is replaced with a glass window.

Astrid steps forward first. Fingertips on the glass, she looks down at something on the other side. I can't tell what it is. From here, it looks like a blank orange wall. She twists to face Sulien, jaw dropped.

"He *is* keeping an eye on them."

Sulien lets go of the painting and comes to her side. "Kazi keeps an eye on all of us."

The questions are starting to mount. Who's Kazi? Why is he

keeping an eye on anyone? But I remember Astrid's warning to keep my mouth shut and bite my tongue.

Astrid turns her head to me. "Come on. Have a look."

Cautious, I step forward. The orange wall sinks down, revealing a tall room. It's probably a full three stories down to the floor. The walls are dirtier too. Cracks in the sheetrock spider downward, crumbling off massive chunks, revealing raw stone. At the bottom, rebels sit on ragged furniture or the floor, eating from bowls and reading books. A few of them pace the room while others lie on lopsided cots.

Nothing stands out. What on earth does she want me to see? I don't know these people. I don't know why I'm—

A man lying on the cot coughs then picks at the bandage on his bulbous nose. He winces, like the injury under the bandage still hurts.

And it should still hurt.

It's the injury I gave him days ago.

This rebel isn't a rebel at all. He's the user who attacked me at the fueling station. The one who tried to force me into his bed. I tense and search the room. More and more of their disgusting faces are familiar. Horribly, repulsively familiar.

Before I can stop myself, the words tumble out my mouth. "What are Freeman's pushers doing here?"

"I KNEW IT!" ASTRID CLAPS HER

hands beside me. "There's no faction in South Austin. Kazi's a fool to let them in here."

"Watch it, Ris," warns one of the brothers.

I'm not sure which brother says it. I'm too busy staring down at the men who attacked me a few days ago as they walk about freely in a rebel base. They're the same men who tried to jack the rigs and murdered Astrid's boyfriend. Only, she doesn't know Mac is dead. I wonder if I should tell her. I'd want to know if it were me. Then again, the boys next to us don't know I'm a shipper. I can't reveal details of Mac's death without giving away my employment.

Why are the pushers here? How can they be here?

What if they ingest Freeman's again? My necklace is back with Dax on the hill. I can't stop anyone from going on a rampage. Maybe the rebels can, but they're the ones who let them in here. Right now, I can only trust Astrid.

"We have to go," I say in a hushed voice I hope only she can hear.

"Watch what?" She either didn't hear me, or completely ignores my plea. "I told you these guys are pushers. They probably work for Orange Pipe too. We have to tell Kazi the truth."

"What makes you think he doesn't already know?" Sulien asks. I turn from the window to look at him. "The man has an eye on everything in RAD."

Astrid flares. "You're suggesting Kazi did what, let them in on purpose? That he's willingly housing dome drug dealers? That he's a traitor?"

"Whoa, Ris," says Cadoc, stepping between the two of them. "He's not saying that. You're not saying that, are you, Sully?"

"I'm saying we have to be careful. If Kazi knows they're pushers, then there's probably a good reason he's keeping them here without a tribunal. We can't jump to conclusions."

"Jump to conclusions?" Astrid storms around the couch and makes for the door. "Freeman's is a disease. We let one ounce of it in here, and it'll destroy everyone."

"Where are you going?" asks Sulien. He navigates to the opposite side of the couch.

"To do something about this. Those creeps know something about the cure, and I'm going to find out what." Without another word, she disappears through the door.

"Wait, Ris, you can't just—" Sulien runs to the door, then nods to his brother before following Astrid into the hall.

Cadoc bends down, messes with something on his side of the painting, then rushes around the couch and out the room to join his brother.

I know I should follow Astrid. She's my ticket out of this place. But it all happens before I can blink. The next thing I know, I'm standing in the odd room by myself while the painting starts to shut behind me. It closes slower than it opened when the two brothers pulled it apart manually.

I stretch my head to look down one more time before I go—make sure I wasn't mistaken, and the guy really is a pusher. Same guy. Same thugs I saw on the other rig murdering Cyrus's crewmate too.

Wait. What's that?

A puff of pink hair pops up over a stack of boxes in the corner. *Tori?*

My hands slam on the windowpane. *Tori?* I press my face against the glass, but all I see from this angle is hair. It could be anyone. But the shade is the same hot pink, that and the curls, and—the painting collides with the sides of my hands. *No!* I push against it. It keeps closing. I try to hold it off. It pushes harder. I can either keep looking or lose my hands. I let go. It slams shut.

I rush to the side of the painting and search the bottom of the frame. My fingers brush a protruding mechanism. I push it, twist it, try to pull it out. It does nothing. Great. Maybe it needs two people to open it from both sides. But how am I going to—

Footsteps and muffled voices sound down the hall. I freeze. My ten minutes are up. The people Astrid got rid of are back, and there's nowhere to hide. If I run out the door, they'll see me. There's no room under the couch. I back up against the wall and touch something soft and velvety—a curtain. I didn't notice the floor-to-ceiling fabric before since it's so dark in here and it blends in with the walls. I wrap myself in the jet-black folds, hold my breath, and will my body to stop shaking.

I don't see anyone step into the room, but I hear them. There are two, maybe three. I can barely tell. Their shoes click and clack over the wooden floor, moving in opposite cadences. Unlike Astrid and the brothers, these people are in no hurry. And I think I found the source of the smell. Both the B.O. and cleaning solution odors have intensified.

". . . ran after that homing bird girl like they wanted to join the flock," says a man with a deep, jovial voice.

The other men laugh at what might have been funny in context. The couch creaks as one or two of them sit.

"Close the door," another man says, cutting through their laughter. His smokey voice is void of humor. That makes four men in here with me now.

The door clicks shut. My chances of walking out of here alive plummet.

"Tell me you're not considering their deal, Kazi," says one of the men on the couch.

There's a long pause before the other man on the couch, who I'm sure is Kazi, answers. "I'll consider what I'll consider."

"Come on, you can't be serious," the man says, still laughing. "They're not from another branch. The bug-eyed one couldn't even form a sentence without space cadetting. I'm telling you, they're pushers. We'd be idiots to trust them."

"Really," Kazi says. His one word sends chills down my spine. He strains each syllable until the word morphs into both a warning and a dare. Anyone with a clue or an ounce of self-preservation would shut up and back off.

But the man keeps on. "So they knew the entrance codes. What does that prove? That they tortured someone in the northern branch till they spilled the codes? Any bombing plans from a pusher is lunacy. They're probably here to raid the arsenal or jack some of our kids for their labs. Sooner we kick them out the better."

"Is that so?"

This time, the man keeps quiet. I can picture realization crashing over him like a bucket of ice water. His boss knows something he doesn't, and he should have stopped talking a long time ago.

"You're right about two things, Marcus," says Kazi once the room is thick with strain. "They *are* pushers. And their deal is crazy. But that's not the reason you won't shut up about them, is it?"

"I . . . I . . ."

"Out of words?" A slow slurp burbles through the room before Kazi speaks again. "Here I was, thinking you're the man with all the answers. Or maybe I had that wrong. You're not the man with the answers."

There's a clink of a teacup then a strange noise, like grinding metal. It sounds like he pulled out a knife from somewhere to sharpen it against another blade.

"You're the man with the loose mouth."

A sharp whistle splits the air. There's a sickening *thunk*, then a man's scream shakes the room. I jolt, knocking into the curtain. I freeze. The curtain still ripples in the aftershock of my bump. I fight the urge to still it, knowing I'll only make it worse.

The man's screams muffle. Either he's covered his own mouth, or someone covered it for him. I want to know what happened. But I'm too terrified to move or blink or breathe. What lunatic people did Astrid leave me with?

"Listen closely. I'm only going to ask this once." Kazi's voice slides from creepy and on edge to pure venom. The other man doesn't answer. But I still hear a moan, so I assume he's still alive.

"I know you're the mole," Kazi continues. "I know you've been selling us out to the Pipe for years. Just like you feared, your pusher friends ratted on you the minute they arrived. The only reason that knife is sticking out of your hand right now and not your throat is I still don't know why they're really here. But I have a feeling you do. So tell me, Marcus. What are those pieces of city trash doing in my house? What are they planning?"

There's a second where Marcus's moans become clearer, like someone removed their hand from his mouth. "Kazi, you've got to understand . . . I had no choice . . . I–"

"I don't have to understand anything. How many of our own are sitting in Quell prisons because of you? How many never came home to their families? Show an ounce of respect and tell me what I want to know."

There's a long stretch of silence until Marcus speaks in intermittent hisses of pain. "Okay, okay, but I want your word. When I tell you why they're here, promise you'll let me go."

Kazi grunts. "Always looking out for number one, aren't you? All right, you have my word."

"Have you heard of the . . . ?" He says something I can't understand through his hissing. I lean forward again but try not to touch the curtain.

"Yes," Kazi answers. Apparently, he understood the man. "It's a myth. Made up to give Grid children hope."

"Except it's not a myth. The pushers have seen it, and they're tracking the girl who has it. She's with the shippers on their way to the Scar."

My body goes frigid. It's like I'm trapped in a bizarre dream. Are they talking about me or one of the other shippers? Does it even matter?

"I wasn't kidding about the artillery," Marcus goes on. "Shippers don't give up easy. If the pushers want to steal that girl from those monster rigs, they're going to have to go in loaded. They're here to rob you."

"Are they." Kazi's response is more a statement than a question. "Well, that's going to be a problem. See, I've never liked it when people take what's mine. Be it supplies, or guns, or secrets." He says the last word with as much punch through his teeth as if to soak Marcus in spit. And maybe he yanked the knife out of Marcus's hand too. There's a squishy unsheathing sound followed by a man's piercing wail.

"Take him out of here." Kazi's voice returns to the creepy calm of earlier.

There's a shuffling of feet as the other men walk, and likely drag Marcus out of the room.

"Oh, and Breck?" says Kazi.

"Yes, sir?"

"Make sure to get the bloodstain out of the couch when you get back."

"Yes, sir."

"And, Breck?"

"Yes, sir?"

"That traitor doesn't get past the outer wall without a couple of bullets in his head."

"Yes, sir."

I wish that were the end of it. But he doesn't leave. I'm almost sure everyone else did, but their ticking-time-bomb leader is still in here with me. Worse, he moves to the picture frame near me and messes with the switch. His back faces me, and I only see his undercut brown waves and his pristine gray and white clothes. He twists the knob some way I didn't try, and the painting slides open. With his back turned on me, I pull some of the curtain fabric closer and hide deeper within its folds.

Kazi puts both hands on the glass and looks down. I can see him in profile now. His sun-weathered skin sports a cropped beard with streaks of gray throughout the umber brown. There are a few angled scars below his eye, over his cheek, and down his neck. The scars are in synthetic patterns. He must have had city-tech ripped off his face before he came out to the Grid. I bet he's one of the purged ones Dax told me about.

He whips something from his pocket so fast I flinch, thinking it's a gun or some other weapon. But the small cloth flops down while he dabs his face, and I relax. I think I might have let out a breath, though. He stops his wiping then turns slowly.

Breath lodges in my chest.

He steps closer. And closer, his eyes narrowing.

"They're here," a woman's voice says at the doorway. Kazi turns from the curtains to face her. "Outside the northern gate."

Kazi wipes the cloth over his face. "I'll be right there." He flicks the bottom of the painting and walks out as it closes.

Tension releases from my body like a snapped wire. I bend over my knees to regain composure, but stay behind the curtain for a minute to make sure I'm alone. When I think the coast is clear, I peek out. The room is the same as before, except for the hand-sized bloodstain on the arm of the couch. I try to ignore the crimson spot and remember the clean-up crew who will find me if I don't get going.

I dart out from behind the curtain, around the couch, and down the hall the way I saw Astrid go. I'm not sure which way to turn down these halls. If Astrid went to confront the pushers, she probably went down a couple flights. I keep my eyes open for stairways or steps or anything that will get me to her.

A few people walk the halls. I must appear whaler enough that they let me pass with barely a glance. I try not to look at them—just keep my head down and get out of here. It seems to work for a while. I even find a stairway. But while I search for the next set of stairs, someone grabs me by the arm and pulls me into a dark alcove in the wall.

I whip around to fend off my assailant.

"There you are," Astrid whispers tersely. Her hair is more disheveled than when she left the painting room. Wisps of black stick out in all directions, like she's been pulling hard on the roots.

Whatever she was doing, it can't be near as stressful as my past ten minutes.

"Where did you think I'd be?" I ask. "Hanging out in that room where you left me with your knife-wielding rebel boss?"

Her face slackens. "You were in the same room as Kazi?"

"Well, he didn't see me. But yes, I was in there with him, his men, the guy he stabbed—"

"He *stabbed* someone? Great. Of course, he's in that kind of a mood. It's a good thing he didn't see you. In fact, we need to get out of here before *anyone* sees you."

I cast her a sideways glance. It's not that I don't agree and want to leave the base as fast as possible, but it's this girl's fault we're still here to begin with. It's odd she's all gung ho to split now.

"Why? I don't look like a whaler anymore?"

Astrid shakes her head then ushers me out of the alcove. When she speaks next, her voice is so hushed I have to bend my head close to hear her. "It's not that you don't look like a whaler. You do. It's that the pushers are plotting to kidnap a blue-haired shipper girl. And you look like her too."

I STOP STONE-COLD IN THE HALLWAY.

So, the pushers *are* looking for me. But why? What do they want, to finish the job they started in the fueling station? Or worse, do they want to do to me what they did to my parents? The thought drags up memories of that awful night six years ago. The images burn strong within me. I can't help but relive every detail right here in the rebel base.

"Why are they chasing us, Mama?" My eleven-year-old self asked, tears blurring the dark alley into a black and neon mess. Mama's grip on my wrist stung as she dragged me through the streets of the Plex behind Dada. We ran and ran. I struggled to breathe the normally comfortable night air. The facial mask Dada insisted we wear didn't help the situation. I could breathe through it, sure, but I'd do better to rip the thing from my face.

Dada pulled us into an alley. Hugging the edge of the building, he watched the street to give us a second to rest.

"Your father and I made something, Sweet," Mama said, tugging the black mask off her nose to speak to me. She tucked my blonde hair behind my ear like she always did when she had important things to tell me. "Something the Pipe doesn't like, and they want to stop us."

"But you work for them. Why wouldn't they like what you made?"

She twisted the satchel around her chest to the front and dug through it. "Do you remember the day your dada and I tried you out on that new medication?"

I felt my heart sink. We were going to talk about that *day? We never talked about that day. Mama always teared up, or Dada* changed the subject whenever anyone brought up my six-year-old near-death experience. Especially if I brought it up.

They always said it wasn't my fault. That everything didn't change because of that day. But I knew better. The day after Dada snatched me from the window's ledge, they became more guarded. Refused to let me take any upgrades or visit them in their lab. They took off time from work and got side jobs. Their co-workers who came by every week for dinner stopped coming altogether.

The first time she wanted to talk to me about the day I almost fell out of a thirty-story scraper, we were being chased. And chased by the same men who used to wave hello to me in the lobby of their work. Mama had no tears in her brown eyes. Dada wasn't butting in to change the topic. Something was definitely wrong, and it was my fault.

"This is about the potential enhancer? I'm sorry, Mama, I didn't know what I was doing. Can't we tell Mr. Blakeman and Mr. Frasier I'm sorry?"

She dropped whatever she was digging for in her satchel and put her hand on my arm. "No, they're not mad at us for helping make Freeman's."

"Though they should be," interjected Dada from the building's corner.

"They should be," Mama agreed. She pulled a triangular rock free from the satchel and held it up by its chain. "They're mad at us for making this. It's a crier stone. And it is the only thing that can reverse Freeman's effect. It's coded to respond to our voices. Tell it to cry as close to the stone as you can, and it will counteract Freeman's in any user within a fifty-foot radius. But it also generates hallucinations and excruciating headaches in any user in range. The user will no longer be bound to Freeman's addictions—"

"Unless they use again," Dada added.

"Right. Free of addiction, unless they use again, but they will always be subject to the stone." Mama slid the necklace over my head.

My brain ached, piecing together her explanation of the black rock around my neck. My parents always did this—long, drawn-out descriptions no matter how bad the timing.

"Keep it on you always," Dada said. "And use it only if you have to.

Let's go before they find us." He crept away from the edge to lead us further down the alley.

We ran hard and fast through the ground streets of the Plex, avoiding city patrol and keeping our hoods and masks up to guard us against facial scanners. Wherever Dada wanted to go, we'd reach it much faster if we took a port. But Dada was certain we'd get caught the second we touched a porting dais.

Soon, the streets grew familiar—the digital wall murals, the Twisted Circles Bar. Since I walked only one neighborhood at ground level, I knew exactly where we were.

"We're going to Uncle Trek's apartment?"

"Uncle Trek knows people," Dada said. "He can get us out of the city."

And he could have. Had we made it to my uncle's home, we might have all survived that night. If the Plex didn't have other plans for us.

A man emerged from the shadows in front of us, his eyes and limbs glowing in circuit-board patterns of teal. Dada spun us around. Another man walked out of the bar to block our way. Then another, and another. Every path we took, there they were, users upon users. Until finally Mr. Blakeman pushed his way to the front of the mob. Behind his decorative glasses, his bulging eyes blazed blue.

"There's nowhere to go, Conway. Hand over the stone." Mr. Blakeman towered over Dada and Mama on normal days, both in height and girth. With Freeman's juicing his system, just one of his arms surpassed my entire body size. In the Pipe lobby, he always dressed in nice suits. Out in the streets, he wore nothing to cover the hexagonal metallic upgrades crossing his pasty chest and massive gut.

"The Plex won't have it. I won't let them." They were the last words I remember my father saying before he lifted me off the ground. He pulled a stone from beneath his shirt and whispered the activation code over its frame.

The sound triggered something within me. My body slackened in my father's arms. I don't know what happened in the real world after that. Everything melted into a loopy vision of the past.

When I woke, darkness surrounded me. The metallic taste of

blood filled my mouth. My legs cried out in pain, but I couldn't move them. Something heavy pinned me down on all sides. Where was I? Only a tiny flashing light lit my surroundings. I tried to push up. Whatever lay beneath me was solid but squishy. Same with what hovered above. There was a steady dripping sound by my ear, and the pungent smell hit me full force.

I struggled to breathe. Then I saw what I was on, and I . . .

"Hey, you awake in there?"

Astrid's voice shakes me from the past.

I blink away the mental fog, unsure how long I stood there staring into space. It felt like hours, but I'm sure it lasted only seconds.

"Yes," I respond. "Let's go." We take off down the hall quickly. When we reach the pigeon courtyard, I notice our lack of company. "Where are the brothers?"

She dodges behind the shed housing a flock of gray birds then pulls out a journal. It's identical to the one Nova constantly scribbled in back in the kart. Snatching a pencil from the messy table, she does the same. Like we have time for that.

She doesn't answer me until I snap my fingers.

"Oh. Uh, they're cleaning up a little mess I made." She doesn't look up from her notebook and waves in the air like she's shooing away both me and my question.

I suppose she can't be bothered while she writes in her diary. Silly me. Here I was thinking we're in a hurry.

"What mess?" I ask.

She looks up at me, exasperated, then shakes her head to switch gears from whatever she's doodling. "I had to get the pushers to talk somehow. The one who did is going to have trouble seeing out his right eye for a couple of days. Sully and Cadoc are smoothing it over with some people who saw it happen while I try to get us out of here. But if I don't let Nova know what to expect, the switch will blow up in her face. She deserves some payback, leaving me here so long and all, but Kazi's wrath is hot right now. I don't know what he'd do to her. So, give me a second."

I blink. I'm not sure how to digest all that. She goes back to writing, and I pace the courtyard. Anxious jitters work their way across my arms. The longer she takes, the more I fight the urge to ask her to hurry it up or nudge her or something.

Then, out of nowhere, she slams the journal shut and stuffs it in her jacket. "All right, let's get you back to your kart."

"There's no one behind us. You can lower your rifle," Astrid calls out, climbing the hill ahead of me. Though I know Dax was aiming a gun at the base before, I couldn't see him on the way back. I still don't see him until he comes out from behind a tree a couple of yards from the parked kart, holding his rifle.

He lowers the barrel and slides the sling over his shoulder. "Took you long enough. Thought we were going to have to drag you two out."

Astrid laughs. "Right, 'cause Kazi would just let a shipper stroll in there no problem."

"He let Juna in," Dax counters.

I flinch. It's weird hearing my real name on his tongue. It's also weird that he called me a shipper. I suppose I have been one for three days now, but I didn't think he'd consider me part of the crew so soon.

Nova climbs out of the kart and runs to her sister. Both girls look almost the same as they hug—high black ponytails, matching beige ponchos. The only difference is their tatt—wait, no, Nova's neck and arms are covered in tattoos. The exact same grayscale tattoos as Astrid. Same astronaut lady on her shoulder, same row of planets on her neck. Was she wearing some kind of makeup to cover them before?

Dax comes up behind them to hug his sister too. Astrid accepts the embrace, but she's much more restrained than when she hugged Nova.

"Is that why I've been in the dark with RAD for months?" she asks when he releases her. "You couldn't find a recruit they wouldn't notice?"

Dax rubs the back of his neck. "I'm sorry about that. You know I would have come to you if I could. We got into some bad situations. There weren't few recruits, there were none. None until Juna."

"You could have sent a bird," she says. "You couldn't do the switch, fine, but c'mon, Dax, let me know you're still out there."

"Oh, right." His voice takes on an edge. "We could do that. Send a pigeon every time we want to give you an update or say 'hi.' Hope no one else is there to receive it. Or better yet, let's increase your chances of getting caught and send one every week."

Astrid puffs out annoyance at his sarcasm. "I'm not asking you to send one that often. But was there really something that bad going on that you couldn't clue me in by bird at least once a month?"

Dax goes silent, and Nova looks at the dirt. An unease settles between us. Astrid looks back and forth between her siblings. Then she turns her gaze on me. I look up at a lone cloud. There's no way I'm going to be the one to tell her about Mac. I did my duty there. It's up to the siblings to deliver the blow.

"Astrid," Dax says, voice quiet now. "There's something I need to tell you."

"But he's going to let me do it," interrupts Nova. She tosses her sister a jar of something then leads her away to the kart.

Dax and I stay behind near the tree. I can't imagine what it would be like to break that news. Dax moves further away to give the sisters more space. Grateful, I follow.

"As promised," he says and reaches beneath his poncho, "one world-changing necklace." He takes out my crier stone, dangling from the golden chain, and holds it out to me. It's strange seeing the small black pendant I've had around my neck for years offered to me. Not only that, but offered by the one who tried to convince me to give it up hours ago. I still don't know what he or Hatcher or any of them want to do with it, but he's offering it freely now.

"You're just going to give it to me?" I ask. I should take it instead of questioning. But I'm curious.

"What? You don't want it?"

I regret my words.

"No, I do." I reach out my hand, and he lets me snatch it from his grip.

"You held up your end, now I'm holding up my end," he says.

I rub my finger over the pendant I haven't held in days. It feels like it's been longer than that, months even. I hang the chain around my neck then drop the crier stone into my shirt. It fits naturally against my chest like I was born with a space carved out between my ribs to cradle it tight.

"Out of curiosity," Dax says, "where'd you get it?"

I look over at him. He's not paying attention to me whatsoever. Instead, he's sitting down on a nearby log and staring at his sisters. Nova moves back and forth, speaking to Astrid, who leans against the kart, applying tan cream from the jar to her skin till the tattoos start to disappear. It must've been the same cream Nova wore on the farm to cover her ink. We can't hear what they're saying, but the exchange weighs on Dax. I can't tell if he wants to know the answer to his question or if he's trying to distract himself from the bomb about to drop on his sister.

Either way, I have questions I'd like answers to before divulging anything about my past.

"I'll tell you, if you tell me first," I say, sitting beside him. "Why do you and Hatcher want my necklace? How do you even know about it?"

He turns to regard me. "All right. You earned that." He looks back toward his sisters. "I've known about the stone since I was a kid. Most Gridders say it's a myth, though. A device on a chain some scientists made to stop the effects of Freeman's. It's something people talk about but don't believe exists.

"Some of us were taught differently. We knew there's a remedy and kind of what the stone looks like. We knew if we found it, we could do something to stop the drug lords from destroying our cities and wrecking the Grid. So, some of the farmers and shippers have been keeping a lookout for it.

"We didn't know the necklace belonged to you. I had a hunch, but at the station, I thought finding it near you was a coincidence. Then you tried to hack into Hatcher's office. It was easy to connect the dots from there."

I recoil. Guess I wasn't as slick as I thought. I want to deny my poor hack job, but he already knows what I did and isn't threatening any consequences.

"So, you're going to let me have it? You've been searching for this necklace your whole life and now you're going to give it back?"

"Well, I'd like to know why you have it, but I'm not a thief. Besides, I doubt a girl who jumped in a vorgle pond to save a farm girl she just met, or risked herself against a sand monster for my sister, is going to keep the stone from those who need it."

His statement throws me in so many directions it's hard to know what to ask about first.

"You know about the vorgle incident?"

"Everyone knows about the vorgle incident," he says. "Especially when a city girl saves a farm girl in the Grid." He gives me a half smile that's both genuine and a little shy. It's a strange expression on him.

It makes me curious. "If I didn't go into the rebel base, would you have given me my necklace back anyway?"

He coughs like he's choking. "What's it matter? You did it, you're all out, and no one's cover is blown. Mission accomplished." He stands.

My jaw drops. "You would have. You would have given me my necklace back whether I went in there or not."

His lips tighten. "Said I wasn't a thief, Princesa. But that doesn't make me an angel."

He grabs the strap of his gun to climb up the hill. By the kart, Astrid and Nova are in more animated conversation. Astrid drops the skin cream then slides down the side of the kart till she sits on the charred grass below. Nova falls to her knees and embraces her sister. Dax sees the exchange and goes still.

He may not think he's an angel for bribing me to go into the base, but I don't know. Right now, watching his sister's heartbreak rattles him in a way he must have known it would, and he still chose to tell her in person . . . he seems a little angelic to me.

"I got it from my mom," I say to his back.

He slowly turns and stands, waiting until I go on.

"Those mythical scientists who made the necklace. They were my mom and dad. They gave me the pendant the same day Orange Pipe operatives murdered them in the Plex and buried all three of us under piles of debris."

WE DRIVE TO THE SCAR IN JERKY,

uncomfortable silence. Astrid rides in the back beside the kart where she asked to be alone. Every now and then, her sniffles rise over the rumble of the engine, but otherwise she makes no noise. She has made hardly any noise since she heard the news about Mac. Nova isn't with us. She trekked back to RAD's base on foot, all tatted up. There, she'll pose as Ris, the girl both sisters take turns impersonating to spy on the rebels.

Which leaves me alone with Dax up front again.

He glances over at me every few seconds when he thinks I'm not looking. We haven't spoken beyond basic marching orders since I revealed my past to him. I think he wants to say something about it but doesn't know what.

I mess with the straps on my bumblebee uniform and wish I had Slate here to buckle everything back in place. There are a few straps on my neck I can't reach. I guess I'll deal with them later. For now, I fiddle with the buckles around my waist and pretend not to notice Dax noticing me.

It's not working.

I can't put my finger on it, but our dynamic changed outside the base. I hardly know this Glasses Guy, yet I've shared one of the most secret parts of my life with him. Outside my family, Tori, and some councilors, he's the first person I told the story of that night. It seems strange to share my past with him. And yet, it docsn't feel wrong, just—relieving, somehow.

He cracks his neck. I look over to catch him looking at me and not the road. He immediately turns away so fast, I get whiplash watching him.

"You alright?" I ask.

He shrugs and taps the wheel. "I'm fine. Why wouldn't I be?"

"I don't know. You look distracted."

He shrugs, but after a minute or two, he clears his throat. "I've gotta ask. How did you get buried alive and . . . you know, you're not . . ."

"Dead?" I offer.

He nods. I chew on my bottom lip. I'm not used to talking about this with anyone. My aunt and uncle already know the story, so I never bring it up around them. I only spoke of it to Tori once, and she tiptoed around the subject whenever it came up again, so it's not like I've talked about it a lot.

"Are you sure? It's kind of messy."

"I can handle messy."

"Okay," I say and lean back, thinking. "How I got down there is still a blur. I remember people from Orange Pipe chasing us through the streets. But I don't know how I ended up under the rubble. I can't remember an explosion, or falling, or any of it. My uncle thinks someone tossed a live ground imploder near us.

"Whatever it was, when I came to, I only saw slivers of light. Something heavy sat on both my legs. I couldn't move my lower half, and it hurt like crazy when I tried. There was a rotten and metallic smell. I wanted to cover my nose, but my hands were pinned.

"When I tried to wiggle free, I realized what I was sandwiched between"—my voice hitches—"my dead mother on top and my dead father beneath. I lay there trapped, soaked in their . . . soaked in their blood."

I keep my eyes focused out the window. The image of my dead parents isn't an image I like keeping in my head for long.

"I don't know how long I was down there," I say. "My uncle said it was a couple of days before he found me. I yelled till my voice went raw, he heard me, and got me out. I couldn't walk for weeks. When I could, we left the Plex. I never looked back." I turn to him.

"You said a girl like me wouldn't keep the stone from people who need it. Well, my aunt and uncle might be called to forgiveness, but I'm never setting foot in that city as long as I live."

Dax doesn't say anything for a long time. When he does, his voice is gentle. "I'm sorry, Juna."

Unsure what to say in response, I watch the landscape dip into twilight. If Tori were here, we'd laugh. The guy I wanted to punch in the face three days ago is now the one I'm sharing deep secrets with. Not only that, he's not making fun of me. He seems to care. I muse over the irony. And rub the chill on my arms at his use of my real name again.

Outside, the last golden spindles of sunlight grace the edges of the wasteland. Their thin rays outline vine-covered buildings, sideways trees, and streetlights bathed in blue. Soon, ancient cars litter the ground. Scattered over the side of the highway in odd angles, the mangled vehicles come in all shapes and sizes. Some are huge like shipper trucks with their narrow trailers punctured with massive holes in their walls. Others are tiny by comparison. I doubt they could hold more than two people. Some are smaller still and resemble skycabs with wheels. At least if skycabs were smashed under trucks, sliced in two, charred to crisps, or upside down every twenty feet.

"Here we are," says Dax, "home sweet Scar."

I give him a look. "Home?"

He shrugs. "Okay, it's not a five-star room in a dome hotel, but it'll do for tonight."

I follow his gaze out the window. In the distance, San Antonio's city lights flicker against the dying sun. There's a faint outline of its transparent dome arching across the sky.

Dax brings the rig to a stop. He flicks a switch to open the channel between rigs. "Looks like the Flux is leaving us alone for the evening. We'll start on the salvage at first light. Fledge, you, and the delivery team can head out. Slate, you're with me."

The drivers on the screens agree and nod while Dax unbuckles and leaves his seat.

"Where are you going?" I ask.

He bends around his chair then opens the driver's side cab door. He beckons to me. "Come on. There's something I want to show you."

For the first time since I put it on, I'm grateful for the bumblebee suit. The air isn't as frigid as the night of the blizzard, but it's loads cooler than it was outside the rebel base. If I didn't have the thick, long sleeves of the suit, I'd be shivering as I follow Dax into the dark. His low-tech flashlight shines over broken concrete and a jungle of waist-high weeds.

Slate walks between us. A long tube with a strap is strung across her chest, and she carries a duffle bag over her shoulder. Both she and Dax walk with purpose. She shines her flashlight beside him rather than behind him. Wherever they're leading me, they've been there before.

Though the sun hasn't set, the thick trees around us block out most of its rays. There aren't any broken cars this way, nor are there any buildings. Just trees and more trees. Then something large and metal sticks up above the silhouetted treetops. I can't make out what it is, arched up there like half a gigantic dinner plate stuck in the earth.

The closer we move to the massive thing, the more it really does look like a piece of broken china. We pass between a few trees until it blocks our way entirely. Now I see the metal thing is white and curved, more like a shallow bowl than a plate—a bowl that could fit several shipper trucks in it easy. There are long cracks on its upper part with huge chunks missing, exposing the bars of its metal frame. It's held off the ground by a short metal building with some ladders flanking its sides.

"What is that?" I ask.

Dax shines his light at the structure's underbelly high above our heads. It covers the space between the trees like an opaque dome. "An old satellite dish. You ever seen the stars?" he asks.

I look at him like he's gone nuts. "Of course I've seen the stars. Who hasn't?"

"Anyone living in the domes for the past couple hundred years," Slate answers for him as she adjusts her bags and climbs up the ladder of the short building.

I want to argue. I've seen the same constellations out my window many nights before bed. The cities track exactly where the natural stars are in space. They display their images across the dome without fail. They might be hard to see if I'm in a super bright place, but I can still spot Orion and the Big Dipper. Without Weather Fluxes, I've probably seen more of the stars than Gridders exposed to constant storms. But I hold my tongue.

Dax just grins. "Follow me. You're going to love it."

I try to stick close to him and his flashlight as I climb the ladder. It's so dark, I can barely make out the rungs. The sun has either gone all the way down, or it will any moment. The top of the ladder soon dead-ends with the bottom of the dish. Slate is first to reach it. She turns a latch above her from right to left. There's an echoing click, and she pushes a door that opens into the dish. A pale light spills down from the square hatch. Slate climbs further then hoists herself into the other side. Dax is quick to follow, and I do the same.

I pull myself up and out of the hatch to sit on the edge. Dax extends his hand to me, and I take it. When he lifts me to my feet, I look into his face. I wish I could see his eyes. I wonder what color they are. It's weird he's still wearing sunglasses when it's this dark outside. Who does that?

"All right," he says, putting his hands on my shoulders. "Look up."

I don't at first. Instead, I take in everything around me. The dish is what I thought it'd be a huge worn, concave plate we can walk on. Slate unpacks poles and tubes from her bags a few feet from us. She brushes her burgundy hair behind her ears and smiles too, like they're both in on a joke. Beyond her, four metal rods as wide around as I am jet from four edges of the plate to meet high in the center above us.

And then I see it.

A sea of spilled electric salt, strewn across the heavens.

The colors are unreal. Blues, browns, purples, and golds. Burnt umbers in balls of dust smashed into aquamarine clouds. I'm used to the night sky drenched in black. This is far from that. Violet and crimson stars flicker like billions of tiny dancers in a cosmic ballet. I can make out Orion—its familiar three-star belt shines brilliant above the rest. But it's richer now, joined by legions of light that fill in the gaps.

My knees go weak, and I start to buckle. Dax catches my other arm.

"Whoa," he says, and holds me upright.

I can't believe I almost collapsed like that. It's not like I haven't seen the Milky Way. I've seen plenty of pictures taken by ancient space explorers in science lectures. I just didn't think we could see anything like that while standing on the earth. And those pics were all static—not teeming with life like they are here in the Grid.

"I, um, thanks." I stumble through my gratitude and ease away. "Why does it look like that?"

"It always looks like that." He strolls across the dish. "At least on nights without Fluxes. With no city-tech in the Outer Grid, we're not steeped in light pollution like the domes."

"We can see how the sky's meant to look," Slate puts in. She assembles whatever it was she had in her bags, placing a white metal cylinder onto a tripod then angling it to the stars.

"What are you doing?" I ask.

She pulls out a notebook from her bag and jots something in it before digging through her bag again. "Practicing my navigation skills."

She doesn't explain further, so I look to Dax for answers.

"The satellite dish is the highest place around here. The rest of the Scar is jagged and sunk low in cracks from the earthquakes. So, it's the best place to view the stars."

"There's also not a rowdy shipper boy in sight," she adds.

"Hey," Dax protests.

"You don't count," she says, looking up from her bag. "You don't pick fights or knock over my telescope while wrestling to see who can pin whom in less than five."

Dax grins. "I lost twenty bucks on Rook that night."

"If the oaf would have paid attention to where he was instead of trying to drop Zane, he wouldn't have tripped over my bag and lost. The klutz still owes me a replacement lens for the one he cracked." She switches her focus back to the bag and digs with more agitation. "I can't find it."

"Find what?" I ask.

"My spare lens." She sighs. "I thought I packed it in with everything else, but it's still in the rig. I've got to get it. I won't be able to see anything with this cracked one."

"We'll go back with you," Dax offers.

She shakes her head. "No, I don't want you to miss the team. I'll only be a second anyway." Without waiting for his agreement, she picks up her flashlight and makes for the hatch. She's down and gone in seconds, leaving me alone with the wind, croaking grid beasts, and this shipper who held me in his hands before showing me the stars.

I spend a few minutes looking up while being painfully aware of Dax's closeness. He's a good three or four feet from me, but it's close enough to make my insides feel loopy. Of all the ways I expected to be treated after sharing my deepest secret, kindness wasn't one of them. Avoidance. Contempt. Pity. That's how all the synths would treat me. It's exactly how the counselors treated me after the incident.

But not Dax. Instead, the first thing he does is bring me here—to a place so beautiful, I want to cry.

I try to talk about something else before I do. "What does she mean miss the team?"

The second my eyes land on at him I regret it. Pointing the flashlight on the dish with one hand, he props his head back in the other. The way he looks then makes me suddenly wish I wore something an ounce more feminine than this bee suit.

"That's why I come here," he says. "The satellite has a great view of the stars and the best view of that."

He points past the treetops at the hills in the distance. A trail of yellow dots climbs the spruce-blue hills. They're attached to four vehicles that look all too familiar to me.

"Shipper trucks," I say. "Is that the delivery team?"

"Sure is." He reaches inside his pocket and pulls out a small, black box with a long rod sticking out its top. Clicking a button on its side, he puts the box to his mouth. It makes a crackling fuzz sound before he speaks.

"What's your status, Fledge," he asks the box.

There's another crackle before the box talks back. "No signs of trouble, boss," says the voice of the delivery team's lead driver. "Should arrive at the storehouse within the hour."

"Ten-four," answers Dax. "Have the guys keep an extra eye out. We'll see you on the other side of the city."

"Roger that. Same to you."

I'm thrown back at Fledge's words. *Arrive at the storehouse*? Now?

"How are they getting into the city after sundown?" I ask. Everyone knows domes aren't open at night.

"They aren't going into the city," he tells me. "See that small group of lights out there?" He points to a tiny orange glow between the shipper trucks and the bright dome in the west.

I nod.

"That's one of the Grid towns still out here. They're made up of descendants of the purged ones who don't mind shippers. City doesn't know it, but we've been trading with them for years. Delivering to them can be dangerous. Sometimes the rebels make trouble for us. Most of the time, though, it's Freeman's users making trouble for the town. They destroy town after town out here and the Quell don't lift a finger."

I cringe. "Because the Quell are here to keep the purged ones out of the cities, not the users out of the Grid."

He nods. "There's nothing I can do but be ready to help if our guys need it. Users outpower us, all juiced up. You saw what happened to Boone, and to Mac. That's not even half of it. There's experiments they run on kids. And what they do to the whaler tribes they capture. Now that the Plex is legalizing Freeman's, it's only going to get worse. We need a way to fight back."

I fiddle with my pendant. He means my necklace. He wants me to hand it over and teach him how to use it. Only he wouldn't be able to use it. It's programed to respond to my family's voice alone, and I have no idea how reprogram it.

"Dax, I—"

He's watching me. "Look," he says, "I know the stone means a lot to you, and I understand. I'm not asking you give it to us. You could . . . maybe use the stone with us? Join the crew long-term."

His suggestion startles me. *Join the crew long-term?* He's not asking me to give up my pendant or even teach him how to use it, but he wants me to join him? To wield the stone against the Pipe as a permanent shipper. Could I do that?

The Grid is all kinds of dangerous. I'd miss my aunt and uncle to pieces, not to mention Tori. But what happens if I don't join? How many shippers could end up like Mac?

It's not what I felt told to do. But it will still help people, just not the people in the Plex. And don't the shippers deserve help more than the losers who murdered my parents? If I'm helping people, that should be enough. Then again, I've only known Dax for three days. Can I put my whole future in his hands? I haven't even seen his eyes once.

"Do one thing for me, first," I say.

His face brightens but shadows with a hint of hesitation. "Okay, what?"

"Take off your glasses."

"MY GLASSES?"

Dax brushes the edge of his frames. His brows dip behind the silver lenses till they disappear. I realize my request is out of the blue. But I don't know how easy it will be to trust someone who constantly hides part of their face. If he wants me to join his crew and risk my life, I want to see his eyes.

"Yes. It's so dark out here, we can see more of outer space than I knew existed, but you're still wearing those things like the sun's out. Why?"

The first time I asked about his glasses he made a joke out of it. This time he rubs his jaw like he's about to give me a real answer.

"It's a long story. I don't think we'll have time before—"

Almost on cue, the dish's hatch pops open and Slate climbs through.

"Sorry," she says. "Zane thought my lens bag was his sock tote. He put my bag on his rig and left the tote back at the farm. So now I have my lens, but that guy is going to stink for days."

Dax bends close. "I'll show you later, okay? Promise." He straightens and claps his hands. "Let's see some stars."

I don't usually eat dinner with more than two people. So sitting around a fire with ten shippers while they tell stories and crack jokes is new. I helped Zane and a bearded guy named Cure set up the seating. They pulled in red-and-white-striped barriers that have seen better days and a couple of logs to sit on. I unfolded a few chairs from Dax's rig and placed them in the empty spots around the circle. The rest of the shippers either worked on the fire or prepped food in metal pots.

The smell of peppered meat, diced potatoes, and sugary baked beans rises over the campfire's smoke. As another solid bite of natural food glides down my throat, I can't help the surrealness setting in. Never in my life did I imagine myself eating this much real food with this many people.

Dax sits across the fire from me, making his dinner into a wacky concoction. Whatever it is, it probably tastes amazing. I can't hear what the two guys on either side of him are saying, but they snicker and point at his food, so it's not hard to guess. Dax takes the teasing in stride. He says something to them with a big grin on his face, making them burst into laughter.

Next to me, Zane stands in front of Cyrus, Cure, and Magnus. He acts out an encounter he had with a grid beast during a wind Flux. His arms flail and wave with elaborate, and probably exaggerated, detail. I try to figure out what animal he's describing. A balderwatt? A jackware? None of the animals Glowen showed me at the farm fit. Whatever it was, the creature met its match in Zane. Or so he says.

Slate sits on the other side of me, cross-legged on the ground. Her straight back grazes a striped, red metal barrier behind her. Next to her slouches Rook. His tree trunk legs stretch out on the dirt to end mere inches from the firepit. A deep frown etches his normally cheery face. He pushes potatoes across his plate but doesn't take a single bite. Instead, he grunts and sighs over Zane's tall tale.

"What's wrong?" Slate asks him, placing her plate into her lap.

"Told you, I'm fine," he mutters then goes back to shoving his food back and forth.

One of the guys is yelling at Dax.

"You're not going to eat that!" cries the other and makes gagging sounds.

Zane stops telling his story to turn his head, then skirts the fire to where Dax sits. "All right, boys and girls," he booms. "It's that time again! Time for what's in Dax's gross sandwich. Let's see if any of you picky wimps will try a bite this time."

He bends over Dax's shoulder. Without a hit of annoyance or hesitation, Dax indulges him, handing him the sandwich so he can open it wide. Seems like they do this often. Zane lists each ingredient. The rest of the crew shrug saying, "I'd eat that" and "It doesn't sound so bad," or shudder and groan. The longer he goes on, the more each shipper heaves in disgust.

To be honest, some of this combo makes my stomach queasy. He has the same meat, potatoes, and beans everyone else is eating plus strawberries, blue cheese, some dandelion leaves, and mustard. All stuffed between a bagel. He said there's something else in there, but it's hard to hear over the clamor. I stand.

"I'll try a bite."

All eyes land on me.

I walk toward Dax. He slowly straightens as I near him. Some of the crew jeer me along the way, but I don't care.

I reach Zane and look directly into his eyes. "And if I do, then you have to take a bite too."

Zane looks like I punched him in the gut. The shippers *ooh* and clap and shake him by the shoulders. He shakes them off.

"Okay, new girl," he consents. "I'll play. On one condition. You have to swallow the whole bite without gagging or wincing once."

So he's calling my bluff. I hold out my hand to take the sandwich. "You're on."

Dax's smile is broad, dimples and all, as he hands me his creation. Without waiting to savor the shock on Zane's face, I bring the sandwich to my mouth and take a hefty bite.

A range of flavor dances in my mouth. Smoke from the peppered meat and potatoes hits me first. I don't expect it to be so remarkable since I just ate a plateful of the same stuff. But the other ingredients enhance the char I hadn't noticed without them. A tingly shock works its way from my tongue to my brain when the tart berries mix with rich explosive cheese. I shut my eyes to savor each second until it's gone.

When I open them again, Zane is staring at me, slack-jawed.

"Your turn," I say, holding out the sandwich.

The shippers yell, holler, and the ones nearest slap him on the back.

"Okay, okay!" he shouts, calming them down. "Said I'd do it, so I'll do it." He sucks in a breath and then another, then rips into the sandwich with a giant bite. His eyes stay pinched shut while he chews. We never said *he* didn't have to wince, but he doesn't. Instead, he finishes his mouthful, swallows, and eyes the sandwich and Dax in awe.

"Not so bad?" asks Dax.

Zane doesn't even answer, just goes for another bite.

"Hang on. Let me try that!" Cyrus snatches the sandwich from Zane and chomps down. There's a pause, his eyes widen, then he slaps his leg before passing it to the guys beside him. "That's one tasty sandwich!"

Dax leans back on his log. He eats the other half of his dinner with amusement on his face. Then he gazes at me intently. Like when we watched the stars together, strange feelings bubble around my chest. I wish I could see if he's actually looking at me but am glad I can't because I'm sure he is.

I turn so I can't see him in my peripheral vision and watch the shippers relish his sandwich. Well, most of them relish it. Magnus takes one bite, grimaces over the mustard, then shoves it back to Cyrus. To which Cyrus says he wouldn't know what good was if it magically made him less ugly. Magnus insults him right back and they both laugh. It's amazing how much these shippers enjoy each other's company. Cyrus even gives me accolades, pointing at the sandwich and grinning in thanks for getting him to try it. They're so unlike the synths in the cities. It's every man for himself there.

Here, they're a tight-knit family. A tight-knit family that ripped open a seam to weave me in.

Maybe I *can* join the crew. Use my necklace and become one of them.

"I said I don't want it." Rook's voice rises above the chatter from across the fire. He's still slumped on the barrier where Slate is offering him a small part of Dax's sandwich.

I take it as a cue to move away from the odd sensations Dax stirs in me. As I do, I spot Astrid, standing in the shadows in Nova's shipper uniform. She leans against a skinny tree, a deep scowl on her face. I guess I can refer to her as Astrid instead of Nova now that the delivery crew is gone. Dax doesn't trust the few ex-rebels in their crew with his sisters' secret.

"What's your problem?" Slate asks Rook. "You've been in a bad mood since we left."

Rook shrugs. "Just waitin' for the second shoe to hit us square between the eyes."

Slate rolls her eyes. "Not this again."

"Y'all can be sick of me sayin' it, I don't care," he goes on, stabbing and releasing his potatoes. "But I'm tellin' you, this whole trip don't feel right. The Quell taking Zane, the whaler path, users at the station, Mac, Boone. If this ain't the eye of the storm, I don't know what is."

Slate doesn't say anything in response.

No one says anything. Every shipper goes silent.

"He's right." Astrid slinks out of the shadows. Coming to a stop between me and Rook, she wipes her bloodshot eyes with the back of her hand. Black mascara smears across her cheeks like a splatter painting of heavy sorrow. "There's only one way to stop what's coming." Her voice is shaky.

She stretches her upturned fist to the fire and uncurls her fingers. Sitting within her palm are a pile of black stones. Each stone has a letter or two written on top in white.

Maybe I imagine it, but there's a collective gasp from the crew.

"Are those—" Slate starts.

Dax jumps from his seat and I barely see him move before he's in front of Astrid closing her fingers back over the stones.

"I thought you were going to bed early."

"I couldn't sleep. Death will do that to you."

Dax's face tightens. "Where'd you get those?"

His sister shrugs. "Found them in one of the trucks."

"This isn't going to bring him back, Astrid."

"I never said it would," she counters. "But if we don't stop the chaos storm now, more of us could join Mac. You want that guilt on your shoulders, Brother?"

Dax doesn't reply.

"Let her roll them," Cyrus says. All the merriment in his features gone. "Those were Boone's storm stones."

All eyes shift from Cyrus to Dax.

Mac's words track through my mind. *We roll these stones to see who ticked the cosmic force off. When we find the guy, we maroon him.* Is that what they're doing? Rolling stones to see who we maroon? My heart pounds.

"Is that what you want?" Dax asks. "A bunch of rocks determining if one of you keeps or loses their job? Is that what Mac would want? Or Boone?"

"No," says Rook, standing to his full height. "But they wouldn't want blood on their hands for doing nothing."

Dax runs his fingers through his hair. "Fine. Do what you want. Just do it without me."

He turns away from his sister then moves past Rook toward the rigs. I want to follow him. But my feet are cemented to the ground. It's several minutes before anyone says anything.

The first one who does is Zane. "So, are we going to do this, or not? Anyone ever used storm stones?"

"Once," says Rook. "Easy enough. Heads sides have one letter that stands for each of us. First two letters for Cyrus and Cure or the likes. Tails up, you didn't cause the storm. Heads up, it might have been you. We keep dropping all the heads-side-up stones till they either all land on tails or we get the source."

I guess by *the source*, he means the person they're going to blame for the chaos storm.

"What happens to the source?" I ask, using up the sliver of hope that Dax was wrong and that they don't maroon someone based on tossed stones.

No one answers. Instead, their faces grow more solemn by the second. Like they've changed their minds and marooning someone on superstition is a bad idea. Some even start to head toward where Dax disappeared.

But then Astrid stops them. "For Mac," she says as she throws the stones on the ground. They crash against earth and rock, bouncing in all directions. Some roll mere inches from where they fell. Others fly near the fire. No one touches them. If any stone comes near them, the shippers step away to let it stop where it will.

Once the stones still, we lean in to read their verdict. The first one I see sits by my foot, blank side up. Tails. I look around. There's a stone a few feet from me—same story. Tails. Then another, and another.

"Anybody see any heads?" asks Zane.

"Naw," says Rook. "Nothin' but blank rocks."

"All blank?" asks Cyrus.

I spin and search. They're all blank. Every rock I see is tails.

Every rock, except one.

Behind me, away from the firelight and the shippers, is a single stone heads side up. The white chalk on the rock is unmistakable, but I'm not sure what letter is written on it. I slink forward, afraid someone will see it before me. When I stand over the stone, the letter is clear. I've never hated my name as much as I do when I stare at the "J" marked in white.

"WHAT IS IT, JUNA?" SLATE'S VOICE

startles me.

"I . . . it's . . ." I can't think straight. Can't form a complete sentence. How is it that every single storm stone is tails up except the one with *my* letter etched on its surface? Just when I thought I'd make a home with the shippers, they're about to maroon me here. Why is this happening?

I wish I didn't know. But I do.

The first time I watched the Plex burn was the first full night I slept in months.

The second time, I thought it was a side effect of my trauma.

The third, fourth, and fifth time, I knew the reoccurring dreams were a sign from God. At first, they brought me peace—a sense of justice when the flames scorched the dome. That city fractured my heart. They could lose their precious buildings.

But then a couple weeks before, the dream changed.

As I stood outside the dome walls, wind at my back watching the licking inferno, I heard a voice. A low, hushed sound. Words I tried to forget.

"Go. Cry against it."

Unsure what it meant, I foolishly went to my aunt and uncle for advice. I'd never told them about the dreams before. The moment the words left my mouth, I knew I shouldn't have said anything. Aunt Marna's face was tight with worry. Uncle Trek held her hand to calm her.

"That bill they're passing on Freeman's," she said to him. "Cry

against it? Trek, you don't think . . . my sister's crier stone . . . Does He want us to use it to save the city?"

Save them? Save the people of the Plex? The ones who murdered her sister, my mother, in the street? My aunt and uncle didn't see my dreams as comfort or justice. They saw them as a warning. A warning to go to the Plex and stop whatever fiery judgement was about to fall on that dump. And they wanted to take me with them.

But I thought I escaped that plan.

I look down at the stone with the white "J" chalked in its center. Who am I kidding? I haven't escaped anything.

"What's wrong, Juna," Slate asks again. I'd forgotten she was there.

I keep my eyes glued to the rock as my options flash before me. I can kick it into the dark. No one would have to know a stone landed here at all. But they could count and know mine is missing. I could flip it over. Pretend it was always on tails. One little nudge with my foot and this would all be over.

My foot taps the edge of the stone. But I hesitate. I can't do it. What good is lying? If I'm the cause of everything going south for them, then don't they have a right to know? Besides, if this is God's will, they'll find out sooner or later.

"You okay?" Slate steps up beside me. She looks at me then down at the stone. There's no hiding it now. "Ahh. I see."

I wring my hands as the words blurt out. "I'm sorry, Slate. I shouldn't have come. I put everyone in danger. It's my fault we're in this—"

Slate inches forward then flips the stone over with her foot. "Whoops. Oh, well, look at that. Tails." She leans near the fire, beckoning for the other shippers to join us. "Here it is! Found the last one."

I look at her in amazement. Why would she do that for me? No one has ever done something like that for me.

"Storm stones are stupid," she says in a quiet voice as if reading my thoughts. "I saw what you did for Nova in the course. I'm not about to let her sister repay you with a death ticket." When Rook approaches, she points to the rock. "There it is, same as the rest. Looks like it's no one's fault after all."

He sighs when he picks up the stone, but deflates as he turns it in his hands. "Guess you're right. You're always right." He winks at her before he walks back to the others.

Maybe it's a trick of the light, but I swear Slate's cheeks glow right along with the fire. She notices me staring and ducks her head. "Come on, let's set up your bedroll."

Morning light breaks over the Scar hours earlier than I want it to. Yesterday felt like it stretched on for years—the obstacle course, the rebel base, the storm stones. Its effects run through my body in a stiff ache in my legs, back, and neck. That, or sleeping on rocks did me in. Whichever, I'm exhausted when I wiggle halfway out of my bedroll.

The sky is blood red. Purple clouds zoom by in a silhouetted race. Flock after flock of black birds follows them, cawing against the dawn. It's both breathtaking and chilling. In the distance, the crew makes noises like they've been up for hours. I don't see any of them, but their knocks, bangs, and hollers drift into the camp. The fire a few feet from my bedroll is long out. Its ashy white remains don't hold a flicker of warmth. I pull the bee uniform closer around my shivering body. Though the sun is up, it's not near as warming as the fire or the covering I slept under. I have half a mind to crawl back into that rocky bed and sleep the day away. But none of the crew's bedrolls are out except mine. And not even eight hours ago they were ready to maroon a crewmate for causing them trouble. I don't want to test them with laziness.

I crawl the rest of the way out and fold everything Slate gave me last night. She said she got my bedroll out of Dax's truck, so that's where I head to put it away.

It doesn't take long to find his rig or to climb into the back trailer. But it does take a while to find where all this stuff goes. The whaler kart strapped in here doesn't help. Dax has its driver's side almost flush with some of the storage bins. It's impossible to pull them out without hitting the kart's frame.

I pull on the one furthest away from the kart. It comes about three-quarters of the way out before clanking against a bar on the kart. The clank resounds through the trailer, causing my pulse to jump. I cover my heart with my hand till I calm down.

I lean in to dig through the bin. There are some boxes of storage bags, some miscellaneous cutting tools, three or four—

Clank!

I drop the tools I'm holding and spin around, searching the trailer for any movement.

There's no one in here. Maybe the sounds of the crew are drifting in. I pull my bedroll close and shut the bin. I move on to the next bin. It has a little more space between it and the kart, so I can open it all the way. It opens with a screech, but what's inside is more promising—a few blankets, a pillow, and—

Clank! Clank! Clank! Clank!

I shove the bin closed and press my back against the trailer wall. It's not out there. It's in here. Something is in here with me.

Clank! Scratch! Scratch! Clank!

Where's it coming from? I look down the row of bins and see it. A bin three away from me, pinned by the kart, shakes with each clank. Then it stops, shakes once more, and stops.

I start to tiptoe as far from whatever is in that bin as possible on my way to the exit. I'll get Dax, he can deal with it. But the second I touch the door, a squawk rings out from the bin. A *very* familiar squawk.

Oh, no, no. No!

The squawk turns shrill, louder and more panicked. I don't want to, but I move to the space between the kart and the bin and shimmy in there with my back against the kart's bar. When I reach the shaking bin, I push my back against the kart and my feet against the trailer wall. After the third shove, there's enough space to tug the bin open.

Two-Heads flies out.

He flaps his red and orange feathers as he soars above my head. I sink down, dropping my forehead into my hands. Two-Heads not only escaped his pen again, but he followed me onto the rig. I can't get rid of him. I'm not sure what the crew will do if they see this bane-of-my-existence bird following me around the Scar. Dax's words haunt me.

I may not believe in marooning someone based on a mythical bad luck bird, but you'd better believe my crew does.

How can I hide this from them? They might have kept me around last night, but if they see the mala suerte bird, they'll maroon me for sure. Slate can't save me from this.

Squished in the tight spot, I look up at the bird, disdain coursing through me. He's perched high up on the kart's top light. His left head picks at his back, while the right coos like he doesn't have a care in the world.

"You're welcome," I mutter.

He shakes his long tail in response.

"You didn't need my help at all, did you? It's all to bug me. Go on. Stay up there and pretend nothing happened."

I shake the kart because I'm mad. He flaps to balance, but does nothing else, all oblivious and happy like I don't exist.

If you take them to a high enough spot, they get comfortable and forget their mark.

Glowen's revelation back at the farm rings in my mind, followed by Dax's voice.

The satellite dish is the highest place around here.

A new determination fills me. I pull myself up, out, and head for the door.

"Come on, you. We're going on a walk."

The ladder to the satellite dish is much easier to climb in the daylight. Even with the thick clouds dimming the sun, I can see each rung perfectly as I scramble to the top. I have no idea how long it'll take to get rid of Two-Heads, so the faster I get there, the better.

I don't have to coax him to follow me. He sits on the highest rung, squawking, before I'm halfway up. I shoo him out of the way once I reach the top to open the latch.

The dish is stark white with a red tinge from the morning light. Slate's telescope and bag are draped with a blue tarp with weights holding it down. She said she'd stargaze as long as the Fluxes would allow, but didn't want to haul the scope back and forth each night. Other than that, everything is exactly as we left it. The beautiful, hilly Grid below is a perfect spot for Two-Heads to fly away and find a less annoying purpose in life.

"Okay, bird. Shoo."

He flaps his wings but doesn't take off. Instead, he hops over to me and rubs his heads against my legs.

"No, no! Go away. Be free!" I shake my leg and back away. He follows. I fling my arms up in exasperation. "Dumb bird!"

This isn't working. Slate might have something in her bag I can use to chase this bird away. I untie the tarp enough to get to the bag beneath. I dig through the bag, hoping for I don't know what. Maybe apples to throw. But there's not anything helpful in here. Unless he's spooked by telescope equipment.

Wait a second. This might help. I reach in and snag a pair of binoculars. They're not exactly like their virt-game counterparts, but I can figure them out. I put them up to my eyes. Though everything is closer, it's also blurred. There's no tap screen, so I'm not exactly sure how to . . . *oh, there it is, on the side.*

I turn the knob until I can see clearer. Once I can, I search for the best place to entice Two-Heads. If I shoo him in the direction of something he's interested in, he might like it enough to stay and leave me alone. I scan the area for somewhere leafy, high up, and growing fruit.

Ten minutes in, I see nothing that fits. Twenty minutes in, I'm about to give up. This place is nothing but hills of broken buildings, and sparse trees. I check one more time, then I almost drop the binoculars.

What is that?

I rub my eyes before putting the lenses back over them. A few seconds of searching later, I find the same weird moving clump as before coming over a hill in the distance. I adjust the focus. No, it's not a clump. It's a group of people heading this way. Not only are they heading this way, but I know them.

The men up front are the users from the rebel base on their way to kidnap me.

Which is bad enough. But nothing prepares me for who I see taking up the rear of the group. Looking worn and ragged is the blonde girl I rescued in the substation.

And Tori.

29

MY BEST FRIEND STUMBLES ACROSS

the wasteland behind a pack of kidnappers, and all I can do is stare. She's supposed to be in her home. Zane told me she left with people she knows. Why? Why is Tori out here?

She wears the same gray shipper uniform she put on back in Austin. It's torn at the knees and her left sleeve is ripped clear off. Mud cakes her cheeks and lumps in her pink hair. I see a few scratches where she's bare-armed, but find no other visible wounds. I hope there aren't any other wounds. But from what I know of the Freeman's pushers she's with . . . Bile rises in my throat.

I can hardly keep the binoculars still in my shaking hands. Why do they have her? *How* do they have her? I can't believe I trusted Zane. That liar!

Beside Tori, the blonde girl from the substation trips on a rock. She lands on her palms and knees, probably scraping them up. One of the men yells at her, though I can't make out what he's saying. Tori gives him a scowl then helps Blondie up. I'm most confused by the substation girl's presence. She's supposed to be long gone in Baton Rouge by now.

Then I think of what the men are here for.

Me.

If they picked up Tori to find me, they must have kidnapped Blondie to find me too. What better way to track someone than through their holo-cuff? Except I gave my cuff to Metal Hair in Austin. Blondie must've gotten it back and tried to return the cuff to me only to get abducted for her trouble. It's my fault she's here. It's my fault Tori's here.

The mala suerte bird was right to choose me. I'm nothing but bad luck.

But I'm also someone who's going to do something about it.

I take the binoculars from my face and throw its lanyard around my neck. I know the stupid bird will follow me if I leave. If the shippers see him with me, so be it. There's no escaping this chaos storm. If I'm the one who caused it, I've got to help fix it.

"Come on, Two-Heads," I call out, racing to the hatch. "We need Dax."

The Scar is a rough place to search for someone when you're in a hurry. I stand on jagged cement right on the edge of a steep drop-off. Weeds and vines grow through broken cars piled every which way. I can't see any human movement, but I hear the crew. They're louder with their clanks, buzzes, and chatter than they were at the campsite. Some of their machinery pulls up huge sheets of metal from the pit below.

The longer I search up here, the dizzier I get. I take a long breath to steady my anxiety. The ground breaks off into layers below me. It's like standing on a roof looking down at the stories of a scraper that had its outer wall ripped off. The road I'm on slopes almost vertical a few feet from me. It covers the layers of stone and earth like a slide. On the other side, concrete within the layers goes off in every direction. Some lines of concrete head toward the dome, and some disappear into the Grid. They must have been roads once, but there's no driving on them now.

One of the shipper's machines sits atop the opposite side of the Scar from me. It's the one I saw pull up sheet metal. A crunching sound pulsates from its engine and overtakes every other noise in the Scar. Though I don't see anyone in the big yellow machine, I should start looking there for Dax. If only there wasn't a gigantic chasm between me and it.

I scan the area for anywhere quick and safe to cross the pit. How did they get that huge thing over there in the first place? I scan the layer the machine is on far to the right until I see something blue and blurry the distance. I lift the binoculars to my eyes. It's a bridge. A bridge that's nowhere close to me. The crew must have risen early to go that way. It'll take forever to get down there and back. Who knows where Tori will be by the time I find Dax?

Dropping the binoculars, I search for anything else. As soon as my eyes land again on the machine, it stops its rumble and Dax's voice rises from the pit.

"Let Rook take that piece back to the rigs with Slate. We won't fit anything else on the trailer with that thing on it."

I see him now inside the yellow cab of the machine. He finishes speaking and puts headphones over his ears.

"Wait! Dax! Dax!"

There's no way he can hear me. He cranks the machine back on. It roars over everything. I can't even hear myself call him. I wave my hands, but he doesn't see me. If I head for the bridge now, I might make it in time. And I could lose my best friend if I take the safe route.

I look down at the road slide beside me. On the edge of the drop-off, there's a speed limit sign sticking up and spinning with the wind. Someone spray-painted a black skull and the words *Scar of Death* on it that alternates with each spin. Two-Heads sits on its pole, cooing. The sign might as well say *come this way and die*. I should heed its warning. I know I can't.

The slide of concrete is mostly flat all the way down. It doesn't extend all the way to Dax, but the space between where it cuts off and his level's edge looks jumpable. From there, it's a short climb up some cement covered in vines. No problem.

"Okay," I say to the bird beside me. "But if I fall, you're catching me."

He hops and coos, like he loves it when I make life-threatening decisions.

I take a second to breathe, picture one of Uncle Trek's obstacle courses, and throw myself over the side. I hit the ground hip first. Gravity snatches me by the ankles and takes me further down. Concrete rubs hard against my palms, slicing my skin as I slide. It hurts like crazy. The sides of my feet slow me a little, but I can't stop.

I have little time to think and less to react. The drop-off comes on me fast. The momentum builds in my body like a runaway subtrain. Once I hit that ledge, I'm either jumping up or jumping off. There's no in-between. As I slide closer, the distance in the gap grows. But there's no turning back now. I run out of real estate and momentarily halt right on the edge. My momentum hits my toes then pushes back, propelling me into the air.

I soar over the gap.

The distance is farther than I thought. I miss the ledge but hit the level below. My feet land first on the wall. Then my fingers grip the edge. Pain spikes out from the cuts in my palms. I wince but pull myself over the ledge.

I grab the vines on the cement above me and climb. It's uneven and covered in leaves, but other than that, it's exactly like Uncle Trek's cargo nets. Which would be great if my hands didn't hurt. I pull myself up onto one slab of concrete then the next till I'm right at the edge of Dax's level. One more slab to go. I reach for the last vine, and the plant is slick in my grip. My hand slips through, and leaves poke out between my fingers. I fumble to get a better grasp of the vine, but the pain is unbearable. Everything I touch stings. I panic, lose my footing, and start to slide down the stone.

But then something strong clamps down on my hands, pinning me to the rock. I look up. It's Dax. He's bent halfway over the ledge with both hands covering mine. It's amazing where he has the tendency to show up.

"You out of your mind?"

"Dax!"

He helps me up and off the ledge. After making sure I'm steady, he runs over to the machine to shut it off. He must have left it running in a rush to catch me. I'll have an army of thank yous to owe him when this is over.

He jumps out of the machine and heads toward me full fury. "There's a bridge right there. What possessed you to jump the Scar when you could've just—"

"They have Tori," I blurt. He's right. That jump was stupid. But I had to do it.

He shakes his head like I dropped an ice bucket of confusion over his anger. "What? What are you talking about?

"My best friend. The one the Quell took with Zane. They have her. They're on their way here to take me too."

"Slow down. Who has your friend?"

"The Freeman's pushers." I'm unable to control my frantic arms. "From the station. They followed me here. Somehow, they know I have the crier stone, and I think they're using Tori to get it from me."

Dax rubs his forehead. "Crier stone? You mean your necklace? Why do you think the pushers are here for you?"

"They were at the rebel base. Astrid told me she overheard their plans to kidnap a blue-haired shipper girl. It's not hard to figure out who they mean. I didn't tell you because I thought the rebels had them locked up. That was until I went to the satellite to see if I could get rid of him"—I look over my shoulder at the bird behind me—"that I saw them."

Dax follows my gaze, then groans when he spots the mala suerte. "I know it looks bad."

"It doesn't *look* bad, Princesa. If the crew sees him, they'll—"

"I know. I know." I hold up the binoculars. "That's why I went to the satellite. To get rid of him. But then I saw the pushers on their way here with Tori. They'll be here any second."

Dax stops staring at the bird and focuses in on me. "The same pushers who went down when you used the crier stone before?"

I nod. "I'd use it on them now if I could, but I can't. The crier stone works on anyone who's used Freeman's ever. Which includes me. That's why I passed out along with the pushers. Even if I manage to throw it near them without being caught, I can't escape its sonic range. I won't be able to free Tori. The pushers will wake the same time I do and then they'll have me, her, and the stone."

Dax rubs his neck. I'm not sure what's bugging him more—the pushers on their way here, or that I'm technically a Freeman's user.

"Then give me the stone," he suggests. "I'll use it to save your friend, then we'll get out before they wake up."

If only it were that easy. "That won't work. The stone is programed to my voice and passcode only. I can't deprogram it. That's why you and Hatcher couldn't get it to work. I *have* to be the one to use it."

He tilts his head as my plan starts to make sense. "And you want me to pull you out after you pass out."

I answer with a short nod.

He bites his lip then heads back over to the machine. Picking up a microphone attached to a wire, he brings it to his mouth. Bending out the window, he looks out at the dark clouds that have now covered the sky. "Pack it up, boys and girls. Zane's right. That's a Flux out there."

He replaces the mic and climbs out of the machine carrying a roll of white bandaging. "All right, Princesa. Let's ruin those drug dealers' day."

AFTER WRAPPING MY HANDS WITH

the bandage, Dax leads me through a safer path than the way I took. I'm sure it's also faster than if we'd have taken the bridge. It would have been nice to know about before I jumped over a fifty-foot drop. I told him the general direction I saw the pushers take Tori. He takes us around buildings and trees I'd never thought to navigate without him.

Before I hear anything other than our own footsteps, Dax holds out his hand to still me. He hears something I don't. I go silent. The wind rustles through the branches above us, but that's the only noise around. He searches through the trees, then locks on to something in the distance.

"There," he whispers, pointing to some trees ahead. "How close do we have to be?"

I look around. I don't see anyone near us. "Closer than this."

He winces. Maybe we're closer than he wants, but I need to make sure this works. I can't throw my pendant at a voice he thinks he hears.

"Okay, you'll have to be silent then. No more walking on sticks. You ready?"

I thought the light drizzle around us covered my not-so-dainty footfalls, but I guess not. Even Two-Heads, who's usually a chirp-box, is quieter than me. I pull out my necklace from under my bee suit and clench the pendant with my fist. "Okay."

He moves fast and swiftly ahead of me. I try to do the same, careful to avoid any sticks this time. We reach a broken-down bus with trees growing out its engine, and he has me duck behind it. That's when I hear the voices.

". . . already started raining, idiots. Shippers never stay put during a Flux. You want to lose them in that dome?"

The voice is male and stomach-turningly familiar. I'll never forget the fishy stink of his breath or the way he offered to take me to his bed back at the fueling station. I press my back against the bus, wanting to hide behind it forever.

"Shut it, Ivo," says a different male voice. "We're not going to lose them."

"Oh yeah?" the Ivo guy retorts. "And who's going to chase those trucks on foot during a Flux? You? Your boy over there? All this ammo ain't worth puke next to steel cages going eighty into a dome city."

The other man sighs in loud distain. "Is robbing someone your answer to everything?"

"It is when there's a whaler tribe over that ravine, and we're packing enough heat to get the job done."

Packing heat? Not only did these guys kidnap my best friend, but I'll bet they're loaded with weapons they stole from the rebels. I look over to Dax. He nods at me to use my necklace now. I almost have the chain over my head when the pusher's next words stop me.

"Fine. We'll steal some whaler rides if it'll shut you up. But the girls stay here. You know the orders when it comes to them."

"Yeah," complains Ivo. "I know. Hard not to when you remind me every time I blink. Now come on, I saw some stragglers fly off this way."

I stay frozen while I listen for rushing footfalls to disappear off to my far right. Then I nudge Dax. He's stretched up next to me, peeking out through one of the bus's windows.

"I can't believe it," I whisper. "They just left them here?"

"That's what it looks like," Dax whispers back when he returns from the window. "All five of them went off that way. Loaded. Why would they leave the girls? Something's not right."

I shrug, not about to take the one time something works out in my favor for granted. "Or there's nowhere else in the Grid to go, so they thought they'd stay put. Does it matter? Now's our chance to save them without using the stone."

I stuff my pendant back in my suit and stand.

"Juna, wait. I don't think we should—"

I don't hear what else he says because I leave the covering of the bus and head to my friend. I already messed up by bringing Tori out here. I'm not messing up more by waiting for Dax to feel right while armed men are on their way back soon. It's now or never.

"Tori!" I whisper, urgency edging my voice. "Tori!"

She sits on a log next to Blondie, facing away from me. Her clothes are worse up close than they were through the binoculars—torn and muddied. She wears her hair in a single braid down her back. Twigs and mud stick out of it in odd places, making me wonder if she fell or was pushed to the ground. When she hears my voice, her head swivels to search for me. Sheer relief washes over her face when her eyes land on mine.

"Juna!" she cries, her voice cracked. Her face shakes with emotion as she gets to her feet. She hobbles forward.

I run to her and wrap her in a tight hug. She hugs me back, burying her face in my shoulder. I never want to leave this moment—holding her tight, keeping her safe. But I know if we stay like this, she won't be safe for long.

I pull back to get a good look at her, both hands on her shoulders. Black makeup stains her cheeks as crocodile tears spill from her eyes.

"I can't believe you're here," she sniffs.

"I'm so sorry, Tori. I—I thought you went home with your parents. If I knew you were still in the Grid, I would've looked for you. I would have found you."

Her forehead creases, puzzled. "Why aren't you with the shippers? How did you escape?"

I take her hands. "Escape? I didn't—I just left them for a second to find you. Come on, we can go back there and—"

"Go back?" Repulsed, she rips her hands from my grasp. "To the shippers? I thought you hated them. Hated Dax."

I wince. My attitude toward Dax when we first met is nothing like what I feel for him now. A strange sensation spins in my belly. What is it? Admiration, friendship . . . something else? Whatever the emotion, it's not hatred. And it's awkward hearing my previous feelings voiced when I know he's a few feet away listening.

"I don't hate—"

"No, Juna," she cuts me off. "You need to stay away from him. He's dangerous."

I stand there, stunned. Why would she want to stay away from Dax? Sure, she only knew him when he was being a jerk, but even that's got to be better than the pushers.

"What are you talking about?" I ask. "Dax isn't dangerous."

"Has he taken his glasses off around you? Even once?"

"No," I say the word slowly, unsure what she's getting at. "Does it matter?"

"It matters because he's keeping things from you that could get you hurt. All that talk about leaving our high-tech back in Austin. Those glasses have tech dampeners in them. They keep the Quell off his back. 'Cause if they knew what's under them, what he really is, there's no way they'd let him back in the Grid."

I lower my voice and hope she'll do the same. "And what is he?"

Her next words quiver with more passion than I've ever heard, and she doesn't lower her voice.

"A weapon."

I'm sure Dax heard her. It takes every ounce of control to keep from darting my eyes to his hiding spot. I make a face and give a slight shake of my head to beg Tori to stop, but she keeps going.

"He was bioengineered by the Plex. The second those glasses come off, he'll kill anyone nearby. Don't go around him. Don't trust him."

A weapon for the Plex? This is a joke. It's got to be a joke. Any second now, Dax is going to jump out from behind that bus and tell her she's wrong. He'll take us back in the rigs and we can leave this place.

Then Blondie stands. She pulls her sleeveless jacket closer around her chest and rubs mud off her umber arms. While she's not in the same outfit I saw her in back in Austin, she's wearing exactly what I saw her in at the rebel base . . . when she was at the base walking around freely. The same unease I'm sure Dax had sinks into my bones.

"How do you know any of that? Even if any of it is true, who told you?" I don't wait for an answer before I turn on Blondie. "And how are you here? Aren't you supposed to be in Baton Rouge with your sick granny?"

"I—" The girl's eyes go wide. She looks to Tori in panic.

In a bizarre response, Tori lifts her chin and straightens her back. "All you had to do was stay with your family," she says, completely unlike herself. "Everything was ready to go. I was one day away from ending my assignment. One day! But no, you had to go rogue. Like you always do."

"What are you talking about?"

"I even set up a Plan B," she goes on with her rant like I have any clue what she's saying. "It was a good Plan B too. I knew your savior complex would come in handy. And I was right."

For a long second, I stare at her, baffled. I'm sure she's speaking gibberish. But then, even though I can't see the full puzzle yet, some of the foggy pieces come into focus.

"Are saying you two set me up at the subtrain?"

Tori takes a step forward. I take a step back.

"If you went back home, none of this would have happened," she says, avoiding my question. "You'd be in the Plex, and Circe and I would be promoted. Not chasing you around the Chaos Grid with a bunch of gross Freeman's pushers." She takes a breath. "What's done is done. I don't have my tracker anymore. The Quell smashed my inhaler the second they noticed the city-tech. I was stupid to take it. But my people still know where your aunt and uncle are. If we hurry, we can get you to them before anyone else has to—"

"Back to the Plex? Tori, have you lost your mind?" I struggle to compute anything she says. She's the reason I didn't make it to Baton Rouge? Bright specks invade my vision. "You worked with people, to what, spy on me and my family?"

"It wasn't like that," she says, hands up in defense. "Okay, so it was like that at first. But I'm your friend, Juna. I want what's best for you. You don't like the Plex, okay, but it's not that bad. I've been there loads of times—"

"How long have you been spying, and who do you work for?"

She blinks at my interruption. "I really don't think it—"

"How long and who do you work for?"

Deep shame shrouds her face. I silently beg her to answer me with any name other than Orange Pipe. Any biotech company who didn't murder my parents will do. But we both know only one group would care enough to hire people to spy on me.

"Tell me it isn't the Pipe." I barely hear my plea.

She responds by dropping her gaze to the dirt.

Who is this girl? I don't know her at all. Not even a little bit. A sharp pang spikes in my chest. I hid my pain from almost everyone but her. How many times did she watch me cry over Orange Pipe?

Something rustles in the bushes behind me. I don't know if it's Dax or the pushers. I don't move, turn, or flinch, numb to any danger.

Tori reacts in a heartbeat. "Circe, grab her hands!"

The cry snaps me awake. Blondie jumps the log. I spin around to face her. She grasps my right wrist. I step to the rear and bring my left elbow up, dodging her grab for that arm. Her side is exposed. I slap my palm flat on her neck. When she bends forward at the impact, I pop my wrist from her grab, twist her arm, and push her elbow forward. She lands chest down on the dirt. Gripping her arm, I kneel on her back and look up, just as Tori rushes in with a big stick. She swings, and I duck too late. The stick only grazes me, but pain still sears my lower back. Adrenaline pushes me on. I grab Tori by the thigh and pull. She loses balance, falling hard.

Circe pushes up from beneath me. I hit the ground beside Tori.

I roll till I'm on my back facing the sky. Circe is on me in a split second, straddling my sides. She grabs my wrists. I bring my elbows in tight against my body, step one foot on the outside of her leg, lift my hips and roll. She falls off me. I jump up and back, trying to catch my racing breath.

They're both down. But who made that noise? Someone else is here.

A huge male arm grabs me around the neck from behind. On instinct, I tug his meaty forearm to gain some space to breathe. When I do, the stink of rotten fish attacks my senses. Ivo.

No. No. Please not him!

I lower my center of gravity and prepare to break his hold—a trick Uncle Trek had me perfect every night for a summer. But right as I'm about to shift my weight and stomp on his ankle, I hear a click and feel the press of cold metal on my temple.

Every self-defense move, tactic, and principle flies from my mind. All I can do is stare at Tori who is now standing. Her betrayal manifests into a gun pressed against my head.

"Look who it is," Ivo snarls in my ear. "The girlie everyone's looking for. Checking back on those two was a good idea after all." He strokes the barrel across my cheek. I flinch. He pushes the gun harder against my face.

"Don't hurt her," says Tori. A weird request coming from the girl who slapped me with a stick.

Ivo ignores her. "If I knew how much corporate is dropping on you when we first met, I woulda handed you over then. Too bad I've got to give you over now. You're just my type."

"Don't look like her type to me." Dax's voice sounds on my left.

I look over to see him saunter out from the forest. Both Tori and Circe scramble away.

Ivo takes a small step back and pulls me with him. With his gun still pressed against my temple, he laughs. "Ha, well, if it ain't TARSH's finest shipper. Or should I say, the Pipe's missing lab rat. You here to stare at me to death?"

Dax continues forward. "Something like that. Drop the gun and let her go."

"Or what? I don't care what you've got under those rims. No way you can take them off without the Quell knowing your secret. Only the stone is a better prize than you, and that's 'cause it can't be tracked. If they pick up on you out here, say goodbye to your shippers, the Grid, and anything else outside a Pipe lab. Don't think you'll bother me. It ain't worth it."

Ivo slides the gun from my temple to under my chin. He leans in close then licks his disgusting wet tongue up my cheek. Fear of the gun alone keeps me from vomiting right there.

Dax clenches his jaw and plants his feet. "She's worth it."

Lightning fast, he tears his glasses from his face. A quick flash bursts from behind them. I wince. When I look up, the world moves in slow motion—literal slow motion.

Everything, from the trees to my captors, moves ten times slower than normal. Everything except Dax. He runs up to Ivo, rips the gun from his hands, and slides it in his back pocket. Freeing me from the sicko's grasp, he lifts me in his arms. I catch a clear view of his eyes as he pulls me close. I'm shocked by the stunning shade of electric indigo. From this angle, I watch the irises adjust and swerve like the insides of a machine. It's unnatural and yet also the most handsome pieces of high-tech I've ever seen.

"Didn't mean for you to find out this way, Princesa," he says as we flee into the clearing. "A time-still doesn't last long, so there's no time to explain what I'm about to do. But trust me, I won't let you go no matter how crazy it's about to get."

I want to question him, or cry, or scream, or say anything, but my jaw is so slow in responding, it's like I can't open it at all. Dax turns his head to look between Ivo and Tori. He breathes in deeply. Then, before I can beg him to stop, streams of sizzling blue electricity explode out of his eyes.

TORI! PLEASE, NO!

My mind races at the inferno between the two girls and us, begging me to do something about the nightmare ahead. But my body reacts like a slug. Whatever Dax did to slow us with his synth eyes, it doesn't affect the bonfire he laid down. The flames lick the sky between me and my ex-best friend at normal speed, taunting me and my powerlessness.

I'm mad at her. Eyes burning, fists shakingly so. Our entire friendship was a lie put in motion by the people I hate most in the world. I want to shake her, yell at her, make her tell me why she did it. But I don't want to watch her die in a fiery blaze before my eyes.

I command my body to leap from Dax's arms. It responds, but not nearly as fast as I push it. So instead, I tumble forward, and he catches me before I go anywhere.

He sets me down and gathers his glasses to replace them over his eyes before picking me back up. "Don't worry. They'll be fine."

I wonder if his eyes give him mind-reading abilities, too, as we take off toward the rigs. Rain intensifies around us, unaffected by Dax's eyes. It takes me forever, but I look up. Above, Two-Heads flies through the shower. I have no idea how he did it, but Dax pulled his *time-still* trick only on the people in that clearing.

Dax keeps his focus on what's ahead and the sky. I look over his shoulder at the flames behind until all I see is smoke rising from the trees. I hope he's right. Betrayal rips at the wound in my heart, but I don't want her dead. Tears join the rain on my cheeks. I still care for my friend. I want to see her again. I want more time with her. And then I hear the voice pierce through my bleeding heart.

Are those I wish to save any different?

I know this means the Plex. I can't deny the hand pushing me back there—that this chaos storm is an act of God. Everything about the disaster raining down on us is Him telling me to go.

But I can't. I can't think of going anywhere near that city without steel encasing my heart. The Plex didn't just murder my parents, they sent people to befriend and spy on me. With my whole being, I want to watch it burn.

Dax leaps over an enormous crack in the ground, landing on the paved road. He hits the cement hard, and I flinch, gripping his shirt tightly. My quick reaction surprises me. I start to look up at him, but he sets me down then grabs my hand.

"We don't have much time now."

We start to move, but after a few strides, he stops cold.

"What's wrong?" I ask.

He puts his finger to his mouth. That's when I hear it. High-pitched squeals whizzing by both ears, one after the other.

Whaler calls.

"That's not—" I start, but I know exactly what it is. We're out in the open during a Flux, being chased by pushers, and smack dab in the middle of a terra cetus hunt.

He tightens his hold on my hand. "Hurry!"

He pulls, and I follow. We sprint through the Scar, dodging cars and leaping over fallen limbs. The moment I know it can't get worse, the heavens open and empty on us. Thunder and whaler calls battle like gunfire in a war.

Then a line of lights shines over the broken cars. Rumbling and roaring, the shipper trucks barrel our way. I squint through the harsh light to see Rook hanging off a ladder on the side of the lead truck. Higher up, leaning over the railing near the cab is Slate.

"There!" she cries, pointing and shaking her finger at us. "Zane! They're over there! Three o'clock. Get us close!"

"Get the lead out, you two," Rook hollers, stretching out his hand. "This storm's madder than a mule with a mouth full of hornets!"

We run, harder and faster than I've ever run in my life. My legs burn and my chest heaves. Behind me sounds something mechanical breaking free of the trees. I don't turn to see what it is, eyes focused on the rig ahead.

Rook looks up at Two-Heads soaring above us. He pulls his hand in only for a second then adjusts himself to stretch out further. Dax jumps. He grabs Rook's hand, and the bigger man hauls him onto the ladder.

Dax wastes no time, turning to reach for me.

I jump and miss.

"Come on, Juna!" he cries.

Engines roar behind me. I look back to see three whaler vehicles fly over the car graveyard. All three are on single passenger hover bikes chasing us. I don't look long enough to tell if they're real whalers or pushers who stole their bikes. I turn back and race for Dax's hand.

He leans out further. I leap. He grabs my forearm and jerks me to the ladder. I pull my legs in until I'm on the same rung as him. Both of us drenched, he pulls me close.

"Told you I wouldn't let you go," he says against my soaking cheek.

It could be because we ran a huge distance at breakneck pace, but my heart drums in my chest.

"Orders?" asks Rook. I glance up to see him standing by Slate, eyeing the sopping mala suerte bird perched on the rail. If he wants to maroon me now that we're in the heart of a full-on Flux, he doesn't hint at it.

"Hey," Dax says soft against my ear. "You okay?"

"Yeah," I answer between heavy breaths. "Considering."

"Good. Because when this is all over, I'd like to take you on a date."

"A what?" I slip, but he catches me. My heart thunders.

He grins at my reaction, full dimples. After setting me on the ladder, he climbs the rungs and turns his attention to Rook. "First, we have to get out of that whaler's path. Tell Zane I'll be right there!"

Once he's gone, I take a second to rub away the heat in my cheeks then climb the ladder after him.

Suddenly, bright light sets the sky ablaze. I shield my eyes from the glare with my arm. When I look again, the light is still there, holding longer than any lightning flash. My eyes adjust, and the worst possible sight pierces the clouds.

Quell ship after Quell ship descends on us. They must have picked up on Dax's high-tech like Ivo warned. They're here to take him.

They pick up on you out here, say goodbye to your shippers, the Grid, and anything else outside a Pipe lab forever.

One by one, the oblong ships descend on the Grid like massive raindrops. Their red-light-encased bodies turn the road into an unpredictable obstacle course. One lands. The rig dodges. Another lands. The rig slips on the slick road. I grip the rungs tight. Our rig slides to a stop.

A Quell ship, a couple hundred feet away, opens its door. Hardsuits spill out. They're here to take him. They're going to take Dax away and experiment on him in a Pipe lab for the rest of his life.

And it's all my fault.

Only the stone is a better prize than you, and that's just 'cause it can't be tracked.

I look up. Dax is at the rail. He sees them too. Rook and Slate argue with him. I can't hear them over the noise of ships, the storm, and whaler calls. Dax yells and taps his glasses. Rook shoves him, pointing back in the cab. Dax shoves the bigger man away and tries to make for the ladder.

I know what he's going to do. He'll sacrifice himself so his crew can escape. And he's right. Once the Quell have the source to the high-tech they detected, they'll leave. He can do it. It will work. But so will my plan.

And I'm closer.

I drink in one final look at the shipper captain I will never see again. The first synth who cared for me, a basic. The Glasses Guy who drove me crazy with his arrogance and bluntness. The boy who told me I was worth risking everything for and showed me the stars.

I mouth the words, *I'm sorry.*

And then I jump.

I hit the ground hard, scraping my knees and slapping my palms flat on the slick cement. Dax calls my name. His voice is wild and raw. It does something to my heart, but I run for the Quell ship. I've got to be close enough for them to see me. But they can't pick up on the stone's tech. If they don't see what it does, this won't work.

The three whaler hovercycles swerve around the ships. Ivo is on one and two men I remember from the station ride the others. Good. Freeman users are exactly what I need to show the power of the stone.

I reach deep into my suit and grab my pendant. In one quick move, I pull out the stone and tear the chain over my neck. I make it midway between the rig and the Quell ship and stop.

The ground beneath my feet shakes. I clench my eyes tight and try not to think about what's beneath me. When I open them again, I'm resolved. Focused. I put the stone to my mouth and whisper a word to set things right.

"Cry."

The triangle reacts in my hand, twisting, shifting, rearranging. I waste no time, reach back, then throw it as high as I can. The world slows like I'm caught in Dax's time-still.

Three things happen at once.

Two-Heads soars above me, circling his wings till he's hovering over my head.

A gargantuan terra cetus breaks through the earth. Its head, the size of two shipper trucks, opens an inky mouth right above me.

And the crier stone releases a burst of sound, trapping me in its song.

My bones shake in terror. Two-Heads lands on my shoulders, shielding me with his wings. Darkness encases me. My stone pulls me under as I'm swallowed by the terra cetus.

EMPTY.

Dark and alone.

Light flashes through the void. It crashes in waves against my throbbing skull. One flash. Two. Hundreds. Growing brighter. Over and over. An inescapable strobe. Flash, flash, flash! Pain worms around the backs of my eyelids. Squirming, twisting. Biting, eating. Why is it so bright? I can't move. Slime and stink everywhere. I can't breathe. In. Out. In. The air is soup. Rotten, foul, dying soup. It hurts. It hurts! I break.

Sizzling into nothing.

Numb.

"JUNIPER."

The sound of my mother's voice is soothing balm to my ears. I crack open my eyes to a blurry golden light. Everything is fuzz. I bat my lids till the haze turns to shapes. A bed. A window. A curtain billowing a soft dance. Dawn spills in through the fabric's rhythm, licking the air with rays of sunlight.

I study the familiar hexagonal shape of the window then push down on the bed. It sinks on the left side like it always did. I know this place. I turn to see the rest of the bright room. It's my bedroom. I'm back in my childhood room in the Plex.

I blink, and everything rushes back to me. The Flux. The shippers. Tori's betrayal. Dax's eyes. The terra cetus. The crier stone.

I'm having a hallucination.

But how am I hallucinating? The terra cetus . . . it swallowed me. I know it did. I'm dead. I should be dead. And yet, here I am, still existing.

I look down at my fingers, expecting small hands. But they're not small. They're the same seventeen-year-old hands I came into this illusion with. Same chipped, pastel-blue nail polish and everything. But how? I'm never in my older body during the stone's effect.

"Juniper," my mother calls again.

I push off the bed and cross the room to the window. The fresh smell of brewed coffee sweetens the air. I pull back the puffed white curtains to see my mother sitting on the window ledge, sipping a steaming cup.

She's as beautiful as I remember. Her golden hair falls in waves over her shoulders. A crisp white shirt and matching pants hang loose over her thin frame. It's a stark contrast to the worn, muddy shipper suit I'm in. Why am I in this? The hallucinations always reenact past events. Never anything new.

"I think it's time," she says. Her honey-sweet voice floats through my room with an ethereal echo. It reminds me of everything good and pure and whole. I can't stop the tears spilling out.

"How are you here?" I ask. "How am I . . . ?"

She sets her coffee on the table beside her before answering. But when she does, she looks past me like I'm not there.

"She's asleep," she says, smiling with a hint of sadness in her eyes. "We can do it if we hurry."

"What are you talking about, Mama? Who's asleep?"

Mama breathes in, deep and shaky. "I can't. I can't do this, Mit."

I turn and see my father in the room, coming up beside her. Dressed in his favorite black pj's, he takes Mama's hand and caresses it with his thumbs.

"It's okay," he says. "You're doing great. The rest will be easier, and we won't have to do them until tomorrow. I'll even edit this part out if we have time."

Edit it out? This isn't a memory. It's a recording.

How did my parents slip a recording into the stone to play in my mind? Is this only playing in my mind? And why is it playing now?

Mama breathes out a long, steadying breath. "Okay then, this can be a test run. How much time do I have left?"

Dada checks his holo-cuff. "A couple minutes. Let's run the Orange Pipe vid. You did that one the best in practice."

"Orange Pipe?" I ask, but they can't hear me.

After shaking her arms loose, Mama starts in with her speech. She gazes at where I stand. It's as if she's actually with me, talking to me.

"Welcome back, June Bug," she says. "Today I want to talk to you about the people your father and I work for. I wish I could say they're kind. At least, I hope you never have to hear these recordings and I can tell you in person who they are and why we left. But since you're here now . . ." She pauses to bite her lips. "Since you're here now, things didn't work out how we'd hoped."

She stops and puts her hands over her face.

Dada touches her knee then gives her a few seconds before whispering her name. "Lira?"

"Just a minute." She shakes her head before going on. "Not everything works out the way you hoped. And that's okay. Sometimes it's for the best. Sometimes you go down one path, thinking you're doing what's right, but . . . but it led somewhere else. Somewhere dark.

"The question is. Once you find out you're on the wrong path, what do you do? Do you keep going that way? Or do you turn around? Do what's hard, no matter the cost. Not because it will make you feel better or happy. But because it's right. And good. And worth it. And it's in those moments we find out who we truly are."

She rubs her head and leans into Dada's arms. "That wasn't in the script."

"No," he agrees. "I might leave it in anyway. You up to record another one?"

She nods. Dada stands and moves to stop whatever device he used to record this on.

"No!" I cry. This will be the last time I see them. I don't want to go back. Not now. Not ever. I may not be dead inside the terra cetus, but I will be soon. "No, Mama, no. Don't leave me. Not again. I need you. Dada, please. Stay."

He locks his ice-blue eyes on mine, reaches up, and touches something inside me. The scene is sucked inward, into all-surrounding darkness.

I WAKE TO A FIT OF COUGHING. MUCK

and grime coat my throat, my mouth, my nose. I can't get it out fast enough. Each hack burns my lungs. They twist and shrink like wrinkled garbage in my chest.

When I finally get myself under control, I try to open my eyes. They're glued shut. My arms are so heavy. It feels like they're covered in thick mud. But I manage to rub my eyes till they open. When they do, it's as if they're still shut. Darkness enshrouds me.

Where am I? Is this death?

I clench my fists, and they close. I flex my toes, and they move. No. I'm not dead. I take a deep breath. The smell of rot and decay knocks into me full force. It's ripe, sour, and I can't keep my stomach from reacting. I turn to the side and wretch.

Acid burns my throat. My eyes drip tears.

Where am I?

The ground I sit on, slimy and soaking, moves up and down in a wave. I try to stabilize myself, laying my hands flat on whatever's beneath me. I'm either sitting in a pile of mush, or I stuck my hand in my own vomit.

I begin to weep. I cry till my chest convulses with hiccups. I cry, making my nose clog and breathing painful. The tears stream until I don't have any more to give.

Then, I sit in silence.

I stare at nothing for minutes.

Hours.

A lifetime.

I miss my mom.

I miss my dad.

Then my world shakes. A deep moan vibrates through everything around me. It shakes me to my very bones. When it stops, I can no longer deny reality. I'm not dead. But I am inside a terra cetus.

Panic bubbles up inside me, hot and wild, but I force it down. What good is panic here? What will it do for me in this pit? Nothing.

I don't know why, but here in the dark, Aunt Marna's songs ring through my mind. I listen to them, sweet and comforting. She sings of beautiful sights. Of waves and mountains. Of One who will save her when her life is fainting away. I join her in harmony, my voice shaking.

As the song stops, I have the dream I haven't had in days.

I stand outside the dome of the Plex, watching as all its scrapers burn in a great fire.

Then I know. I know why I'm here.

"You are right," I say into the dark. "I was wrong. I don't know how I'll do it. I don't have the stone anymore. But it doesn't matter. I'll go. I'll do what you want."

I close my eyes, and nothing happens. My breathing slows. I stay that way for a while when light swells around me. I open my eyes to a blazing inferno. Pain rips through my retinas. I shield myself until I can see. When I look back, Two-Heads is lit aflame, flying in the space between where I sit and the roof of terra cetus flesh. It doesn't look like I'm in the mouth. While the gunk around me is disgusting, I don't think it's stomach acid. Maybe I'm stuck somewhere in the esophagus?

Two-Heads hacks and coughs out his left head until something black shoots out his beak. It falls toward me, and I catch it before it hits the bumpy muck I'm on. When I uncurl my hand, I can't believe my eyes.

My crier stone.

That crazy bird ate my crier stone. It's then I know, deep in my soul, somehow, someway, we're getting out of here.

I look back at Two-Heads and see him coughing again. This time it's from his right head with much more violence than before.

As I reach out to soothe him, he expels a small black thing with such force I barely see it. It lands beside me then slides back. On instinct, I grab it before it disappears into the belly of the beast.

It's covered in so much slime, I can't tell what it is. I wipe it clean with my shirtsleeve until I make out a flat metal box. My heartrate triples at the sight.

"Two-Heads," I cry. "You little sneak! You aren't a bad luck bird. You're the luckiest bird that ever hatched. Prepare yourself. We're getting out of this beast!"

I RUN MY THUMB OVER THE CASE OF

Glowen's revolter and thank God for the weird fire bird that swallowed it. I'm sure the piece of high-tech would have been picked up by the Quell long ago had it not sat in the belly of the mala suerte. I don't care if those hardsuits pick it up now. The more people coming to get me out of this earth fish, the better.

I do care that I push the button at the right time. One second too soon, and the terra cetus could expel us somewhere deep in the earth. One second too late, and I could end up free-falling from who knows how high. I have no way to judge. The best I can do is pray.

Please, get us out of this pit.

I shut my eyes, wish I had something to hold onto other than this tiny device, and smash the button on the revolter. It makes a soft click, but nothing else happens. There's no flash of light or loud noise or anything.

I open one eye, and the terra cetus convulses. Its low, guttural moan swells until it's deafening. I look over at Two-Heads as he lands beside me. Still burning bright, he doesn't seem affected by the revolter in the slightest.

"All right, buddy. Let's hope he doesn't spit us out somewhere worse."

The flesh of the terra cetus I'm sitting on jets up, pushing me forward and backward. Forward and backward. Forward and backward. I about lose what could even possibly be left of last night's dinner. The beast beats me to it. Huge rocks and chunks of fleshy who-knows-what join Two-Heads and me.

We're not in the putrid gunk long before we're pushed forward by the beast and expelled out of his mouth. Like I feared, he vomits us mid-jump. I keep my eyes locked on the ground beneath us. It's yellow, rocky, and coming at me fast. I tuck my legs and arms in my chest. The beast's lunch falls faster, and some of it hits before I do. I land on some nasty gunk. Whatever it is breaks my fall. I roll to the side and immediately look up. The terra cetus isn't directly over me, but it's close. My body aches, but I push through, running till I no longer see shadow.

The ground shakes as the terra cetus submerges into the earth, spiked headfirst. I slip on some gunk dripping off my body and fall on my side. I look back. Massive chunks of earth fly from the beast's entry point. I cover my body with my arms. Some of the smaller rocks pelt me relentlessly. A larger rock speeds right for me, but Two-Heads flies between us, his feathers blazing red. I slam my eyes shut and curl myself in tighter from the heat.

Moments later, the world stills. I remove my arms from my face one at a time. The hot sun shines down on wherever I am from its spot high over my head. There's not much out here—yellow dirt, scraggily trees, cactuses, and two giant terra cetus holes. I look around for the one other thing that should be out here, but I don't see him anywhere.

"Two-Heads?" I cry. "Two-Heads!"

He's nowhere. Not flying above me or injured on the ground. It doesn't look like he was here at all. How is he gone? The only friend who can help me in this wasteland is gone. Exhaustion overtakes me and I collapse on the dirt.

"Can you believe that? I've never seen anything like it!"

I crack open my eyes at the girl's voice ahead. I see nothing but a fuzzy haze of heat on the horizon.

"Careful," says a boy's voice, cracked and familiar. "Don't get too close. It might come up again."

"It's not going to come up again. Terra cetus aren't known to do that. At least not the ones I read about in—Oh! Do you see that?"

"See what? Wait . . . is that . . . Hey! It's a girl! Berries?"

Two figures stand in the haze. The one a little taller than the other rushes toward me. Reaching me, he bends down close. For a second, he hesitates then moves around me and puts both his hands under my arms. Gently, he lifts me till I'm sitting up. It's a boy—a teenager like me, though younger, with dark sepia skin, and—and I know him.

"Milo?" I croak.

"It *is* you!" Holding me up with one hand, he motions to the girl. "Hurry, quick, it's Juniper!"

The blonde girl drops whatever she was holding and runs toward us. Her pigtail braids bounce behind her.

"Glowen?"

"What . . . ?" she says, kneeling beside me. "What happened? How are you out here, and what's all over you? Aren't you supposed to be in San Antonio with the shippers?"

Relief floods over me, relaxing my whole body. If Milo and Glowen are here, then we must be close to the farm.

"It's a long story," I say weakly. "One I'd love to tell you after a hot shower and something to eat. How close are we to the farm?"

Both Milo and Glowen give each other a strange look. Milo's eyes somber, and Glowen takes a deep breath.

"Juniper," she says before delivering the blow. "We're not close to the farm."

"We're a few miles out of San Angelo," says Milo. "Glow and I were out tracking an endangered nightcrux on our monthly animal excursion. You know, we go on those now and again. Don't like to tell her family about it. They don't like her being in the Grid and all. When our rover broke down in Eola, and—"

He keeps going, but I stop listening, stuck at his mention of San Angelo. The northwest town is a gigantic distance from San Antonio. Much further than the farm. I know it won't take too long to travel the distance by truck. But a terra cetus had to be going slower and at a less consistent rate.

"Hang on," I say, holding up my slimy hand. "How long ago did the shippers leave for San Antonio?"

"They left before we did," says Glowen. "Four days ago."

Four days! That means I've been in that beast for at least three. Three days of slime, gunk, and promises made. But how am I going to get all the way to the Plex from San Angelo on foot? Not that it matters. I made a promise. I am not going back on it now.

"So, if your ride broke down, what are you going to do?"

Milo smiles wide, and Glowen rolls her eyes. "Oh, no, here we go again," she mutters.

"It just so happens," he says, chest out. "You are both in the presence of a terra cetus migration expert. As those beasties head up to the Plex for their natural breeding grounds, guess who follows them? That's right, whalers. And who are the best mechanics on the planet? Whalers. It's a genius plan. If all goes well, we'll be back at the farm by dinner."

I look at the two farmers and smile. I hope he's right and they're both back on the farm by dinner. But as I think back on everything that happened, the storms, Mac's death, Tori's betrayal, I know I can't join them all the way. If I go back on my word, I'll only bring destruction.

I hope the two of them won't mind making an out-of-the-way pit stop once their ride is fixed. If not, I'll try to hitch a ride with the whalers. It's a long shot, but what other choice do I have?

I pick myself up off the ground and try to wipe off some of the dirt and slime from my hands. "All right. Let's find some whalers."

Whatever happens, I know one thing for sure. I'm on my way to the Plex.

I'm done running.

ACKNOWLEDGMENTS

DEAREST READER, AFTER FINISHING the last few chapters, I cannot imagine what you are feeling. Sometimes I wish I had my own porting dais so we could hang out to discuss what happened. For now, I will tell you my own feelings—ones of deep gratitude. Not all novels are read to the very end. The fact you chose to finish this one brings me great joy.

I started writing Juniper's story when my middle child was a baby. He is now nearly fully grown with a chin covered in facial hair. When my twin boys were born a few years into pitching a different series, I hit a low point in my writing career. I not only received many rejections, but hundreds. Years' worth of them. I remember one night slamming my computer shut with tears streaming down my cheeks for the umpteenth time. It was that night I gave up for good. I wasn't meant to be a writer. I would focus on other things. These stories would stay with me alone.

Then, two full years later, God called me to pick up *The Chaos Grid* again—to finish it and seek publication. To which I said no. It was only halfway written. I had no clue how to end it. Besides, I'd already made my plan. One that didn't involve writing.

But, though I gave up, He remained faithful. Timing is something I didn't understand then, and I don't understand now. Yet, through this publishing process, I'm more convinced that beauty can be made from our ashes. And reader, I'm thankful to share that journey with you.

To Johnny, my husband, best friend, and solid rock. You've been by my side since that first day in youth group, when I was just a fifteen-year-old girl with a crush on the boy sitting next to me. Thank you for reading everything I've written. Not only did you tell me when the story worked, but you also gave it to me straight when it didn't. It's an understatement to say I wouldn't be published without you. When the world told me no, no, and no again, you inspired me to press on. I'm honored to share life with you.

For the five sharp arrows in my quiver, Aria, Ransom, Caspian, Digory, and Emeth. I started writing this story when some of you were in diapers. Now you are growing into young adults I'm proud to call my children. I wouldn't trade my time with you for all the accolades, treasures, or published books in the world. You five are blessings by which the future is pierced.

To mom and dad. Thank you for instilling in me a love of reading, writing, and jazz music. All three resulted in hours spent in coffee shops and this book in your hands. Thank you for showing me the magic of books and ingraining the notion that when one is in the mall, one must stop by the book section. Your love and support mean the world. To Alison and Eric for loving me as only siblings can. I'm grateful for your friendship through the years.

Many thanks to my amazing beta readers, Aria, Cerys, Mary, Rob, Amanda, and Rachel. Your feedback was vital in rounding out my worldbuilding. And to Aria, I'm sorry for all the cliff-hanger chapter endings, especially the one that made you mad at me in the coffee shop and on the ride home. You know the one. Watching you read those pages then almost drop your phone in shock but still love the story was worth it.

To Kathleen Baldwin for offering valuable insight the moment you heard I received a contract offer.

To Mary Weber for your detailed query and synopsis magic! Your edits fixed that jumbled mess and gave me the confidence to submit my manuscript one more time.

Steve and Lisa Laube, thank you for bringing Juniper's story to the world despite the terrible title I originally gave it. Lisa, your edits not only smoothed out the novel's rough edges, but also elevated the Texas flare I hoped would permeate the pages. Thank you for pulling this book from the slush and being its champion!

A tremendous thank you to everyone working on the Enclave Team. To Trissina for keeping me on track after the many e-mails I stuffed in your inbox. To Jamie for letting me geek out about maps and printing specs at Realm Makers. To Lindsay for gently guiding me through the editing jungle. To Kirk for the action-packed thing of beauty on my cover. To the other members of the team that I haven't met but know are doing a fantastic job, well done!

To my fellow Enclave debut authors, Katherine Briggs, Rachelle Nelson, Candace Kade, Clint Hall, L. E. Richmond, and Sophia Hansen, thank you for treading the waters before me with overwhelming support. Not only are your stories AMAZING, but you are also a group who back up what you believe, seeking out this new author to welcome her into the fold.

And finally, thank you to my Lord and Savior, Jesus Christ. I wouldn't have thought to write a novel if it weren't for You. You have always been my favorite Author. Though I walk through the many plot twists of life, I am not afraid. Because of You, I know how the story ends!

ABOUT THE AUTHOR

LYNDSEY LEWELLEN IS A YA SCIENCE fiction and fantasy author. Her stories are filled with adventure, wonder, and journeys toward redemption.

As a struggling reader, she never imagined she'd one day become an author. Growing up on comic books and punk rock music, she was convinced she'd spend her life illustrating superheroes or singing on stage. Words didn't jumble together in drawings or songs like they did in novels. It wasn't until her mother convinced her to read *The Scarlet Pimpernel* in high school that she fell in love with the written word. She battled through each paragraph, reading them over and over till she understood. But with promises of swordfights and sweeping romance, she kept reading through to the last page. It was then she discovered that experiencing the beauty found in stories sometimes takes perseverance.

Reading didn't get easier overnight, but the worlds she unlocked were worth the fight. Soon, her love for science fiction and years working in a comic book shop translated into an appetite for speculative novels. It was that love combined with her time teaching teen girls the Bible that inspired her to write encouraging stories for teens young adults. She hopes her novels will spark a love for literature in both avid readers and late-bloomers like herself. Her stories feature bold characters who aren't afraid to take risks. Overcoming many mistakes, they grow and fight for what matters.

When she's not writing, reading, or whittling down her endless TBR, she designs covers for novels and paints on shoes. She lives on a small Texas farm with her best friend/husband, their five children, and what some might call a zoo of animals (especially after meeting the peacocks).

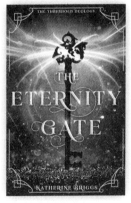

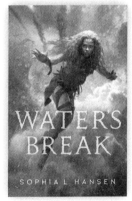